The Secrets We Keep

A BY THE BAY NOVEL

Visit my website at www.jlberg.com

Cover Designer: Devin McCain, Studio 5 Twenty-Five www. studio5twentyfive.com

Editor: Jovana Shirley, Unforeseen Editing

Proofer: Katy Nielsen, Once Upon a Proofread

ISBN: 979-8-9893204-6-2

ALSO BY J.L. BERG

THE WALLS SERIES

Within These Walls

Beyond These Walls

Behind Closed Doors

The Cavenaugh Brothers - A Box Set

THE LOST & FOUND SERIES

Forgetting August

Remembering Everly

BY THE BAY SERIES

The Choices I've Made

The Scars I Bare

The Lies I've Told

The Mistakes I've Made

The Secrets We Keep

By The Bay Series: A Box Set (Books 1-4)

STANDALONES

Fraud

The Tattered Gloves

The Affair

For Ember,
For always believing in me… even when I couldn't.
I love you kiddo.

PROLOGUE

Macon

I t was so damn hot.

I brushed the sweat off my brow, wishing like hell I had chosen to take my lunch break somewhere air-conditioned rather than in the belly of my cruiser.

But as much as I hated the heat, I loved the silence.

All five minutes of it.

The eager tourists disembarked from the ferry in droves. I watched as each car rolled off, their wheels hitting the hot pavement as they made their way onto Highway 12. Soon, they'd descend on our little town, buying everything from tacky keychains to local artwork.

Right now, however, they were doing their best to ignore me, and they were hoping I'd do the same.

Everyone always recognized the standard blue and white hues that embodied Ocracoke's patrol cars. When I had been young, the sight of it alone made me stop in my tracks.

Of course, in my family, it was never me they chased after.

But that had been a long time ago, and now, I was the one behind the wheel.

The tourists continued their way down the highway, every one of them driving with extra caution.

They had nothing to worry about. I wasn't here for them anyway.

Leaning back in my seat, I gazed across the bright blue sea, hoping to catch a glimpse of the other side. I squinted, trying to turn my attention away from the many tourists and their minivans.

Away from this island and all its bullshit.

But all I saw was water. It was all I ever saw. Nothing but fucking water.

Letting out a sigh, I took another bite of the turkey and rye I'd bought from a local place down the street and tried to settle my thoughts.

I'd known moving back here would be an adjustment.

But recently, it had been like living in my own personal prison.

After high school, the military had seemed like an obvious choice. It gave me the only thing I wanted more than anything—a way out.

My pivot into the police force had been a strategic choice and I'd never really planned on ever returning to my hometown.

I'd grown up here. I knew what it was like.

But I'd come back anyway.

For a while, it'd been good.

Real good.

But now, here I was, staring out at the ocean, eating a dry sandwich, wondering what the rest of the world was doing, while counting down the hours until my shift was up.

Usually, the busy summer months kept me fairly occupied. But lately, even the tourists had been on their best behavior.

Everyone was thankful for a safe town, but the days were really starting to drag.

So far today, I'd given a couple of warnings to some kids who had been cruising down the main drag in a golf cart they were clearly not old enough to be in. I'd received a call from a local woman, complaining about a renter's dog and the unwelcome presents it was leaving in her yard.

And I'd given a lift home to a teen who was having a rough day.

I'd been back for two years, and every day was pretty much the same.

We had our fair share of hurricanes. But aside from that, nothing bad ever happened in Ocracoke.

I thought it'd be different this time around.

I thought I'd be different.

But you know what they say about coming home again…

It fucking blows.

I watched the last of the tourists head down the highway toward the shops and restaurants and wondered how it would feel to drive down those streets and not know all its dirty little secrets. To get off that ferry and learn about the history and beauty of this place without feeling the burden of keeping it safe.

But I was not a tourist. I was not native, and when I looked around Ocracoke, all I saw were memories and regret.

I opened a bag of chips and started to pull a handful out when, out of the corner of my eye, I saw a familiar car pull into the lot and park.

Well, try to park.

The car had sort of haphazardly scooted into a parking spot, barely making it between the lines, before coming to an abrupt halt.

I watched with a curious gaze as a man I recognized from town got out and started to fiddle with his keys. He looked down as if he'd never seen them before, going through each of them, one by one.

Finally, he picked the one he wanted, holding it out in front of him, inspecting it for much too long.

What the hell is he doing?

He turned back toward his car, and his hand moved

toward the door handle. He shoved the key in, a vain attempt to lock it, but it wouldn't budge.

"Wrong key, asshat," I muttered as I watched him try again and fail.

I grumbled under my breath, knowing it was now time for me to intervene. Setting the remnants of my lunch aside, I let out a groan and pushed the door open.

This guy was an old friend of my dad, and while, in most families, that might make this a pleasant exchange, in mine, it just made it fucking awkward.

My dad didn't really have actual friends. Just drinking buddies and people he weaseled out of money.

And usually, they were one and the same.

I'd said I was bored, but this was not what I'd had in mind.

Stepping out of the car, I ran a hand through my sandy brown hair as the wind tried to toss it in my face.

I made a point of shutting the car door with a bit of force, hoping the sound would alert him of my presence. I didn't like sneaking up on people if I didn't have to.

It seemed to work. His eyes turned and found mine, and although he tried to hide it, I saw them widen ever so slightly.

"Hey, Raymond," I said, nodding my head in his direction.

"Oh, hey, Macon. Um, Green—I mean, Deputy Green."

For the older folks who had been around since I had been a kid, they never knew how to address me. Some still called me by my first name. Others tried to show me respect and called me by my official title. It was technically Captain Green, but whatever. I honestly couldn't give two shits what any of them called me as long as they didn't end up in the back of my cruiser.

Unfortunately for this guy, he had done just that on multiple occasions, and I was afraid he was about to get another stamp on that imaginary frequent flyer card he seemed to be working on.

I folded my arms across my broad chest as his eyes tried to avoid mine. "Saw you having a bit of trouble with your keys. Figured I'd come over and see if you needed some help. You haven't been drinking again, have you?"

I'd learned to not beat around the bush with Ray. He was a world class expert in bullshit.

"Oh, no, Macon. I'm clean," he assured me. "Been so for a long while."

I gave him an appraising look that told him I wasn't so sure I believed him. "So, what's with the keys?" I asked, and then I pointed toward the car with my right hand. "And the shoddy parking job?"

"Oh, well, you know how it is. Dang car has been giving me trouble for weeks. Couldn't get the thing started, and now, I'm running late."

"Late?"

He motioned toward the ferry.

I nodded, remembering he had been hired as a captain a while back. My dad had been a captain once. I still remembered the look on his face when he'd told me the good news.

"Things are gonna be different for us, Macon. You just wait and see."

He had gotten fired four weeks later.

Things were not different. They never were.

"It's a good job, Ray. A lot of responsibility." He audibly swallowed. "So I'm gonna ask again, you sure you're okay?"

I knew he'd said he was off the booze, but I'd rather have him come clean now so I could drive him to the local AA meeting than find out about it later and have to take him to the station.

"Just a rough day," he said before adding with a bit of hesitation, "I'm sure you understand."

My jaw tightened. "What is that supposed to mean?"

His face blanched as he took a step back. "Nothing, Macon. Really. It's just with your wife—ex-wife, I mean," he stammered as I stared him down, "and the sheriff being on their honeymoon. I thought—"

Thankfully, his words were cut short by the sound of static on my radio.

"Unit 2, this is dispatch. Can you please provide your current 20?"

Raymond looked at me and then toward the ferry while my mind was still hovering around that comment he had made about Kristy.

Did everyone know they were on their honeymoon this week?

I looked up at Raymond, noticing the way he looked at me.

Of course they did.

This fucking town and its fucking gossip.

I let out a frustrated sigh, scrubbing a hand over my face. I didn't want to deal with any of this today.

You don't have to stay…

"Better hurry up then. You don't want to be any later than you already are."

He visibly relaxed, his head bobbing up and down in agreement. "Will do!" he said adamantly as he scurried off.

"Oh, and, Ray?" I hollered.

He turned, his eyes wide again.

"Bring that car round my place soon," I said. "I'll take a look at it for you."

He hesitated but nodded before turning back around.

As I grabbed my radio and responded to our dispatcher, I watched Raymond board the ferry, and my eyes drifted back to his car.

Why do I feel like I just made a huge mistake?

CHAPTER ONE

Marin

How stupid do they think I am?

I tried to keep a straight face as the two of us continued down the hallway. The black dress I'd picked out for my failed birthday dinner felt tight around my rib cage, but in reality, it was probably just nerves.

God, why was my family like this?

Curtis was currently on his third apology. Or maybe it was his fourth. I'd lost count somewhere between the restaurant and the elevator, and I thought he had, too. I could see the sweat starting to bead along his temple, and his neat brown hair now had deep trenches from his fidgety hands sweeping through it.

"Marin, I truly am sorry. I thought for sure I'd made the reservation for tonight, not tomorrow night. I mean, how could I possibly mix up the date?" He let out a nervous laugh. "It's your birthday after all. It's not like I didn't know the date, right?"

He'd said all of this before in his first three apologies, and I'd played along then, too, telling him it was all fine and I didn't mind in the least.

"It's not a big deal," I'd said. "We can just eat in. I don't mind frozen chicken nuggets or ramen as long as I'm with you."

And he'd smiled—a genuine one this time. I'd laughed it off and tried to change the subject.

But then, after a few minutes of work talk and the changing Virginia fall weather, somehow, we'd circle back to the fact that it was my birthday.

And then the apologies would start all over again.

He was like a broken record.

I wasn't sure who had decided my shy, introverted boyfriend should be in on this little secret, but they were either clueless or diabolical because the man was a whole-ass mess.

"I even had it on my calendar!" he said, referring to the botched restaurant reservation. But I knew there was never one to begin with.

He was acting like a cheating spouse who'd just gotten caught with the nanny.

I can't handle it anymore.

He's suffered long enough.

Grabbing his hand, I pulled both of us to a halt right in the middle of the hallway of my downtown apartment building.

His confused expression met mine.

"I know," I said, raising my brow in an obvious sort of way.

"You know what?" he said casually as tried to look at anything but me.

He was *really* bad at this.

Rolling my eyes, I threw my hands up in the air. "I know, Curtis. Okay? I've known for about a week. Maybe more. You guys aren't exactly subtle. Texting my mom while we're watching a movie, Curtis? Really? You never talk to my mom." I tried sounding annoyed, but it was actually kind of cute.

His eyes widened before his face broke out in a grin. "I thought you'd fallen asleep!"

"And miss seeing Ryan Reynolds? Never."

"Who?" He furrowed his brow.

Until we'd met, the man hadn't even owned a TV.

"The actor from—" I paused. It was like he was an alien. Or a time traveler. "Never mind."

We both stood there, staring at each other, until one of us cracked—the laughter spilling from my lips milliseconds before his own filled the hallway.

"You've really known that long?" He grinned.

I merely nodded.

"You seem to be a better secret keeper than the rest of us then."

"Well, their fatal flaw was including you in on it."

"Hey!" he said. "Okay, you're probably right. I've been in a perpetual state of dread since your sister called me. Why does your family insist on these things?"

" 'Cause my dad loves them. But he seems to forget that after one, it's a little redundant."

"Well, it is sweet. Stressful, but sweet. And they do love you."

"I know they do. But this is the fourth surprise party we've had. I'd be more surprised if we didn't have one."

"Well, try and act like you don't know; otherwise, they're going to blame me. Your dad might not be able to throw any punches anymore, but your mom?"

"Yeah, she's a beast."

———

"Surprise!" the crowd shouted as everyone popped up from their various hiding places around my apartment.

I'd had no idea this many people could fit in here.

I'd played my part well, sauntering in with a slow gait, doing my best to ignore the subtle movements as everyone shifted in the dark. And even though I had known it was coming, I actually had jumped a little.

I scanned the apartment, seeing my parents and siblings. My best friend and her boyfriend were sitting on the couch, although they were sitting so far apart, you could practically fit the entire state of Texas between them.

Things between them had been a little rocky. I made a mental note to check on her later.

A few of my coworkers huddled in a tight group in a corner, like they were all glued together for moral support.

Honestly, I didn't blame them.

My family could be a little overwhelming.

"Happy birthday, *liebling*," my mother greeted me. My parents had affectionately called me their *liebling* or *darling* so often, it was a wonder my friends didn't confuse it for my actual name. Even after decades in the States, my mother's German accent was still just as strong as I remembered it as a child.

Curtis took that as his cue and wandered off to grab a drink.

"Thanks, Mama," I replied, giving her a warm hug. The subtle smell of her perfume reminded me of my childhood. "I had no idea."

She pulled back, giving me a stern look, to which I rolled my eyes. I could never lie to that woman. It had made my teen years incredibly frustrating.

"Okay, fine. But why couldn't we, for once, try going out to dinner, like normal people? We did this three months ago for Margo."

"Your father insisted," she said in a sort of exasperated tone. "You know how much he loves a party."

She patted me on the back and went to go grab a glass of red wine, and as much as I wanted to follow her, I knew I had about a dozen or more people to greet. Searching the room, I found my very uncomfortable boyfriend, trying to make small talk with a few of my coworkers. His eyes met mine, and he gave a half-hearted wave.

We'd met in an elevator over two years ago. He worked as

an accountant on the third floor. I worked as a graphic artist on the sixth.

For weeks, we'd step onto that elevator in the morning, and he'd give me a shy smile and then bury his head in his phone.

For weeks, I'd say hello, and he'd say nothing.

Finally, when I was beginning to wonder if there was something wrong with me, I'd heard a timid voice behind me ask, "Do you like sushi?"

It had been three years since my husband had died, and up until that moment, I hadn't even thought about the idea of another man.

But for some reason, I felt safe and comfortable with him. So, I'd said yes to sushi and then to another date after that, and we'd been together ever since.

"You are definitely a better actor than me."

I turned to see my younger sister sliding up next to me with an extra glass of red wine. She handed it over without even asking.

She was officially my new favorite sibling.

"Well, thankfully, I don't think Papa even noticed," I said, pointing toward the man himself.

He was near the kitchen, his wheelchair parked at the small dining room table. His loud, thunderous laugh filled the tiny space.

"Alex had him fooled when he walked into his party and made that ridiculous face." I tried to mimic the expression my brother had made that night, rounding my lips into a comically wide O.

Margo laughed, shaking her head. "Oh, no, that was real. He didn't have a clue."

"You're lying," I said. Now, I was the surprised one.

"I was supposed to keep him away from his apartment that night, but I had to work late, so I asked a friend of his. They took him out, and, well, they pre-partied a bit too hard."

I covered my laughter. "I knew he was drunk!"

"I was just waiting for him to give a speech, like that episode of *Friends*."

"I would have filmed that and posted it on the internet so fast." I snickered.

After a bit more chitchat, Margo headed off to find the food table, and I started my rounds, making sure to say hello to everyone and thank them for coming. I was grateful my parents had asked everyone to bring food instead of presents. Nothing was more awkward than unwrapping a gift and finding something hilariously inappropriate, only to look up and see your very traditional mother staring down at you.

After about thirty minutes, I'd managed to grab a plate of food and talk to nearly everyone. After I refilled my wine, I headed over to give a little moral support to Elena, who, by the looks of it, was clearly having an emotional crisis.

"He's just so..." She struggled to find the words, motioning with her hands, as if the movement would conjure the missing letters from thin air.

"But you guys were so good," I said as I sat next to her.

We'd taken residence on my beige sofa. I'd just dropped a fortune on it last month, and I was trying not to focus on the dozen or more people scattered all over my apartment, balancing red wine and cocktail sauce.

"I know. But now, we're—"

"What?" I asked, trying to understand where she was coming from. "Maybe you're just overthinking it."

"No, we're stagnant, Marin. Like dead in the water."

"What? Really?"

"It's just—" She stopped mid-sentence again, but this time, it seemed she'd paused herself on purpose. Her brown eyes met mine, and they were round and wide and reminded me so much of her brother's.

"What?" I asked before saying, "It's okay. You can say it."

"You and Daniel always had this intensity about you, you know?"

My lips pressed together, keeping the emotions at bay. "Yeah, we did."

She took a slow breath. "I just keep thinking about this one night when the three of us were out. Before I met Chad and I used to tag along as your third wheel."

"You were never a third wheel."

"Yeah, I'm sure Daniel loved always having his sister around on dates," she said with a shadow of a laugh.

"You know he loved spending time with you," I said. "And besides, had it not been for you, we would have never met."

"I still remember the way you looked at him when we went to do our college tour at Duke."

I smiled, remembering that moment, too. "I'd been secretly staring at pictures of him at your house forever. If only you'd moved to Richmond a year earlier."

"There was nothing secret about that." She laughed. "I don't think I could have handled you two dating in high school. And besides, you probably would have hated high school Daniel. College Daniel was much cooler."

"If you say so, but meeting him was so much better than I'd thought, and I almost put my acceptance in right then and there."

"Your mom would have killed you." She laughed.

"When we had an amazing art program right down the street? Absolutely. But that didn't stop me from driving down to visit you every chance I had."

She gave me a dubious look. "Me, huh? Sure. And whose dorm did you use to wake up in?"

I gave her a half-hearted slap on the arm, making her grin. "Don't say that too loud. I know I'm an adult now, but my mom still scares the shit out of me. Besides, I think we got a little off-topic. We were talking about you and your supposed boy problems."

"We were, and you're right. And they are not 'supposed' problems—they are very real. We are headed toward something neither of us wants to acknowledge. I just don't want to hurt him, you know?"

"Then, what makes you so sure it's the right thing to do? If you're so bothered by the thought of it, shouldn't that be a clue? I mean, I've never seen you even the slightest bit mad at him. For anything! He's always treated you well, and you guys seem—"

"Happy?" she interjected.

I nodded.

"See, that's the thing. I always thought I was happy. But I think I was confusing the feeling of being comfortable and safe with being happy. He's easy to talk to, and I enjoy spending time with him, but I keep thinking about you and Daniel—and that night I mentioned before."

"When you were our third wheel?" I said, grinning.

She rolled her eyes but continued, "You hadn't been dating long, maybe a couple of months, and I was still a little leery of you two being together."

"A little?" I scoffed, knowing that was understating it by a long shot. "You made your feelings perfectly clear on the matter when Daniel and I came to you."

"Up until that moment, we'd always had the same taste in guys. And then you all of a sudden fell in love with my brother? Gross." She stuck her finger in her mouth and pretended to gag. "Anyway, we were at this little Italian restaurant not too far from campus. Do you remember the one?"

"I remember the beer was cheap. Not sure I'd label it Italian though."

"Whatever, anyway," she said, rolling her eyes. "You got up from the table to head to the restroom, and I watched Dan's eyes follow you as you walked away. For the next five minutes, his gaze constantly drifted back toward that side of the restaurant, searching for you. It was like the two of you were tethered and he was looking for the other half of himself."

Tethered. That was how I had felt when I was with Daniel. And when he had died…

"And you don't think Chad is that to you?" I asked, feeling the emotions weighing heavy on my chest at the mention of my late husband.

Unfortunately, I never got the chance to hear her answer. As soon as her lips parted to speak, the telltale sound of metal hitting a champagne glass had everyone halting their words. As silence fell across the apartment, I let out a huff and turned my eyes toward my father. He was known for his elaborate speeches and would never miss an opportunity to bestow a bit of wisdom to a captivated crowd. But to my amazement, it wasn't him holding the glass.

It was Curtis.

His eyes met mine, and suddenly, I felt a swift sense of dread settle deep in my gut, and I had no idea why. I quickly tried to dismiss it, smiling as he held out his hand for me to join him.

I glanced quickly over to Elena, raising my eyebrow ever so slightly. In best-friend language, this was the equivalent of, *Do you know what the hell is going on?*

Her eyes went wide, and her shoulders shrugged a bit, which translated to, *I have no idea, I swear.*

I swallowed the anxious feeling I had as all eyes in the room settled on mine. Rising to my feet, I smiled and smoothed the satin of my dress as I took a few steps across the living room. My parents seemed unaffected by this impromptu interruption as they both did their best to avoid my gaze.

What's going on? I mouthed as my hand met his.

Curtis was not the kind of man who sought out attention. If anything, he was the exact opposite. During big gatherings like this, he often took breaks, stepping outside for a moment because his social battery needed a quick charge.

And now, that same man was standing in the center of a

room full of people, acting like he was an instructor for Toast-masters.

He blew out a breath from his lungs and turned to me. "Marin, I know it's usually your father who speaks at these kinds of things," he began, giving me a nervous smile. "But he happily gave over the reins for the night when I told him what I had planned."

Out of the corner of my eye, I noticed my siblings passing out tall glasses of champagne.

Oh. I let out a sigh of relief. *He's giving the birthday toast.*

I felt the tense muscles in my body relax, knowing my family always made a big fuss before the candles were lit.

"I know it might come as a shock to most of you, but speaking in front of a crowd isn't exactly something I excel at. In fact, speaking at all to anyone can be somewhat of a challenge. Marin can attest to that; it took me four weeks just to work up the courage to say hello to her."

Several chuckles could be heard around the room as he took the moment to collect himself. I joined in, feeling my nerves kick into overdrive once more.

Seriously, what the hell is going on?

"I thought about doing this in the elevator where we met, but when else am I going to have all of you in one room again? So, here goes."

And then he dropped to one knee.

***

I'd like to say the rest of the evening went off with a hitch.

In a perfect world, the tears that had started running down my face would have been the happy kind, and I would have looked down at Curtis and said yes without a second thought.

But as I'd come to find out, the world was not perfect, nor was it filled with perfect people.

And I was a shining example.

"Can I get you anything, hon?" the nurse asked as she entered through the exam room door. Her badge said *Eve*, and she was covered head to toe in teal.

I cannot believe they took me to the freaking emergency room.

"No, I'm fine. Thanks," I answered softly.

She gave me an encouraging smile, checking my vitals before walking back toward the door. "Dr. Matthews will be in shortly. The call button is right next to you if you change your mind or want to turn on the TV."

"Thank you."

The door clicked closed as I looked around the cold, empty room. I sniffled slightly, wiping my nose and my cheeks for probably the hundredth time. The tears had long since dried up, but the aftereffects lingered. My eyes felt puffy, my chest ached, and my throat was so dry that I could barely swallow.

I probably should have asked for a cup of water, but I already felt like an incredible nuisance for even being here. The ER was for emergencies.

Not…whatever this was.

As I sat there, alone and miserable, having sent Elena off to find coffee and Curtis—

I looked down at my left hand, my ring finger still bare, and felt the quickening in my breath.

The way he'd looked at me.

So sure. So full of hope and love.

And then I…

I can't breathe.

"Oh God. Not again."

The door cracked open just then, and a man entered. He was tall and handsome, and on any other day, I would have given him a second or maybe even a third glance, but I instantly turned away, feeling the panic in my chest.

And then the guilt that always followed.

I can't believe I did this.

I heard a chair drag across the floor.

"Hey, Marin. I'm Dr. Matthews. But you can just call me Logan. I'm a doctor here in the ER."

I let out a ragged breath.

"I know you don't know me, but I'd like to offer some help. Can you let me try?"

His voice was soft and steady, and although I didn't feel any calmer, the cadence in his voice had me turning my head in his direction.

"Good," he said. "Now, I'm going to ask you to focus on something in the room. Can you do that? It can be the tip of my ear, the doorknob—anything that you think you can stare at for a few minutes."

I gave a brief nod, but really, I'd only heard about half of what he said.

Tip of his nose? Ear? Shit.

I went with the whiteboard behind him. The nurses' names were written on it, and I zoned in on the curve of the *E* in Eve.

"Okay, now, I want you to breathe in through your nose for five seconds and then out through your mouth for ten. It might be difficult at first. I'll do it with you, but still try and count in your head. It will help, I promise."

A stray tear fell down my cheek as we began, the guilt still weighing heavy on my shoulders at the thought of this doctor sitting in here with me when there were so many others with actual emergencies.

And then there was Curtis, sitting somewhere out in the hospital…

At first, I could barely make it to one, my breath so frantic that I felt dizzy. My chest heaved up and down, like I'd just run a marathon. But he never wavered. We repeated this exercise over and over, and each time, the staccato rhythm of my breath began to even out until, finally, I looked up at him and felt calm.

Or at least as much as I could in the middle of a hospital, sitting next to a man I didn't know.

"The first time I met my wife was in this exam room," he explained as he looked over the room with a glint of nostalgia. "And as I was explaining something to her, I brought back a memory of her late husband that sent her spiraling into a panic attack."

"And you did this?"

"Uh, no," he answered, visibly embarrassed. "I knew the signs, but I was pretty inept at alleviating the symptoms, so after that, I did my research."

"And did it help her? These exercises?"

He took a breath, angling his head slightly. "The breathing will help, yes. But it's just a Band-Aid. Until you actually heal what's underneath, these panic attacks aren't gonna go away."

"What will help? Permanently, I mean?" I asked, looking down at my fingers as I nervously picked at my nail polish.

"Have you ever spoken to a therapist or a psychiatrist about your panic attacks?"

I turned away. "No," I answered softly. "I went to grief counseling for a while after my husband died, but I've never told anyone about this. Which is why I'm in the ER. I guess when your boyfriend springs a proposal on you in front of all of your friends and family, and instead of saying yes, you—"

Understanding spread across his face. "Oh. Well, now might be a good time to have that conversation," he said before adding, "If you're ready, of course."

I nodded.

"I'll write up your discharge papers, and in the meantime, you're welcome to chill in here by yourself and gather your thoughts, or your family can join you. Either way, it was nice meeting you, and I'm always around if you need anything."

"Thank you," I said before he exited.

I let out a deep sigh, looking around the room once more.

Now, I guessed, came the hard part.

Deciding what I should do next.

CHAPTER TWO

Macon

top fucking looking at it.

I tried to turn away. I tried to focus on the dirty dishes in the sink and the pile of fresh laundry that needed to be folded. But every time I did, my gaze would dart right back to that damn black-and-white print.

Of all the days to read the fucking newspaper.

When I had seen it sitting on my doorstep, I thought, *What the hell?* It was my day off after all.

So, I grabbed a cup of coffee, kicked up my feet, and gave myself what I thought was a few moments to sit back and relax.

The moment I spread those inky-black pages apart, I saw it. I couldn't have opened the paper to the Sports section or World News.

No, it had to land on this.

Sheriff Robert Hayes and wife welcome second child…

I couldn't remember a single word that followed.

My coffee had gone cold as my gaze slowly wandered around the room, looking from one worn piece of furniture to the next. She'd taken all the nice stuff when she left, but it couldn't erase the memories. Those clung to the walls like her old perfume.

Just when I'd thought I'd gotten over it, I'd see her name in the paper, and I was falling back in time.

"Oh, it's perfect, Macon! We can put the Christmas tree here during the holidays, and there's a fireplace for stockings! And when we have kids—"

"Whoa there. Slow down." I laughed, sliding my arms around her waist. I still couldn't believe she'd agreed to leave Charlotte behind so I could take a job back home. Not just agreed, but suggested it. "I haven't even checked to see if we can afford it. This is Ocracoke after all, and I'm not making big-city money anymore."

We'd make a good profit on our home in Charlotte, but I'd have to dip into our savings to make it work.

"Yeah, but you're a captain now, Macon!" She beamed. "I'm so proud of you! And I have a good feeling about it," she said confidently. "Besides, when the two of us set our minds on something, it always has a way of working out."

I shook my head, trying to dislodge the memory from my mind.

She'd set her mind on something all right.

It just wasn't me.

Picking up the entirety of the paper, I hauled it into the kitchen and dumped it in the trash. It landed at the bottom with a loud thunk. The sound wasn't nearly as cathartic as I'd hoped.

"Well, my day is ruined," I muttered to absolutely no one.

I decided to head to the bedroom. I needed to get out of here. I threw on a pair of shorts and running shoes, and after grabbing my wallet, I headed out the door.

The small house I'd purchased with my ex-wife was on the outskirts of town, but that wasn't saying much. Ocracoke was about as big as a postage stamp, and within a few minutes, I was in the middle of town.

I pushed ahead and headed out toward the dunes.

My mind drifted back to the newspaper.

It wasn't that I hadn't known she was pregnant.

The sheriff was my boss after all, and he'd married my wife.

Ex-wife.

He couldn't wait to tell me all about baby number two, but of course, being the narcissistic prick he was, he'd made a big show of it, taking me out to lunch so we could have a "man-to-man chat."

He loved playing the good-guy role, when if reality he was anything but.

Fucking asshole.

My legs started to burn as I reached the ferry terminal. It was mid-October, so the parking lot was fairly empty. Not many tourists visited this time of the year, and it was a much-needed break for the locals—even if it meant a solid dip in income for many of the business owners.

As always, I tried to avoid the massive sculpture that loomed over the water. The one that had been installed years earlier to memorialize the thirteen lives lost out on sea.

But clearly, I was a glutton for punishment today because as much as I tried to look away, I found myself doing the exact opposite.

It wasn't uncommon to find a small crowd gathered during high season. The man who had sculpted it, a main-lander turned local, had garnered quite a following, and people always wanted to check out the memorial created by Ocracoke's blind carver.

This usually suited me just fine on a run because it meant I could turn my attention away from the crowd and focus on the road instead.

But today, there were no tourists.

There was no crowd of fans, adoring Aiden Fisher's work.

There was just one.

I nearly stumbled over my feet when I saw her. She must

have heard the commotion, too, because she turned her head at the sound, her eyes recognizing me instantly.

The elderly woman held her hand up in the air in my direction. It was a greeting, but it held no enthusiasm. As if the simple gesture had taken a monumental amount of effort.

Just keep running, Macon.

I could just wave back, turn my sights back on the road, and never look back.

I mentally groaned, slowing my pace as I turned off the road and steadied my breath. I'd been running for miles, and it showed, but Mrs. Crewes didn't seem to notice.

"Afternoon, Macon," she said, giving a polite nod in my direction. "Nice weather for a run, isn't it?"

"Yes, it is, ma'am," I answered, noticing the fresh flowers at the base of the monument. My stomach churned when I saw the names etched into the stone.

"Today would have been Wade's eighty-first birthday," she said, gesturing toward the flowers. "He wasn't much into celebrating, but I always liked to make a cake. I started bringing flowers round here a few years ago after they put the memorial up, but it's not the same, you know?"

I merely nodded, although I had no idea why.

I didn't have a dead spouse, so, no, I didn't know.

Not even a little.

"The kids say I should make a cake anyway even though he's not here to enjoy it. Seems like a mighty waste of food, but they keep telling me it's important to remember all the happy days and not just the bad."

Realizing I hadn't said anything in a while, I opened my mouth to respond, but she beat me to it.

"Guess I'd better be going. You take care, Macon, and enjoy the rest of that run now."

I watched the old woman walk away, her bright floral dress swaying in the ocean breeze. She got into a late model sedan, the only car occupying the parking lot, and slowly drove off. I took a deep breath, looking down at those thirteen names.

I didn't need to look at them to know who they were.

They'd been etched in my memory since the day it had happened.

Since the moment I'd realized...

I was the reason they'd died.

By the time I made it back to town, it was close to lunch, and I decided to grab a bite to eat at a local place near the harbor. It was owned by a good friend I'd gone to high school with and was one of those rare places loved by tourists and locals alike.

Billy's wasn't formal, and guests were welcome to take a table wherever they could find one. Thankfully, there were plenty today, so I sat down at a small one overlooking Silver Lake Harbor. The moment my body slid into that plastic chair, I sort of regretted those last few miles.

Everything hurt.

"Someone been chasing you again, Macon?"

I turned to see Billy himself standing a couple of tables back, wiping it down with a clean towel. His head tilted up, and I caught a glimmer of a smug grin spread across his face.

"It's called self-care," I replied with an equally smug smile back. "You should try it sometime."

He straightened, looking down at his burly physique as he palmed his dark brown beard. "I think I'm gonna leave that one to you. Besides, my mama always taught me that if you're gonna treat yourself, it should involve chocolate. Or beer."

I joined him in a laugh as he proceeded to take my order, deciding on a double cheeseburger, fries, and a Coke. I'd earned it after all.

He headed towards the kitchen, but was stopped when another customer walked onto the patio. An elderly couple I recognized from town started to make their way to one of the tables nearby, and he made a beeline in their direction to help them out.

"Such a gentleman," Mrs. Joyner said, graciously taking his hand as Billy escorted her to the table. He slid out the chair, assisting her as she scooted into the seat.

"Always happy to help," he said before walking the short distance to the service station to grab two menus.

"Mr. Joyner has always been like that—chivalrous and kind, like you," she explained. "He still opens my car door to this day. Can you believe it?"

"You've got yourself a good man, Mrs. Joyner," Billy answered with a genuine smile.

He seemed used to the random chitchat. He'd owned this restaurant for years, and although he'd been sort of a shy, awkward kid in high school, he'd grown into quite the master of small talk.

"I do," she said proudly, giving her husband an adoring gaze.

Billy took the Joyners' order, and soon after, the restaurant started filling up a bit as some of the locals took their lunch breaks. Thankfully, my food arrived, and everyone left me in peace to enjoy it. The sight of my sweat-soaked clothes must have tipped them off that I was off duty and only to be bothered in case of an emergency.

Well, most of them anyway.

I saw Jake Jameson eyeing me the second he stepped onto the patio.

"What do you want, Jameson?" I hollered.

Everyone's eyes turned, darting from him to me. I couldn't tell if they were gunning for a fight or hoping for the opposite.

Knowing this town, I was going to assume the former.

Jake and I went way back. Even in kindergarten, we'd hated each other. A few years ago, he moved back to town and took over his father's medical practice, married his high school sweetheart and basically became a town hero.

I still hated the guy.

His hand went to the back of his neck, and he walked nearly all the way back toward the entrance of the restaurant before letting out an audible huff. It gave me a great deal of satisfaction, knowing whatever he was here for was causing him this much grief.

Finally, he stormed back in my direction.

I couldn't wait to hear what I'd done wrong now, what atrocity I'd committed against our good doctor, but when he finally arrived at my table, his face wasn't that of a person with a grudge to bear.

He actually looked quite uncomfortable.

"What's got you all upset?" I said, pushing the seat back from the table as an offering.

He looked surprised but took it nonetheless, plopping himself across from me.

"I need a favor," he mumbled.

I held my hand to my ear as a big grin spread across my face. "I'm sorry, what was that?"

He huffed again, muttering under his breath.

Watching him suffer might just be the highlight of my day.

"I need a favor, Macon, and unfortunately, you are the only one in town I can ask."

My eyebrow rose. "Unfortunately?"

"Are you going to answer everything with a question?"

"Depends," I replied. "Are you going to start making sense soon? I thought you went to one of those fancy colleges or some shit. Shouldn't you be able to string two sentences together?"

His jaw twitched, but he carried on.

"It's Molly's truck. The one she uses for the inn. It's been acting up, and now, it won't start. I told her to take it into Ander's last week, but she was too busy with planning the charity gala. Now, she's panicking because she needs to get supplies for the inn and can't."

I folded my arms across my chest and leaned further back in my chair. Ander's was the only mechanic on the island and because of that fact, he was in high demand and liked to charge a fortune. "Why doesn't she just use your car?" I asked.

"Because I need mine during the day for house calls, in case someone can't make it into the clinic. We have a few homebound people on the island."

I had to give that one to him. Couldn't exactly leave people without medical care, and our island was pretty lacking in that department as it was. I couldn't stand the guy, but he was a decent doctor. And when there was an emergency, we worked surprisingly well together.

"It's my day off, Jake," I said, enjoying the sight of him dangling on the long hook I'd cast.

"I'll do anything, Macon. Seriously. She's already taken on too much stress. It's not good for her or the baby."

Hearing that one word felt like nails on a chalkboard to my ears, and just like that, I lost all the will to do any good deeds that day.

Especially for Jake Jameson.

"Sorry. No can do, Jake. Find someone else to fix your problems," I said before rising from the table. I threw a twenty down and began my exit, not planning on saying another word to anyone for the rest of the day.

All I wanted to do was go home and pretend like the rest of this island and its fucking problems and drama didn't exist.

"You headed out, Macon?" Billy said, stopping me mid-exit.

His hands were full of plates, which kept me from maneuvering around him. I didn't exactly want to trip the guy.

"Yep, I left money on the table."

"Oh! What timing!" I heard Mrs. Joyner step up next to

me. "We're just leaving, too," she said casually, as if Billy wasn't standing there, holding forty pounds worth of burgers. He nodded politely while I tried to find an exit strategy. "We're taking the ferry up to Corolla to see the grandkids for the weekend."

"That's lovely, Mrs. Joyner," Billy said, giving me a pointed stare.

Oh, right. I should say something, too.

I fucking hated small talk.

"Great," I managed to reply.

"You know," she said, turning her attention toward Billy, wrapping her arms around her husband, "our youngest granddaughter is about your age. Pretty thing, too. Quiet. What does she do, honey?"

Mr. Joyner widened his eyes a little, maybe surprised by the fact that he had to speak. Or maybe a little taken aback at being put on the spot. Either way, he seemed to gather his senses fairly quickly. "Oh, um, yoga instructor, I believe."

"Oh, yes. That's right. These young people and their jobs."

I looked up at Billy, his usually cool demeanor now something closer to despair as Mrs. Joyner prattled on about her granddaughter and her upcoming trip to the island. When she finally got to the point of asking whether he might be interested in meeting her, Billy faltered. He opened his mouth to answer, but I managed to beat him to it.

I swiveled my head back toward the table I'd just left in a hurry. Jake sat there, his head buried in his phone, no doubt trying to find a solution to his wife's *broken-down car* situation.

"Jake!" I hollered, interrupting the granddaughter discussion completely.

His head swung up immediately.

"I'll take a look at Molly's truck. Tell her I'll swing by in half an hour."

His eyes widened in surprise, but he simply nodded.

I turned back to the Joyners. "Well, we'd best be letting

Billy get back to work now. You two have a lovely time in Corolla and safe travels."

They seemed distracted enough that they didn't bother finishing their conversation with Billy, and he took the opportunity to run off, delivering his dishes to the various hungry customers.

But a few minutes later, as I walked back to my house, taking a much more leisurely pace this time, I got a single text from him that simply said, *Thank you.*

After a quick shower, I headed over to the inn that Jake and his wife, Molly, owned.

By the Bay Inn was one of those iconic places in Ocracoke that visitors came back to time and time again. I was sure when most locals drove up and saw that weathered gray siding, it stirred a feeling of nostalgia and memories of happy days gone by. The McIntyres were known for hosting big cookouts and inviting nearly everyone in the town.

Nearly being the operative word.

My family had never been one of them.

My dad used to say there were two types of people in the world—those who were handed everything on a silver spoon and those who had to work for it.

"They ain't us, son. Don't even bother."

I didn't know why those words had stuck with me for all these years. Most of what he'd said to me, growing up, had fallen by the wayside. But whenever I saw my former classmates, all their happy smiles and successful lives, I heard his words in the back of my mind.

And they stung.

I'd no sooner put my car in park than I saw the front door open, and Molly walked out to greet me.

As she stepped off the porch toward me, I noticed the slight swell of her stomach and the gentle way her hand rested there. The announcement that the town doctor and his wife were expecting their second child had spread like wildfire a few weeks back. It brought back memories of another pregnancy announcement that had been the talk of the town.

One I'd rather forget.

"You're pregnant?" I breathed out, echoing the words she'd just said to me.

"Yes," Kristy answered, her voice timid, as she placed a single hand on her stomach.

"Are you sure?" I asked. My eyes were fixated on that hand.

This could be our chance to start over.

We'd tried so hard, for so damn long.

"Yes, Macon," she answered. "I'm sure. But—"

"But what?" I asked, searching her face for signs of distress. But all I saw was sadness. Sadness and regret.

And that was when I noticed the absence of her ring and the reality of our situation.

I should have known.

"It's—" The words caught in my throat. "It's not mine, is it?"

"Hey, Macon," Molly greeted me, her bright smile distracting me from the brutal memories the day had brought. "I really appreciate you taking the time to help us out. I know—" She hesitated, swallowing whatever she was about to say next. "Anyway, I—we really appreciate it."

While I could give Jake the third degree until the end of time, I couldn't do the same with his wife.

"Jake said you can't get it started?" I said, always feeling a tad awkward around her.

It might not be fourth grade anymore, but she would forever be my first crush, and that wasn't something you forgot.

"Yeah," she began as we headed over to the truck in question. "Jake's been trying to talk me into trading it in for years, but my frugal heart just can't do it." She exhaled a sort of exasperated sigh. "Like always though, I guess he's right."

She did a good job of trying to look annoyed with her husband, but the corner of her mouth turned up just a smidgen. "Well, let's see if we can maybe keep her going a little longer. What do you say?"

Her smile turned into a wicked grin. "I say I might owe you a pie, Captain Green."

"You know I can't take bribes," I quipped back in a mocking tone, which seemed to surprise her. It surprised me too.

I couldn't remember the last conversation I'd actually had with Molly Jameson, let alone one that involved jokes—unless you counted that time in grade school when I'd called her a string bean.

After that, she let me work in peace, running back into the house to check on a few things. It didn't take long to work out the problem, and by the time I was about to awkwardly meander through the front door to find her, she was walking back down the porch with two cold glasses of lemonade in her hands.

"I know it's a little late in the season for it, but I've never been much into pumpkin spice," she said, handing me one.

"Me neither," I agreed, taking a hearty gulp of the lemonade. It was homemade, just as I'd expected, and it reminded me of warm summer nights and cookouts on the beach. "I'll take the cooler weather any day. Makes for a much more enjoyable workday. But the mainlanders can keep the rest of it."

"So, I guess I won't see you down at the hotel for a pumpkin facial then?" She grinned.

"A what? Is that even a thing?"

Molly nodded. "Yep, Lani has a whole fall package printed up for the guests at the resort. Pumpkin facials, spiced cider massage. It's crazy."

Lani and her husband Taylor owned Windows Hotel and Spa, which was a relatively new establishment on the island. Lani was too, but that was a whole other story.

"And people actually pay money for that shit?"

Her head bobbed up and down. "Oh, a ton."

I leaned against the door of her old truck, catching a glimpse of the bay through the trees out back. "There are times I seriously wonder why I stayed after…" My words died, just like they always did when the conversation veered toward Kristy. "But then I hear about shit like that, and I worry I'm not cut out for the real world anymore."

A silence fell between us, and before I could say something about her truck, she spoke up. "I saw the article in the paper today."

My body went rigid as I held my nearly empty glass of lemonade, staring at the water winking in the distance.

She must have seen me flinch because she chose her words carefully after. "I'm so sorry. I didn't mean—" She sighed. "I only meant to say I was thinking of you."

I turned my head and saw the compassion in her eyes. "Why?" I asked, not beating around the bush—I never really did. "We've barely spoken in years, and I'm not exactly on good terms with Jake…or Dean for that matter."

She bit her bottom lip before continuing, "Do you remember when Jake left?"

My eyebrow rose, and I let out a sort of strangled laugh. "Which time?"

She turned her head and glared. "The first time," she said.

I shrugged my shoulders. "You brought it up. Not my fault he's a bit of a flight risk."

Everyone thought Jake and Molly would get married. But, then Jake's mom died during our senior year and he left that summer and never came back. When he finally resurfaced for his father's funeral over a decade later, Molly was engaged to his best friend Dean.

So much fucking drama.

She ignored my jab at her husband and went on, "You were gone for most of those years, so you didn't see the aftermath. I wasn't—" She paused. "I wasn't myself. I was lost. Alone. Bitter."

"I can't picture you being any of those things," I said, having only ever seen her like this—happy and content. Even when she was with Dean, her life seemed perfect.

She shook her head. "I'm a good actress but those first few years, even I couldn't hold it together."

"Why are you telling me this?" I asked, unsure how our conversation had taken such a bleak turn.

"Maybe I'm just trying to tell you not to give up hope."

"Kristy and I are not—"

"*Not* Kristy," she said with an emphasis on the first word. "You're kind of a bully, but even you deserve more than that."

She turned, looking at the truck with appreciation. "Now, what do I owe you? I know you've already fixed it. I saw you lurking around out here while I was changing linens in the yellow room."

"It's on the house." I shrugged.

"Seriously?" Her eyes were wide with shock. "I might need to take that bully comment back."

"It was a quick fix. Nothing major. Just make sure to tell Jake she'll run for a few more years. Knowing he was wrong will be payment enough."

"Oh, I will," she said with a satisfied smirk. "But are you sure there isn't anything I can give you as a show of thanks? I have freshly made cookies in the house."

Still full from lunch, I had to pass, but the idea of baked goods did give me an idea. "No cookies, thanks, but do you happen to have any cake?"

Her brow arched. "Cake? Something you're celebrating?"

"No," I answered. "It's not for me. But the Crewes are. And they're in need of some cake."

CHAPTER THREE

Marin

My car was packed to the gills as I watched Elena try to shove another suitcase in the backseat.

"Just forget it," I said. "I don't need this much stuff."

"You say that now, but you haven't been back there in ages. For all you know, everything could have been eaten by moths. Or alligators."

As we stood on the sidewalk outside my apartment, I couldn't help but grin. "There are no alligators in Ocracoke. And I hired a company years ago to come and take care of everything—the house, the landscaping; it's all been well kept. So, it's not like the place has been rotting down there for five years."

Five years.

I inwardly gulped.

I tried not to think about the last time I'd been there—the last time I'd raced out of our little house, on my way to catch a plane.

I'd never been able to go back.

As if sensing my emotional shift, Elena set the bag down and turned toward me. "Hey, look at me."

I hesitated, but eventually, my eyes met hers. Right after

Daniel had died, I sometimes found it difficult to look into her eyes when they looked so much like his. But now, I found them comforting—especially when he felt so far away. Shortly after we had married, his parents had relocated back to New Mexico, and when he'd died, they'd pleaded with me to have him buried there in the family plot.

I cherished that connection to Daniel. Sometimes Elena felt like the only one I had.

"It's going to be okay," she said. "You're doing the right thing."

I rolled my eyes, wrapping my arms tight around my chest. "Seems like you're the only one who thinks so."

She made a face that told me exactly what she thought of my family and shook her head. "They'll come around."

"And Curtis?" I could barely say his name without bursting into tears.

"He's..." Elena searched for the right word. "Hurting," she finally said. "He doesn't understand. But he will. In time."

"And if he doesn't?" I asked, swallowing the lump in my throat.

"Then, I think you have your answer," she said, referring to the marriage proposal I had yet to even acknowledge.

The night of my infamous panic attack had been brutal. Not only for me, but also for my family, who ultimately felt betrayed to learn I'd been suffering in silence for years. To them, when I doubled over, unable to breathe, they thought the worst.

It was embarrassing for me, but for them, it was terrifying to witness.

Days later, when I'd finally told them what I'd decided to do about it, their response had been less than supportive.

"What do you mean you quit your job?" My dad's eyes widened, his accent growing thicker by the second.

"I needed an extended period of time off, and … well, I didn't have it, so I quit."

"To do what?" my mom questioned.

"I'm going back to Ocracoke."

They both just stared at me. I'd rendered them utterly speechless.

Never done that before.

"I need closure," I explained. "I need to go back to that house and face my fears." I took a long breath. "Figure out why I couldn't say yes to Curtis."

"Have you maybe considered that you just don't like him very much?" my father asked.

My mother made a loud gasp, and gave him a stern glare.

"What?" he asked, looking up at her as she stood next to him. "It's an honest question. I've never really understood the two of you anyway. I like Curtis, but he's not—"

"Don't you dare say he's not Daniel, Papa."

"No, liebling," he said softly. "I didn't mean…" His voice drifted off before he changed the subject. "How long will you be gone?"

"I don't know," I answered. "I guess as long as it takes."

That was a week ago. We hadn't spoken much since.

I'd made arrangements to sublet my apartment and contacted the company that looked after our home down in Ocracoke. They assured me they could have the utilities turned back on and they'd even alert the old lady who lived next door of my arrival.

I didn't want to give the poor woman a heart attack.

So, after that, there hadn't been much else to do but pack.

I'd kind of hoped for more of a send-off than this, but I was just glad to not be alone.

"Okay, you'd better get going," Elena said before handing me the extra suitcase. "Shove it under the dashboard. It will fit."

Just as we were about to say our final good-bye, a car pulled up to the curb behind me. Elena looked over my shoulder, and her eyes widened slightly. I turned to see what she was looking at, and that was when I saw him.

He stepped out of his car, his dark blue eyes meeting mine. Elena stepped back, pretending to have a sudden interest in the landscaping around my apartment. I silently thanked her for the privacy.

"Curtis," I said. "What are you doing here?"

"Seeing you off," he answered. There was a touch of sadness in his voice. "And trying to give you a reason to come back."

He reached into his pocket and pulled out that velvet box I remembered from my birthday party.

I backed away, my eyes wide as I looked up at him. "Curtis, I can't—"

"I know," he answered. "I don't understand why, but I'm willing to wait."

"I don't want you to put your life on pause."

A look of shock blanketed his features. "What do you mean? Are you planning on being gone that long? I thought—"

"I don't know," I answered. "I quit my job."

I hadn't had the chance to explain everything to him. He'd barely returned any of my calls.

"You what?" He looked like he'd just been slapped across the face. "But why? Why would you do something so reckless?"

"It's not the first time," I admitted. There was so much I'd never told him about my life—before. "I need to do this, Curtis. Did you know I used to paint?"

He shook his head.

Of course he didn't. I'd never told him.

"It was my passion—the real reason I went to art school. And I haven't picked up a paintbrush since I left Ocracoke.

Something is pulling me back there, and I need to find out what."

"Something or someone?" He meant Daniel.

I winced. "I don't know," I answered honestly. "Maybe I am going back to try and revive a ghost. Maybe not. All I know is, I need to go. That part of my life feels unfinished."

"I thought *we* were building a life—"

"We were," I insisted. "We are!"

"Are you sure?" he asked softly. "I want to build a life with you—something real and lasting. But, I think the thought of that scares you."

I stared at the ring box in his hand, unsure of what to say.

"So, where does that leave us? Are you breaking up with me?"

He let out a sort of pained laugh. "Do you think I'd be holding this if I were?" He took a deep breath. "I don't want to lose you, Marin. I still want this," he said, his fingers brushing the green velvet. "Take the ring—"

"I can't—"

"You can," he insisted, placing it in my hand. His warm palm enclosed mine. The feel of that precious box in my hand felt all wrong—like I was unworthy of such a prize. "Take it. Put it in a dresser drawer or carry it around in your pocket. Just please take it and think about us and what you want for the future. And when you come back, you can either return it or…"

I can say yes.

He didn't say it, but the words hung in the air between us.

I felt my eyes well up with tears as I tried to will myself to stay. To say the words he desperately wanted to hear—that he was enough, that I would marry him and share every part of myself with him.

But every molecule in my body was telling me to leave— to go back to the place where I had lost everything.

If I was going to rise from the ashes, I might as well go back to the inferno.

And so, I said a tearful good-bye to Curtis and Elena, and then I drove away.

Ready for whatever might come.

I'd forgotten how long of a drive it was from Richmond to Ocracoke.

I'd also forgotten the amount of traffic that could pile up near Virginia Beach, so by the time I made it through that stupid tunnel and crossed the border into North Carolina, I'd been on the road for hours.

My back ached, and my eyes were tired.

And then I got to the ferry terminal.

"Shit," I whispered to myself as I pulled into the little store situated right at the entrance.

I promptly turned off the engine and just stared out at the water and the massive ferry docked at the shore.

Logically, I knew I had to board it to get to Ocracoke. I'd traveled on it many times during the few months Daniel and I had lived here. It wasn't like you could just drive there.

But up until now, I'd been so focused on everything else—from quitting my job and packing to saying good-bye to my family—that I'd completely shut out the pesky little part that involved the ferry.

And to make matters worse, the traffic had made me so late that my only option was the very last ferry of the day.

The same one Daniel had caught when—

I felt my breath start to hitch, and my eyes filled with tears. "No." I shook my head. "Not now. Not today."

Remembering what Dr. Matthews had taught me, I looked around, trying to find something unassuming and solid. I found the car parked in front of me and focused on the Florida license plate, specifically the vibrant oranges in the middle. I drew in each breath slowly, methodically, until I felt back in control.

I never stopped—even as my eyes pulled away from the license plate and I started my car. I pulled out of the parking lot and got in the queue. I felt every ragged breath go in and out of my lungs as I boarded that ferry.

And then I parked.

I'd done it.

I'd made it on the damn boat.

I bit my bottom lip, holding back five years' worth of emotions as we pulled away from the shore. I looked around as people emerged from their cars to go grab snacks and look over the rail at the water until, finally, the fucking dam broke.

Tears poured down my face like sheets of rain.

If anyone heard my sobs, they were kind enough to leave me to my grief.

It felt like another five years went by before we docked on the other side.

But when we finally did, my tears dried up, and I was ready to make my way onto Highway 12. Departing the ferry, I wasn't really sure what to expect.

Would things look different?

Would they be the same as I remembered?

But there was one thing to be sure of—I definitely hadn't expected it to be dark when I disembarked.

But it was.

Pitch-black dark.

I turned down the familiar road on the outskirts of town, remembering the way like the back of my hand.

Pulling into the driveway felt far too intimate, so I opted for the curb. Loose gravel crunched under my tires as I came to a halt and took my first look at the house in five years.

The maintenance company had done everything they'd promised and more. The landscaping was neat and tidy, the grass was cut and—

"Wait. What the hell? Why aren't the lights on?" I said out loud, furrowing my brow in confusion.

I cut the ignition and stepped out of the car, stretching my legs for the first time in what felt like forever. I took a cursory look around, checking out my neighbors' houses.

My two neighbors to the left and right of me were both home, their windows aglow with light.

The curtains were pulled tight, but I recognized the old truck of the middle-aged empty nesters who lived to the left. The wife had always been particularly interested in when we were going to start a family, offering babysitting if we ever needed it.

I really hoped she'd gained a bit more tact since then.

My neighbor on the right, the old lady who had a love for cats and baking, must have upgraded her late-model car because a shiny black SUV sat outside it, along with a sleek black truck.

Maybe she has family visiting?

Reaching back into the car, I grabbed my keys, which were still in the ignition, and my purse and made my way up the driveway.

Every step felt like a lead weight was attached to my heels.

Every step forward felt like a journey further into the past.

"Oh God, what was I thinking?" I breathed out as I stepped up to the door, my hand resting on the cool wood.

"It's perfect!" I said, turning my head toward him.

"You're going to paint that door, aren't you?" He grinned.

"You know me so well." I turned my head toward the boring black door. "What color? Blue? Green?"

"Whatever you want," he told me. "This is your island fantasy. I'm just here for the ride."

I let go of a shaky breath and unlocked the bright yellow door and took my first step over the threshold.

The air smelled stale and stagnant, and I could barely

make out the plastic coverings that remained on the furniture in the dark.

"So much for, 'No problem. We'll take care of it,' " I muttered, as my eyes shifted around the room.

I could make out the familiar shadows of the sofa and the large chair in the living room.

I immediately felt both uncomfortable and at home, all at once. It was like someone had taken all my emotions and tossed them up in the air, and I was still waiting to see which one would land on the ground first.

I walked over to the light switch and said a silent prayer, hoping they'd at least done one right thing. I flipped the switch.

Nothing happened.

I tried again. Nada.

"Son of a bitch," I said under my breath. I turned, unsure what to do, and the moment I did, my purse collided with the lamp on the small table. It fell with a thunderous crash, sending pieces of pottery flying all over the dusty wood floor.

I looked up to the heavens and tried counting to ten.

This is fine. Everything is fine.

I tried to ignore all the memories coming to the surface as I wandered through the dark house in search of a flashlight. I went to the kitchen first but came up empty-handed. And then I remembered Daniel used to keep one on his side of the bed, in case the power went out at night.

Which meant I had to go to the master bedroom.

Taking a deep breath, I headed down the hallway, placing a hand on the wall to help guide me. The small living room had been fairly easy to maneuver with moonlight streaming through the semi-sheer curtains, but the hallway was another story.

I felt like I was walking blind.

I found the first door on the left and entered. Not nearly as dark as the hallway, I was able to make out the shape of the bed and the dresser. There was no bedding. It had been stripped ages ago, and I took a moment to sit on the edge of the mattress, trying to remember the last time we had both been here.

Our time in Ocracoke had been an adjustment, to say the least.

So many nights spent alone in this bed.

The job Daniel had taken to make this possible came at a steep price.

Of course, neither of us had realized just how steep…

He'd called me from the airport that day, telling me he was going to miss his flight. I was so angry. It was our anniversary weekend, and he was going to miss it.

He had driven all night just to catch that last ferry.

"I don't know what I'm doing here, Daniel," I said softly, looking around the room, thinking of all the what-ifs.

What if I hadn't gotten mad at him?

What if he'd just waited for the next flight?

What if we'd never moved here?

The silence gave way until the sound of soft sobs echoed throughout the room.

It had only been a day, and I was already sick of crying.

I sucked in a deep breath, pulling myself together as I took one last glance around the room and rose to my feet.

I needed to find that flashlight. The luggage wasn't going to carry itself in, and I needed to sleep.

But the second I started to head for the nightstand, I heard a noise.

My body froze at the sound of the front door creaking open. I'd always bugged Daniel to fix it, hating the sound it made whenever we used it, but now, I was thanking my lucky stars that I'd had a husband proficient in procrastination.

Because I was pretty sure I had an intruder.

CHAPTER FOUR

Macon

"Do you have a new neighbor?" I asked, peering out the window like a damn Peeping Tom.

If I could shut off that part of my brain—the one that had been trained to notice everything and anything—I would. But I couldn't. So, the moment I saw those head-lights pull up to the curb outside Billy's house, all I could do was stare out his window.

I hadn't heard a word he'd said since.

"Uh, not that I know of," Billy answered, caught off guard by my question. "The house has been vacant since—" He averted his eyes, as his words cut off mid-sentence.

"Yeah, I know," I answered. "I know whose house it is."

Ever since he had bought this house a couple of years ago, I'd tried to pretend like I didn't know who lived next door. Like it wasn't this sad, vacant reminder of the life I'd ruined. Billy knew I hated talking about that day. He probably assumed it was the normal kind of guilt cops felt when they couldn't find a cause for such a senseless accident.

If only it were that simple.

We both got up and went to the window, putting our movie on pause to see if we could catch a glimpse of who had parked outside. But whoever it was, they were nowhere to be seen.

"Do you think they finally sold it?" he asked.

I just shook my head, my phone already in hand. "No houses have sold in Ocracoke this month. Or the month before."

"How do you know that?" he asked, looking seriously impressed.

I gave him a wry smile. "Zillow, dumbass."

"Oh." He gave a goofy grin, resembling the kid I remembered back in high school who could barely string two sentences together. "I thought you might have some super-secret database you could tap into for that kind of stuff."

"Yeah, I do," I answered, unable to help myself. "It's called Zillow."

"Asshole." He chuckled. "Maybe it's the owner. It would be the most logical answer."

"This late?" I glanced out his side window for a better look at the house. "And wouldn't they turn on a light?"

The house was pitch-black.

He shrugged. "I don't know. Maintenance company? I know she uses one. They're over there all the time, mowing the lawn and shit."

"Again, at this hour?"

He let out a huff. "You know, I don't hear you coming up with any viable options."

I peered through the glass, my eyes squinting as I tried to see into the dark landscape that separated the two houses.

"Did you hear that?" I asked, as the faint noise of something breaking pierced the silence. I couldn't remember the last time we'd had a break-in in Ocracoke, but it didn't mean it never happened.

My gut felt suddenly uneasy. The last time I'd let something go...

"I'd better go check it out," I finally said. "I'd hate to have to call the owner up tomorrow and tell her that her house had been broken into and I'd been next door, watching the whole damn thing."

"Well, you wouldn't necessarily have to mention the last part," he reminded me. "You are off duty."

I gave him a dubious stare. We both knew that I was never fully off duty. Not in this town. "I'll be back."

I stepped out into the cold night and swiftly walked across the grass. The car was parked far enough down the curb that I couldn't make out the plates in the dark.

What I wouldn't give for a flashlight right now.

I moved down the walkway, trying to get a look through the curtains, but with no lights on, it made it nearly impossible.

I walked up to the door and turned the handle. The hinges creaked so loudly that I might as well have just shouted my entrance. A few steps inside, and the floor groaned beneath me.

So much for being incognito.

I glanced down just as my feet hit a scattering of broken pottery. My eyes searched through the dark, trying to make sense of it. Looking up at the small table by the entry, I noticed a void.

Someone had broken a lamp.

"Time to come out now," I hollered, in the direction of the master. I hadn't noticed it outside, but now, I could see the faint glow of a flashlight coming from down the hallway.

Well, at least someone has a flashlight.

"You've had your fun," I said, trying to sound approachable and nonthreatening. If it was a teen or someone in need of help, the last thing I needed was for them to get scared and for this to escalate.

I didn't get a chance to finish my thought though because the second I started to open my mouth again, I saw that flashlight round the corner.

And then someone tackled me to the ground.

"What the fuck?" I yelled.

My hands went up, and they collided with the curvy lines of a woman. I pulled them back just as that flashlight came at the right angle.

"Shit!" she cursed.

"Shit!" I echoed.

I recognized her the second I saw her face—those dark brown eyes and silky chestnut hair. I was guessing by the shocked expression she was giving me as she lay frozen above me that she knew exactly who I was, too.

"Shit," she cursed again, finally scurrying off me to rise to her feet.

I did the same, taking a bit more time though as I brushed a bit of dust off my shirt.

"What the hell are you doing here?" I blurted out, so surprised to see her here that my sense of decorum went flying out the window.

"Me?" Her eyes went wide with surprise. "What the hell are *you* doing here?"

Damn, she's still just as hot as—

Nope. Not gonna think about that.

"I saw someone pull up to the house, and considering there were no lights on and I heard a crash, I figured I'd better make sure it wasn't being robbed."

She pulled the cardigan she was wearing tightly around her chest, like a protective shield. Her dark brown hair was pulled into a loose braid down her back, and her eyes were staring daggers into mine.

Marin Mendez.

I never thought I'd see her again.

I never wanted to either.

"They were supposed to leave the lights on for me," she said quickly, the words tumbling out of her mouth one after another.

"Who was?" I asked, confused as I looked around. The house resembled something out of one of those creepy, old movies.

"The maintenance company," she explained. "They were supposed to turn on the utilities, open up the house—you know, remove all of this." She pointed to all the clear wrapping that covered the furniture and all the dust that had settled on it. "And they were going to let Mary and the Floyds know I was coming."

I grimaced. "Well, that would be a little difficult—the last one, that is."

"What?" She furrowed her brow and nervously chewed her bottom lip, which only brought attention to it, and now, I couldn't seem to stare at anything else.

"Uh…oh, um…Mary died," I finally said, turning my eyes upward. "About three years ago. Billy Radcliffe lives there now."

"The restaurant owner?"

I nodded, sort of surprised she remembered him so quickly.

"He used to let Daniel…" She paused, pressing her lips together, as if the task of saying his name out loud was difficult. She audibly swallowed. "Um, he used to let my husband use the restaurant Wi-Fi for his Zoom meetings, back before…" She never finished her sentence.

Guilt gnawed at my gut at the mere mention of her late husband.

"Are you selling the house?" I finally asked, startling her somewhat.

Those dark brown eyes met mine, and it felt like a jolt of electricity running down my spine.

Don't stare, asshole. She's a fucking widow because of you.

"What? No," she answered softly. "I'm…" She hesitated.

I held up my hands, cutting her off. "No need to explain. None of my business anyway. I came over to make sure your house wasn't being broken into, and clearly, it isn't. So, I'll leave you to it."

I didn't wait for her to reply.

I simply headed for the door and walked away.

My only hope was that whatever had brought her here, it wouldn't take long. I did not need another ghost haunting me in Ocracoke.

***

"Fuck my life," I breathed out.

"You can say that again," Billy agreed as we both stood there with our arms crossed over our chests, watching the large patio area of his restaurant get turned into "gala central," as Molly liked to call it.

"And you actually agreed to this?" I asked, turning to him.

I'd been on patrol and stopped by to see how things were going. I'd had no idea I was going to walk into all this.

He shrugged. "Seemed like a good idea at the time."

"Couldn't say no, could you?" I grinned as he nervously watched the craziness unfold.

He took the towel he had swung over his shoulder moments earlier and blotted his forehead before letting out a defeated breath. "It's hard to say no to normal Molly Jameson. But pregnant Molly? She's fucking scary."

"And busy," I added, watching Molly, her sister, Millie, and several of their friends buzz around the restaurant, setting up chairs and tables. "What the hell is this anyway? I thought they were just selling tickets?"

He'd told me all about how Molly had begged him to use his patio space for selling tickets. But this? This was something he'd forgotten to mention.

"They are, but you know Molly. She couldn't just do halfway. She had to throw a bake sale to raise a little extra cash."

"And all the other crap?" I asked, motioning to the tables filled with jewelry, candles, and a bunch of fancy bath shit.

"I guess they figured if they were gonna sell food, might as well sell some other stuff, too. Fuck if I know. I don't even know what half that shit is."

"I thought gay guys were into bath salts and scented candles." I grinned, pointing to where Millie was stacking small tins of something or other on the table.

"That is the most cliché thing I've heard in a long time. And I live in the South."

I laughed before asking, "Hey, how's Eli doing?"

We hadn't gotten the chance to catch up nearly as much as I wanted to the other night. Running into Marin Mendez had put a bit of a damper on my mood, and I'd left after that.

He sighed. "Good, I guess. Travels a lot."

"Still not set on moving here?"

He shook his head. "Would you be? He grew up in the Bronx. I might as well be asking him to move to Mars."

Billy had met Eli a year ago online, and they'd been doing the long-distance thing ever since. I honestly didn't know how they managed when both of them had such busy schedules, but he seemed happy regardless.

Even if he hadn't told a single soul on the island but me.

"Well, this seems to be under control. Guess I'd better get back to"—I paused for effect—"absolutely nothing."

He laughed. "Maybe you have nothing to do because you've done such a stellar job of keeping us all safe."

"I wouldn't be so sure," I said, remembering a time when I definitely hadn't done a stellar job—as Billy called it—of keeping the town safe.

"I'll see you—"

"Macon!" Millie hollered, interrupting my exit.

"Fuck my—"

"Life," Billy finished. "Yeah, we get it. You'd better go see what she wants." He chuckled, his broad shoulders bouncing up and down. "At least you're not bored."

I tried not to roll my eyes before I headed toward Millie's table of…whatever. I found her hanging small, carved ornaments on a display while her husband stood next to her. At his side, there was a large golden retriever, wearing a vest around its chest.

"I didn't realize you'd gotten a service dog," I said to Aiden.

Although he and I barely knew each other, the blind artist seemed to know everyone's voice, and he turned toward me as I stopped in front of them.

"Yeah, about a month ago," he answered.

His British accent always caught me off guard. We didn't exactly have many English folks down this way.

Well, unless you counted the dead ones in the British cemetery.

"Her name is Helen."

Millie rolled her eyes.

Not wanting to get involved in whatever that was, I simply stood there, waiting for whatever reason it was that I had been summoned.

"He named his dog after Helen Keller. He thinks he's hilarious."

"Helen Keller was a badass. You're just upset I didn't take any of your suggestions."

A slight grin tugged at the corner of his mouth, and I tried not to react. I did not want the wrath of Millie McIntyre.

"You hollered," I said, giving her a pointed glance.

"Oh, right. Molly told me not to let you leave without buying a ticket. So, I didn't."

"To the gala?" I said.

She nodded.

"No, thanks."

"But it's for charity."

"I realize that," I said.

"And you're a major part of the community."

"I already give enough to this town," I stressed. "Why would I want to dress up and waste an evening out?"

"To charm us with your award-winning personality?" She snickered while her husband tried to act invisible.

I simply stared.

"Okay, but good luck telling that to Molly." She shrugged as she continued setting up her table.

"What? I just told it to you."

"Look, it was my job to keep you from leaving. And that's what I'm doing," she explained before pointing over my shoulder. "Oh, look. There's Molly! Bye, Macon!"

Every day, I told myself I should just move. And every damn day, I went to bed and woke up and then did the same thing over and over again.

Why do I hate myself so much?

As I was turning my head, prepared to tell Molly Jameson exactly where she could shove that gala ticket of hers, I heard that telltale sound of a female cooing.

You know the sound? The high-pitched noise a woman made when in the presence of a puppy, a designer handbag…

Or a baby.

"Captain Macon!" The sheriff's voice grated against my ears as he began walking to meet me with that stupid shit-eating grin plastered across his face.

"Sheriff Hayes," I said stoically.

I'd forgotten how much he loved showing up at events like these. Since our county encompassed both Ocracoke and part of the mainland, the Sheriff only came to town when it pleased him.

Or when it made him look good.

Today was one of those days.

"Come meet our little one," he said with a slight emphasis on the word *our*.

It wasn't a request.

I gritted my teeth and walked with him, just in time to see my ex-wife turn, her eyes bright with excitement and energy.

"Macon." Her smile faltered.

Well, at least I could still get some reaction out of her.

"I guess congratulations are in order," I managed to say.

"Oh, um, yes. Thank you."

"Isn't he just perfect?" Hayes butted in as he snaked a hand around my shoulder and gave me a friendly pat.

If my job wasn't dependent on this guy, I would punch him so hard that he'd be on the other side of the country with a palm tree stuck up his ass.

I took an honest look at the newborn, and I hated to admit it, but he was quite precious, at least as far as babies went. His cheeks were pink, and he had light-blond hair that matched his mother's.

Thankfully, I didn't have to answer his slightly rhetorical question because Molly chose that exact moment to interrupt our uncomfortable reunion.

I hadn't wanted to talk to her a moment ago, but right now, she was a fucking lifesaver.

"Hey, Macon," she said, walking toward one of the tables. I took that as a cue to follow her. "You coming to the gala?"

"I don't think so. Not really my thing."

"Not going?" someone echoed behind me.

I turned to see Sheriff Hayes hot on my heels.

"You have to go," he said decisively.

I had a feeling the phrase *fuck my life* was going to be the motto of the day.

"I'm pretty sure I don't," I argued. "I've looked at my job description a few times, and I don't recall any mention of mandatory gala attendance."

His arms crossed his broad chest, and he stood a little taller—an obvious attempt to make his authority known. "It would be in bad form for you not to attend, Macon. You and I need to show a united front and make sure the town knows we support them."

Fucking hated it when he used my first name.

We were not on a first-name basis before you fucked my wife, and we certainly aren't now.

"You really should attend," Kristy chimed in, coming to stand next to her husband, which just made the situation all the more uncomfortable. "People will expect it."

My jaw twitched, hearing her try to offer up an opinion on the matter. Like she still had ownership of my life.

"I'm sure no one will care."

Hayes gave me a stern stare before sliding a possessive arm around Kristy's shoulder. A wide smile spread across his face, knowing I'd seen it.

"Come on, Macon. It will be fun. We've got a babysitter all lined up, and I can't wait to put on a fancy dress and—"

Her words faltered, as if she'd finally just realized who she was rambling on to.

Yeah, me. The one you used to dress up for.

"So much fun," Hayes echoed, his smile widening.

"It's not really my thing," I said between gritted teeth. "And besides—"

"Besides what?" Hayes said.

I let out a sigh, hating the fact that they were making me say it out loud. "I don't—"

"He wasn't sure if I could go," a familiar voice said from behind me.

Before I had a chance to see who it was, a slender, warm hand slid into mine. Our fingers wove together, and I felt a zing of electricity.

Who the hell—

"Marin?" Molly said just as I turned to see the would-be intruder from the other night.

"Molly!" She broke our connection to step forward, giving her a huge hug. "It's so good to see you."

"I didn't know you were in town."

"I only just arrived the other day, and this is my first time out," Marin explained.

Kristy gave her an appraising look, and then her gaze shifted to mine.

Don't look at me. I have no fucking clue what's going on either.

"Are you staying long?" Molly asked.

"Oh, um, I think so. I am kind of winging it."

Kristy, still looking unconvinced, chimed in, "And you

and Macon are…" And I saw the side of her I always chose to ignore—the one that gossiped about her friends and threw backhanded compliments to her coworkers—rise to the surface.

"Oh." A shy smile crept across her face as she wrapped her hand back tightly around mine. I felt that same jolt. "It's kind of complicated. We've kept in touch a bit here and there since I moved back to Richmond, and when I got in the other night"—she looked up at me—"we just sort of ran into each other."

More like collided.

She looked back at the three pairs of eyes. "We've been kind of inseparable ever since."

What the actual hell is happening?

Molly, the hopeless romantic, was buying the load of shit she was selling, but Kristy was still giving her an appraising glare.

"And you're going to the gala? Together?"

"Well, I was trying to talk him into it the other night, and then I wasn't sure if I could go," she said and then turned directly to Kristy. "I don't get to dress up often, and I'd love to see this guy in a suit. Wouldn't you?" Her other hand went up to my chest—a possessive move my ex didn't miss.

"Well, I guess we won't hold you two up then," Kristy said in a tone I remembered all too well.

She was pissed.

"I can grab those tickets for you, Macon."

"What?" I said, feeling like my mind was coming out of a fog bank.

"The gala tickets," Molly reminded me. "Or is Marin paying?"

"Oh, no. I got it," I answered, somewhat bewildered.

While Molly and Marin continued to catch up, I pulled out my wallet. So many questions were circling around in my brain as I watched Molly run my credit card and hand us the info about the gala.

"I'm sure Macon already told you, but we raise money for the relief fund in town. It helps out when people need money rebuilding after a storm or—"

"When they need to get to the hospital after a ferry accident."

She gave Marin a warm smile. "Yes, exactly."

"Thank you for everything you did that day," Marin said. "I've never forgotten it."

"I didn't do anything," Molly argued, clearly overwhelmed by her kindness.

"You held my hand on that plane and let me vent. It was exactly what I needed at that moment."

Molly looked like she was going to burst into tears at any second, but she managed to hold it together.

Hearing them talk about the ferry accident was like getting hit with a bucket of ice water, reminding me who I was standing next to.

"I, um," I stuttered, "I need to get back to work."

Looking like a complete idiot, I pivoted around and hauled ass out of there without another word.

Gala or no, the last thing Marin needed in her life was me.

CHAPTER FIVE

Marin

What the hell?

Did he really just run off?

I stood there at the booth as Molly stared at me from across the table, holding out the tickets Macon had just paid for.

"Yeah, um, he does that sometimes," she said with a slight shrug. "Macon isn't known for his tact. Or manners."

I turned back toward the road. There was no sign of him. If this was a cartoon, there would be a trail of smoke behind him.

That was how fast he'd wanted to get away.

From me.

"Oh," I said, plastering a fake smile across my face. "I know. He's, um …" What did I say? I barely knew the guy. "Unique."

Sure, that sounds fine.

We finished catching up, and I did a little shopping at her sister's booth, grabbing a pair of earrings for Elena and a scented candle for me. After five years of being closed up, the house could use a bit of vanilla lavender. After that, I grabbed a sandwich at the corner store and headed back home.

I spent the rest of the afternoon unpacking and trying to settle.

Trying being the operative word.

Around five or so that evening, I found myself pacing around the house.

Why?

Because I couldn't stop thinking about Macon running off.

And it seriously pissed me off.

I'd done that man a huge-ass favor, and he'd bailed on me?

I found the gala tickets sitting on my kitchen counter and looked at the date. It was four weeks away.

Four weeks.

I'd had no timeline when I came down here. No sense of urgency, but four weeks seemed like a lifetime, especially when the last two days in this house had dragged on like an eternity.

I had known it was going to be hard, going back into that house, but the reality of it was far worse.

I'd thought I would feel Daniel everywhere in this house.

I'd thought his presence would be so overwhelming that I would drown in it.

But I'd forgotten how little he was here.

How few memories we'd actually made here.

And now, I felt even more alone.

That was how I'd ended up at Billy's today. It used to be Daniel's favorite place—one of the few benefits he'd gained from working remotely.

Maybe I'd feel his presence there.

We'd only lived here a few short months, but even I knew about the scandal between the captain and his wife. You'd have had to be living under a rock to not hear about how she'd gotten pregnant, cheating on him with the sheriff.

You would think, after five years, they'd leave the poor guy alone, right?

Of course not.

The minute I'd stepped on that patio, I knew I'd just walked into a standoff. Macon's tense posture, the sheriff's wolfish grin.

I might have eavesdropped a little.

Aside from that late-night break-in, I didn't know the guy at all, but this? This was unacceptable.

So, I just reacted. I marched up there, butted into their conversation, and lied my ass off.

And it worked. Macon's ex was pissed.

But then he'd just stormed off?

Without even saying *thank you*?

Well, fuck that.

Ocracoke was small. When you took out the rental properties, it was even smaller. It was easy to figure out where the captain lived.

And it was time to pay him a visit.

I stepped out into the cool autumn evening, closing my door behind me. "He can take those gala tickets and shove it," I muttered.

It didn't take long to get there, especially when I was speed walking.

By the time I got to the front door, I was short on breath, but my temper was as long as they came.

As soon as I held my hand up to knock, the door swung open. Judging by the note of surprise on his face, he had not opened it for me.

"What the fuck?" he said, taking a step back.

His hazel eyes were ablaze with shock at the sight of me. He had a tiny scar over his left eyebrow.

"You say that a lot around me."

"That's 'cause you just keep showing up," he said, still looking confused as hell.

"Well, if you'd stop storming off, maybe I wouldn't have to."

He grimaced slightly. "Look, I don't know why you did what you did, but it wasn't necessary."

"Wasn't necessary?" I laughed. "You were getting your ass handed to you."

That scarred eyebrow rose as he leaned against the doorframe, those muscled biceps slowly folding across his broad chest. "I can assure you, I never get my ass handed to me."

No, I bet you don't.

His voice was as smooth as hot chocolate, and I didn't know why, but suddenly, my legs felt jiggly.

"Well, you don't have to go, but a little *thank you* wouldn't hurt."

He pushed off the doorframe, and it was the first time I realized how tall he was. He had at least a foot on me, and with our bodies this close, I had to crane my neck upward to look at him.

And what a view.

Stop it.

You're mad at him, remember?

"A *thank you*?" He scoffed. "Seriously? You didn't do me a favor. If anything, you just made things worse."

"What?" I took a step back. Now, I was the one confused. "Why? Just find someone else to go with if you're so worried." With a body like that, I was sure he had options.

Does he work out? 'Cause damn.

"Well, in case you forgot in the five years you've been away or maybe you just never figured this little tidbit out since you're a dingbatter—"

"I hate that term," I said, referring to the word people used to differentiate ex-mainlanders, like me, from the real locals who'd been born here.

"Yeah, well, I do, too, in most cases, but Ocracoke is set in its ways. And one thing it excels in is gossip. And it spreads like wildfire. You standing there today at Billy's, telling everyone we're *inseparable*? By tomorrow, the entire island will be planning our wedding."

My eyes widened. Shit, I hadn't thought about that. "I just wanted to wipe that stupid grin off the sheriff's face."

The dark shadow hung like a cloud over him. "I've been trying to do that for years. Never works. He always gets the upper hand."

"So, if you wind up at the gala alone or not at all?"

He shrugged. "Just add it to an already-long list of shit he likes to throw in my face."

"How do you put up with him?" I grimaced. *What a slimeball.*

"He's my superior. Don't exactly have a choice."

I mulled over my next words for a moment before I spoke. "So, then we go to the gala."

His eyes met mine before he shook his head. "No," he insisted. "It's fine. It will blow over in a few weeks, and he'll have his fun. I'll figure it out. Besides, I don't want to be anyone's charity case."

I bit my bottom lip before an idea came to mind. "You won't be."

His eyebrow rose, and I tried not to notice all the wonderful things it did to his handsome face. "I seem to remember you being pretty handy, correct?"

"I fix a lot of cars around town, but I can do pretty much anything. Why?"

"Well, the maintenance company I hired did an excellent job of keeping up the outside of the house, but the inside—"

"Houses don't like to sit around," he stated.

I nodded in agreement. I had a feeling the man standing in front of me didn't either. "I have a laundry list of things that are either not working or on their last leg."

"Like the creaky floor?"

I thought about the less-than-stealthy way he'd walked into my house my first night back. "Yeah, I guess so."

"So, what? You want me to be your personal handyman, and in exchange, you'll go with me to this stupid ball—"

"Gala," I corrected him.

"Whatever." He rolled his eyes.

"Yes, exactly."

"You're forgetting one thing," he said.

"What?" I looked up at him.

"I don't want to go to the gala." He shrugged. "Like, not even a little."

"Not even to make your ex jealous?" I teased.

"What makes you think she'll be jealous?"

I gave him a smug grin. "You haven't seen me in a dress yet."

His eyes heated as he took in the length of my body, giving me an instant shiver down my spine. "And after the gala?"

I shrugged. "I'll go back to Richmond, and we can go back to our own lives. You can say we tried long-distance, or you flat-out dumped me. It doesn't matter, but at least you'll get the satisfaction of seeing your ex-wife's face when you walk in with me at your side. And I'm sure that will drive the sheriff crazy."

"And you think this can all be achieved in one night?"

"I mentioned the dress, right?" I was really overselling this dress that I didn't have. "They'll care."

I waited for him to mull it over, which felt like an eternity. I didn't know why I wanted him to say yes so much.

I didn't know what I was doing.

I really hadn't been sure since the second I'd walked onto the patio.

But it was the most excited and alive I'd felt in a long time.

His intense gaze met mine. "All right, deal."

Turned out that life in Ocracoke was going to be anything but dull.

If there was one thing I had learned about Macon Green in the last twenty-four hours, it was that he was not a sit-around-and-chill kind of guy.

The next day, at promptly eight o'clock in the morning, he was at my door, banging away.

Jolting upright in bed, I looked around the bedroom, still trying to adjust to my surroundings, and quickly rose to my feet.

The knocking continued.

"What the actual hell?" I grumbled, rubbing the sleep from my eyes.

Shuffling down the hall as quickly as I could muster, I went to the door and pulled it open with a huff. "Do you have any idea what time—" I stopped short of finishing my sentence.

Macon was dressed in plain clothes today, his muscly body filling out his tight-fitting T-shirt perfectly. His hazel eyes flared with heat as they slid down my body.

"What?" I asked.

He cleared his throat and finally broke eye contact, looking upward. "Do you always answer your door without pants?"

This time, it was me whose eyes were nearly popping out of my head as I looked down to see my naked legs and a barely there Guns N' Roses T-shirt. "Shit!" I exclaimed, pivoting on my heel to run back to my bedroom. "Make yourself at home. There's coffee in the pantry," I hollered.

I honestly didn't even remember falling asleep, let alone the attire in which I'd done it in. Sleep hadn't been coming easy here.

Too many emotions and not enough time to sort them all.

While I was grabbing a pair of pants, I took a moment to brush my teeth and hair and change out of the shirt I'd slept in. It wasn't a shower, but it was enough for now.

Walking back down the hallway, I found myself stopping dead in my tracks. Macon was standing at the counter, filling the coffeepot with water, his back facing me.

It should have been an odd sight—another man in my

kitchen. But somehow, he seemed like he belonged there. Like he'd been here a hundred times.

"Morning," he said, not bothering to turn around.

"How did you even know—" I'd barely made a sound.

"I might be a small-town cop, but that doesn't mean I'm a bad one," he said before he pressed the button on the coffee maker and turned around. "Besides, creaky floor, remember?"

I blushed a little, remembering the way I'd tackled him the other night, thinking he was a burglar. I had been really glad he wasn't 'cause I wasn't sure what my next move would have been after that. "Oh, right."

"Does the master still have floral wallpaper?"

My mouth opened and then promptly closed. "What?"

He leaned against the counter, and I tried not to stare at him. I didn't know why it was so difficult. It wasn't like I'd never seen a hot guy before.

My boyfriend was good-looking.

Shit.

My boyfriend…

I hadn't even called him since I'd gotten here.

"Horrible floral wallpaper with orange and pink blooms?"

His answer brought me back into the conversation. I'd contemplate my boyfriend situation later.

"You—" How did he know about that horrid wallpaper? It was the first thing I'd changed after we moved in. "How?"

He might be a good cop, but no one was that good.

The corner of his mouth curved upward into the tiniest grin. "A friend of mine from grade school used to live here. I've actually spent a lot of time in this house."

I opened my mouth, looking shocked before I finally caved and broke into a laugh. "Seriously?"

"Welcome to Ocracoke. I'm pretty sure I know the layout of every house on the island for one reason or another."

I guessed that explained why having him here felt so natural. He had a connection to my house.

To the house, I reminded myself.

Not you.

"So, what's up first?" He quirked a brow.

"What? Oh, right." *How could I forget about that?* "The to-do list."

"That is why I'm here on my only day off this week."

My brow lifted. "You only get one day off a week? That's not right."

"We're down a deputy, so Deputy Lucas and I are covering the extra shifts while the sheriff finds a replacement. It's taking longer than usual."

That brow of his rose again, and I realized I hadn't answered his question yet.

"Oh, right. The list." I looked around, trying to remember where I'd put it. As I scanned the room, I caught him looking at me.

Not just looking, but staring, like he couldn't help himself.

"Um," I said in a flustered tone, remembering I'd done some panic cleaning last night when I realized he'd be in my house. "I think it's in this drawer."

I took a step forward, which put me right next to him. I could feel his body heat, and his arm brushed against mine. I quickly pulled open the drawer and rifled around until I found the list.

It wasn't the only thing I found.

Hidden in the back, just out of view, was a certain emerald-green box.

I'd had it in my purse for a while, but then I got scared I'd lose it, so I put it in my dresser drawer, but then I'd realized I couldn't look at it without an immense amount of guilt.

The kind of guilt I was feeling now.

Seeing it sitting there was like a punch to the gut, and I felt ashamed for every lewd thought I'd had since I'd collided with Macon.

This is not why you're here.

I quickly pulled out the list and slammed the drawer closed.

"Here it is," I said sort of abruptly. "Up here are the things that don't work, and down here, I've listed the things that work, but not well."

He took the list and scanned it over quickly. "This shouldn't be too hard."

"Seriously?" I blurted out, taking a step back. I needed some space. Standing that close to him felt like there wasn't enough oxygen in the room. "That list is, like, a mile long."

He shrugged. "It will probably be a matter of finding replacement parts, which will require a trip off the island."

I gulped.

Oh, good. Another trip on the ferry.

As if sensing my uneasiness, he added, "But we can worry about that later. I'll just check things out today and let you know what I find out."

I let out an audible breath and nodded. He took that as a cue to start looking around, but not before filling up a large mug of coffee first.

Once he was gone, I made a beeline to the coffeepot myself and poured the biggest cup I could find, adding two packets of sweetener and a tiny bit of cream. The first taste was heaven, and it had me wondering if there was anything this man couldn't do well.

A few hours later, I was sitting on the couch, going through freelance websites, feeling less than enthused with my options.

I'd quit a perfectly good job.

It wasn't the first time I had done it either.

But at least with the first time, I'd had Daniel.

And Daniel's stable income.

Now, I was on my own, and I knew my small savings account would only hold me for so long, so if I was going to stay down here for an undetermined amount of time, I had to try and find a source of income.

Even if it was some shitty freelance gig.

Just as I was about to hit Send on a mind-numbing job that would no doubt drain the last drop of artistic talent I had left, I heard the door creak open, and Macon burst through.

"We have company!" he announced in a tone I'd never heard him use. It was light and warm and...*weird*.

"We?" I asked before he gave me a pointed stare.

I was about to raise my shoulders in the universal shrug that was the known body language for *what*, but as I did, he stepped aside, and Molly walked in with a giant basket on her arm.

Oh, I see. *We* did have company.

I hadn't really thought this gala gig through when we'd agreed on it.

I'd just really wanted to make his ex pay.

And the free housework? Total bonus.

Everything else, though? Didn't even cross my mind.

Good thing I took that semester of acting in high school...

"Oh my gosh," I exclaimed, rising to my feet to help her. "What is all this?"

"A *welcome home* basket or a *welcome back* basket," she said before adding with a wave of her hand, "I don't know. Pregnancy makes me want to bake even more, so here, take it, before my husband sees it and gets all growly."

She handed it off, and I took it from her and nearly fell over.

"This thing weighs a ton," I exclaimed, setting it on the counter and taking a peek inside.

There were cookies, brownies, and just about everything else in between. My empty stomach growled at the mere sight.

Yum.

"I tried to take it off her hands, but she insisted on being the one to give it to you," Macon said, his tone more in line with what I was used to—annoyed.

I'd been so overwhelmed by the basket that I didn't even notice he'd taken up residence at my side. And it wasn't like he was just casually standing next to me, like two friends waiting for a latte at the coffee shop.

No, he was standing *with* me.

His arm brushed mine, and then, like he'd done it a million times before, he absently linked his pinkie with mine while he spoke, never stumbling over a single word.

Meanwhile, my heart rate skyrocketed, and it took every ounce of my willpower not to look down at our linked hands.

I knew I'd been the first to do this specific maneuver, but he seemed to be the master at it. That single touch set my skin on fire.

"Thanks for making that cake the other day," he said to Molly, carrying on a conversation while I tried to ignore the way his fingers slightly curled, brushing my palm. "I hadn't expected a whole damn cake."

Is he immune to this?

Does it not affect him at all?

"Oh, it was no trouble. I was happy to do it. Did they like it?" she asked.

He absently shrugged. "No idea," he answered. "I just dropped it off at their door with a note."

Molly's mouth fell open. "You just left it at the door? You didn't even hang around to see the look on their face or—"

"No." His tone changed as a dark cloud seemed to loom over his head. "They didn't need me hanging around on a day like that."

"Well, it was generous of you nonetheless."

It appeared, whatever or whoever they were talking about, that Macon didn't seem to agree.

An awkward silence settled between the three of us, reminding me just how little I knew about Molly. I'd seen her around town, but that was all.

I'd never gotten the chance to meet her.

"We should do dinner," I blurted out before I had a chance to consider what I was saying.

Both Macon and Molly looked at me with wide eyes. Molly at least had the decency to recover quickly, replacing her shock with an encouraging smile.

Macon, however?

He was looking at me like I'd just sprouted a second head.

A second head who was inviting everyone to dinner.

"Um…" I managed to say. *Can't take it back now.* "Yeah." I swallowed hard. "Macon and I were just talking about how I don't know anyone on the island."

His eyebrow rose just the tiniest bit, and I knew he was fighting to keep it together.

"And I thought, who better to start with than you?"

Molly stared briefly at me, and then her eyes traveled to Macon.

I could see the indecision all over her face.

Was it me? Maybe I'd overestimated our budding friendship and just made everything super weird?

"That sounds great," Molly finally said, sounding genuinely excited. "But I have to make one request." Her hand rested on her small baby bump, and a sheepish smile formed on her lips.

"Sure," I said. "Anything."

"Let me host it?" she said, and before I could even open my mouth to protest, she beat me to it. "It's off-season, and the inn is almost empty at the moment, and I'm going stir-crazy. This basket is an example of what happens when I have nothing to do. When I say I want to host it, I'm not asking to be nice."

I looked up to Macon, who hadn't said a thing. He still had a hold of my pinkie, that thumb slowly rubbing the skin above my wrist. His touch sent electricity down my spine, and he still seemed completely unaffected.

In fact, since I'd blurted out my idea about the would-be

dinner party, his facial features had gone almost completely neutral.

What is going on up there in that head of yours, Macon Green?

"Okay, sure," I answered, deciding for the both of us.

"Here," she said, holding out her hand. "Let me give you my number. I'll check with Jake tonight and see what his availability is—he goes up to the hospital after the clinic closes sometimes," she explained. "You two can do the same, and then we can pick a date."

I handed her my phone with the Contacts open, nodding my head. "Sure, sounds good."

She left shortly after that, and I followed her to the door. We said our good-byes, and as I watched her car pulling away, I turned to see Macon pacing the floor like a lion.

A really pissed-off lion.

Oh boy.

What had I gotten myself into?

CHAPTER SIX

Macon

"A dinner party?" I said, the words grating against my tongue like sandpaper. "A fucking dinner party, Marin?"

I had visions of Kristy dragging me to never-ending parties, where we'd stand around, listening to her vapid friends and their arrogant fucking husbands.

"You're angry," she said, her voice hesitant as she watched me from across the room. She didn't even bother to form it as a question.

I guessed the rampant pacing back and forth might have given it away.

"I don't remember that being part of our deal," I argued, taming my voice. I hadn't meant to scare her.

"I don't remember it *not* being part of our deal," she countered, her arms folding across her chest as she tilted her head toward me.

I let out a long sigh, grabbing the bridge of my nose as I mentally went over the last hour in my head, trying to figure out how I'd managed to get from there to here.

I'd been outside, minding my own business, working on a long list of parts I'd need to get on the mainland when a car drove up.

That was when Molly and her giant basket of food stepped out.

Instant panic.

What did I do? Did I greet her like I was Marin's boyfriend?

Was I a boyfriend?

It wasn't like Marin and I had worked up any kind of backstory.

Up until that moment, I'd thought we could just lie low until the gala. I'd do her repairs, avoid her as much as possible, and then this would all be over.

But then I remembered where I lived—on an island where the biggest form of entertainment was talking about each other's life.

I was so in over my head.

So, I just went with my gut and greeted Molly like I owned the place, and then I kind of winged the rest. I walked into the house and played the part of Marin's new love interest a little *too* well.

God, I should have never touched her.

In doing so, my mind was swirling, and most of those thoughts were less than honorable.

I should have said no to the whole thing the second she had brought it up. I wasn't even sure why I'd agreed to it.

That wasn't true.

I knew exactly why I'd agreed to it, and it had nothing to do with screwing over the sheriff or making Kristy jealous. Gala or no, I couldn't give two shits what they thought of me.

Saving face wasn't what had made me say yes. It was her.

When she'd brought up that long list of things that needed to be fixed, I knew I couldn't say no. I would have just offered to do it all for her, free of charge, but I had a feeling she would have never agreed to that kind of deal. She was far too stubborn for that.

Call it guilt. Call it atonement.

Whatever it was, I had to do this one small thing for her.

It would by no means make up for what she had lost, but by the end of this ridiculous bargain, at least she'd have a safe house to live in or sell.

But in my haste to say yes, I really hadn't thought any of it through.

And now, we were going to a dinner party.

Fuck my life. Again.

"I'm sorry," she said, her voice still soft and hesitant. "I don't know what came over me. I—" She cleared her throat, as if she were trying to stir up a bit of confidence. "I should have asked you first. I completely understand if you don't want to go. I don't expect you to want to spend time with me any more than necessary."

"That's not—shit." I let out a frustrated breath. She thought I didn't like her?

I flopped down on her sofa, angry with myself for the confusion I had caused. The action apparently surprised her because she stared at me like I was some sort of zoo animal.

Yeah, well, you freak me out, too.

"It's not you…" I tried to find the words, but this woman seemed to make every last one of them fall out of my head simultaneously. "I hate Molly's husband."

Her eyebrows rose, and her lips pressed together until, finally, a laugh erupted. "You what?"

"Jake, her husband," I began to explain. "I can't stand the guy."

"Why?"

"What do you mean, why?"

"Why don't you like him?" she asked, taking a seat in the chair across from me. She tucked her legs under her, fitting into the chair like a puzzle piece. "There has to be a reason."

"There's no reason," I lied. There were lots of reasons. I could make a whole fucking list. "I just don't like him."

She cocked her head. "That doesn't even seem fair. If there isn't a reason, how do you even know if you don't like him?"

"I…" *Fuck.* I really didn't want to answer that. "He doesn't like me either."

A smirk tugged at the corner of her lips. "Kind of childish, if you ask me."

"I didn't." I glared at her.

Her grin widened.

Seriously, stop staring.

"So, what'd you discover? About my house? Is it going to cost me a fortune to fix everything?"

The way she had changed the subject felt like whiplash.

"What? Wait, that's it? No more talking about the dinner thing?"

She shrugged. "I'm not sure what there is to talk about. I already said we'd go. Do you want to back out?"

I gave her a look that said that was exactly what I wanted to do.

She gave me an exasperated sigh. "Look, I'm sorry I overstepped. I didn't know you had such a long, complicated history with Jake," she said, rolling her eyes. "I wasn't really thinking when I asked her. It just sort of came out. I didn't realize that would mean we would have to—"

Pretend.

I looked away, hoping she wouldn't see my reaction. Because as it turned out, pretending to like her wasn't all that hard for me. In fact, I didn't need to pretend at all.

And wasn't that a whole fucking problem on its own?

"But asking her over for dinner did come from a genuine desire to get to know people on the island. That was something I never had the chance to do before."

How long exactly was she planning on staying?

"And Molly seems like a good person."

"She's one of the best," I agreed.

"You just can't say the same for her husband?" she teased with that same note of humor in her voice.

I let out a long sigh. "He's a decent human being. I just—"

"Can't stand the guy," she finished. "I got that part."

I could see how much she wanted this, but I could not be that guy for her. I wanted to; I really did.

And that was exactly why I couldn't.

"I can put up with him for a night," I finally answered. "We manage to not kill each other in a professional setting. I guess we can manage this as well."

"Really?" Her eyes lit up, and I swore my chest tightened at the mere sight.

"The whole town thinks we're dating," I quickly added, my words diminishing her excitement almost as quickly as it had come. "Might as well keep up the charade."

"Right," she said softly. "Good idea."

I rose to my feet and went to the door. I needed to get out of here before I said something I regretted.

"I'm gonna head out, but I'll be back around tomorrow evening to work on a few things."

"Oh, right. Sure. Thanks."

I knew my comment had stung, but that had been the intent.

I was not the hero Marin thought I was.

And no one in the room needed that reminder more than me.

To say work was difficult the next day would be the understatement of the century.

I'd never been more distracted in my life. I hated the way I had left things with Marin.

I shouldn't be this affected by someone I barely knew.

And out of everyone on the planet, she was the last person I should be thinking about.

"Green, did you hear what I said?" Sheriff Hayes barked at me from across the room.

Why the fuck was he even here? There were no events on

the island today. No photo ops or journalists. He'd been texting someone on his phone all damn day.

God, I hoped he wasn't cheating on Kristy.

"What?" I answered him, leaning back in my chair to meet his gaze.

"Did you notice those kids?"

"Oh, yeah," I answered. "By the harbor? I've talked to them a few times before. Lucas has, too. They're harmless. Just bored."

He didn't seem convinced, his arms folding one over the other as he leaned against his desk. It was bare, except for the single family photo by the computer. He never left anything here—almost like he was paranoid and didn't trust me. *Weird.* "Bored kids tend to get in trouble."

I resisted the urge to roll my eyes. It wasn't that he didn't trust all bored kids.

Just these bored kids. The kind who had parents who worked on the fishing vessels or in the kitchens.

Sheriff Hayes was a snob, and to make matters worse, he was a snob with a badge.

"We'll keep an eye out on them," I half-heartedly assured him. "Have you ever considered talking to them yourself? Or their parents?"

"Why would I do that?"

That's why he has peons like me.

"They're part of the community," I pressed. "I know they don't donate to your reelection campaign, but it still might be worth it."

He just scowled at me.

"How is the deputy search going? Find anyone in the last round of interviews?"

"Oh," he began, and somehow, I already knew what he would say. "We had a few promising leads, but nothing panned out."

They'd been interviewing for months now, and nothing ever seemed to "pan out". I knew Ocracoke was a hard position to fill, but I had a sneaking suspicion that Sheriff Hayes wasn't exactly too keen on filling it.

Knowing Lucas and I were both down here, working our asses off, six days a week didn't seem to bother him one bit.

"So, what's the deal with you and that woman?" Hayes blurted out.

I looked up at him like he'd just asked me to solve a complex math equation.

"What?" I asked.

"I just didn't know you were dating. Seems kind of out of the blue."

My jaw tightened. "I didn't know you were dating my wife either. We're not exactly chatty."

Hard lines formed across his brow, and I saw a flash of anger before his expression went back to neutral. "Man, I thought we were over this."

A pained laugh escaped me. "Whatever, *man*," I echoed. "I'm just saying we don't have to discuss our personal lives to work together. We never have."

He held his hands up like he was waving a white flag, like I was the one attacking him. "Fine. You're right," he conceded. "You're right. But…"

There was always a *but* with this guy.

"I only asked because she's the Mendez woman, right?"

"Right." My eyes narrowed as I glared at him from across the room.

"Well, I just brought it up because I wanted to make sure you knew what you were doing. I mean, her husband died on that boat, Macon."

"Don't call me Macon," I gritted through my teeth. "We're not friends."

He stared at me, no doubt trying to decide if he should assert his authority over me.

Go ahead, I thought. *I dare you.*

"I know who she is," I finally said.

"Okay," he simply said. "Just trying to help you out. Seems a little too close to home, you know?"

"You would know."

I was digging myself a real deep hole today.

"I just know how much that case affected you, not being able to find an answer."

He knew he was poking at a gaping wound, and he felt no remorse.

"Thanks for your concern," I said, not bothering to hide my sarcasm.

It didn't matter that what was happening between Marin and me wasn't real.

I was still the reason she was here in the first place.

Here, alone, asking me to fix up a house that had stood vacant for five years.

Because at the end of the day, I had allowed Raymond to get on that boat when every instinct was telling me not to.

And I'd never forget that.

I had told Marin I would stop by after work, but Sheriff Hayes's words were still ringing in my ears.

"…she's the Mendez woman, right?"

As if I needed a reminder of who she was. Those thirteen names had been permanently seared into my memory since the day that boat had gone down.

Unlocking my front door, I threw my shit on the table and went to the fridge. Grabbing a Coke, I headed for the couch and picked up the remote to put on the game.

I needed a distraction.

But after about fifteen minutes, I knew football was not going to cut it. What had I been thinking? Had I really thought fixing a few things around her house was going to make up for the fact that her husband had died because of me?

It'd been five years, and I could barely look at Dean Sutherland's amputated arm without breaking out into a cold sweat.

So many lost lives.

All because I'd become too fucking lazy to do my damn job. If I had just taken my time with Raymond that day…

I should just text Marin the name of a local handyman and tell her I had to work the night of the gala.

I was about halfway through my Coke when my phone rang. Since I was on call, I figured it was the station's dispatcher, but instead, I saw another number altogether.

Marin.

I stared at her name on my screen, trying to decide if I should answer or let it go to voice mail. I could just ignore it. Give her the cold shoulder and be done with this whole thing.

Now or never, Macon.

Finally, at the last possible second, I let out a frustrated groan and hit Answer. "Hello?"

"Oh, thank God!" Her voice was strained and filled with panic.

I instantly rose to my feet, my pulse racing. "What's wrong? Are you okay?"

I wasn't sure why, but I was already grabbing my keys.

"It's been an awful day. God, this house is trying to kill me."

I exhaled a little. She wasn't hurt.

"There are bees in the attic."

"Bees?" My eyes widened. "Like, actual live bees? Why the hell were you up in the attic?"

"I couldn't remember what was up there," she explained, sounding embarrassed. "And then I tried to use the stove and—"

"You haven't used the stove?" This story was getting more complex with every word.

"Um, no," she said. "I don't really like to cook, and when I do…" Her voice drifted off.

The corner of my mouth curved upward. "What's wrong with the stove?"

"I don't know. It won't light. I've tried and tried, but all it does is make that stupid clicking noise."

Shit.

"How long?" I asked, the humor I'd felt from her words dying instantly.

"What?" She sounded confused.

"How long have you been trying to light that pilot, Marin?"

"Um—"

I headed for the door. "Get out of the house," I ordered. "Get out of the house and don't go back in until I get there."

"But—"

"Do it, Marin."

And then I hung up and headed back to the one place I shouldn't—again.

<hr>

When I arrived just a few minutes later, I found her standing outside her door, waiting for me.

Thankfully, that stubborn streak of hers seemed to be lying dormant today.

"You know, I don't appreciate being yelled at over the phone," she said with an exasperated huff the second I stepped out of my truck.

Never mind.

"Do you appreciate your house not blowing up?" I asked.

Her eyes widened. "What?"

I didn't bother answering her. If there was a leak, I didn't want to waste any time. So, I just headed toward the front door.

"You know, I do know what gas smells like," she said confidently as she trailed behind me.

Why is the woman always doing the opposite of what I want her to?

I opened the door and was immediately hit with the pungent smell of rotten eggs.

"Oh, holy shit," she gasped. "It did not smell like that before, I swear."

I didn't believe her for a second. There was no way it got this bad, this fast. If anything, the leak was probably slow enough that she hadn't noticed.

I covered my face with my forearm and turned. "You go back outside."

She opened her mouth to argue, but I beat her to it, placing a single finger upon her lips. "No arguing. Out."

She froze, her eyes drifting downward. Finally, they focused back on me, and she nodded, silently turning to exit through the door.

With the feel of her lips still branded on my skin, I began the process of opening the windows to create as much ventilation as possible. The cool autumn air started to pour in, and I finally felt like I could take a decent breath.

I headed to the stove, and within a matter of seconds, I found the problem.

With a simple twist of my wrist, I shut it off and then ran to the back of the house and shut off the main—just to be safe. I met her out front minutes later.

Her anxious eyes met mine. "The dial on the back burner wasn't off all the way," I said. "It was hard to notice, which was why you probably didn't smell it at first."

"So, no leak?"

I shook my head. "No leak. But you're not gonna want to sleep in there tonight. It will take a while for those fumes to dissipate."

"That's ridiculous. I'm—"

"Don't say you're fine, Marin," I warned her. "You're lucky I'm not marching your ass down to the clinic to get checked out." I was seriously still questioning it.

"So, where the hell am I supposed to go?"

I breathed out a long sigh. "Molly might have a room," I suggested.

"It's ten o'clock at night!"

I looked at my watch. I had forgotten it was one of my late shifts. "Oh, right. Shit."

Don't say it. Don't say it.

"You can stay at my place," I blurted out. Before I had a chance to retract it, I continued, "I have an extra room, fume-free."

"I can't ask you to do that."

"You didn't ask. I offered." I replied. "You're not going back in there tonight, and you don't have much else in the way of options. Now, get in the truck."

Her arms folded across her chest. "Can I at least grab a toothbrush?"

"No," I answered with a smug smile. "But I can."

"Ugh," she grumbled. "Has anyone ever told you that you're kind of bossy?"

"Once or twice. Now, are you gonna tell me where your toothbrush is or not?"

CHAPTER SEVEN

Marin

'd been in Ocracoke for a week, and so far, I'd nearly been chased out of my house by a swarm of angry bees, applied for half a dozen soul-sucking freelance jobs that I hadn't even been selected for—

Oh, and here was the best part: I'd landed myself a fake boyfriend.

Never mind that real one I had waiting for me at home—the one I still hadn't called.

What a fucking nightmare.

And now, to top things off, we were having a sleepover.

I didn't say a single word on the way to Macon's house. Granted, he only lived a few blocks away, so it wasn't an exceptionally long amount of time to not talk, but I was sure he noticed all the same.

He seemed to notice everything.

"We're here," he simply said as we pulled up to his driveway.

I grabbed my things, which only consisted of the toothbrush he'd so graciously gone in to get for me and my purse.

I had seriously considered asking him to grab a few other things, but the thought of him rifling through my clothes to grab me clean underwear had seemed far too personal.

So, I just settled with what I had.

I got out of his truck and followed behind him. I'd only been as far as his porch, having visited him that day he bought the gala tickets. The outside of his house was neat and well kept, the landscaping simple but beautiful.

Kind of like the man himself.

I wasn't sure what to expect when we stepped inside—maybe more of the same simple, clean style—but what I saw was…

"It's, uh…it's not much," he said, his hand touching the back of his neck in a gesture I'd never seen before.

Is he embarrassed?

The living room was sparse, to say the least. It was clean, which wasn't surprising, but everything looked picked over, and what was left was sort of haphazardly placed here and there, like a puzzle with missing pieces.

Had he not rearranged anything since his wife had left?

"It's great, Macon. Thank you," I said, giving him a reassuring smile. "I really appreciate you rushing over to help me."

"It's the least I could do," he replied, still awkward. Still unsure.

"Well, I don't know if that's true," I replied, attempting to lighten things up a bit. "I mean, from where I'm standing, I think I'm getting the better end of this deal. You're working your ass off—"

"It's nothing, believe me," he insisted.

His mood was different here. Quieter, more guarded. Like a whole other version of him existed within these walls.

It was sort of how I thought I'd feel coming back here. I had always thought walking back into that house would be like immersing myself in a bucket of ice water.

Painful and bitterly cold.

But the more I was there, the more I found the space oddly comforting.

"The, uh…the room is just down here." He pointed to the hallway. "Have you eaten?" he asked.

"Oh, um, no. I didn't really get to that part."

The corner of his mouth turned upward, and I could see the effort he made to not smile.

"I'll see what I have."

"Do you want help?" I asked, placing my purse on the table. I tucked my toothbrush inside, grateful he had been thoughtful enough to find a plastic bag in the kitchen to put it in.

I was also grateful I'd moved a certain velvet box and put it back in my dresser. Finding a diamond ring next to my sandwich baggies would have been awkward as hell.

"Do I? You didn't seem too confident around that gas stove," he joked, though I could still see that shadow looming over him like he just couldn't quite relax.

Was he always like this? In his own home? Or did I make it worse?

"I wouldn't trust me with the actual cooking, but I have decent chopping skills. Or at least, that's what my mom has always told me."

"Well, seeing as I haven't been to the grocery store this week, our options might be limited," he explained.

His head was bent forward as he inspected the contents of his fridge, and I had to turn my head to force myself not to stare at the way his ass looked in those rugged pants, or how his tight black shirt accentuated his massive biceps.

I'd seen him around town, wearing a complex black vest that stretched over his broad chest.

It was a good look—I wasn't gonna lie.

"How do you feel about pancakes?"

I laughed. "You don't have much, but you have pancakes?"

His eyes glimmered with amusement. "You really don't know much about cooking, do you? Pancakes have, like, five ingredients."

"Besides the mix?" I was confused.

"I thought you said you helped your mom in the kitchen?" he asked as he began taking items out of the fridge —butter, eggs, and milk.

"I said I chopped things, not help," I clarified, taking a seat on a lone barstool at his small kitchen island. "There's a difference. My sister was the helper."

"So, is she a good cook?"

"No," I shook my head. "To my German mother's utter disappointment, none of us are. My brother is an utter failure as well."

"Are you the oldest?" he asked, appearing genuinely interested as he moved around the kitchen with ease.

I liked watching him.

"Um, yes. Not by much though. My sister, Margo, and I are only two years apart. Our brother, Alex, is seven years younger than me, and very much the baby of the family."

The rapid-fire questions seemed to pause for a moment as he gathered bowls and other items from the pantry, his expression somewhat unreadable.

"Do you have any siblings?" I asked, hoping to keep the conversation going.

I liked talkative Macon. I much preferred him over bossy Macon or stoic Macon.

Although I'd take any version over the sad version I had seen the moment we walked into this house.

"A brother," he answered, averting his gaze from mine. "But I haven't seen him in a long time."

When he didn't elaborate more, I decided to change the subject. Family did not appear to be an agreeable topic.

"Do you like living in Ocracoke?" I asked. "Have you ever lived anywhere else?"

He started throwing ingredients in a bowl, almost like it was second nature. He didn't use measuring spoons and cracked eggs one-handed, and he did it all while carrying on a conversation.

I'd never once found cooking to be sexy in my life.

Turned out, there was a first for everything.

"Well, your first question is complicated. Do I like living here? Sometimes. On the days when I get to run on the beach in the middle of December? Yeah, I love it. Then, there are the days when I have to step into situations I'd rather not know about. Kind of hate it then."

"Oh God." I winced. "I'd never thought of that. How awful."

"It's not great, but—" He gave a sort of shrug. "Someone has to do it."

"Is it weird, being a cop in your hometown? Do people treat you differently?"

"Some do; some don't. I've never really cared either way." The tone of his voice sounded convincing, but the look in his eyes told me something else entirely. "To answer your second question, I have lived in quite a few other places," he said as he started back up with his batter-making. "I left Ocracoke right after I graduated high school. Couldn't wait to get out. The military gave me that."

"What made you become a cop?" I asked.

"Kristy," he said simply. "She didn't want to be a military wife, and I was ready to settle in one place. It was an easy transition for me. I took a job in Charlotte, and we bought a house. I never thought I'd go back."

"But you did."

"Kristy liked the promotion I'd get if we moved here, and her excitement convinced me that maybe I could do something good."

I nodded, watching him intently.

"But the second I got here, I met Sheriff Hayes who was elected while I was gone, and I knew it was going to be hell. He brought me to a bar and told me how things ran in *his* county."

"What do you mean, his county?"

"Let's just say he had a long list of dos and don'ts—real shady shit that had nothing to do with the law."

My heart sank. "So, what did you do?"

"I told him where he could take that *list* and walked the fuck out," he said, the malice clear in his voice.

"I'm surprised you didn't get fired considering what you knew."

"Pretty sure he thought about it, but he would have just denied everything anyway and it's not like I had any proof. Plus, by that time, he'd met Kristy. Couldn't fire me if he wanted my wife."

I winced.

"I'm so sorry," I said.

My words seemed to snap him out of whatever he'd just been swallowed up by.

He straightened a bit and resumed what he was doing. "It wouldn't have happened if she didn't want it to in the first place."

I watched as he poured the first pancakes onto the griddle with ease. It was as if he'd done it a hundred times, and it got me wondering.

"So, why do you stay?" I asked. I immediately wished I could take it back. It was too personal, and we'd only just met.

But he didn't seem offended, just pensive. "The only reason Hayes keeps me here is to torment me. He loves dangling Kristy in my face." He looked over toward the living room like, at any moment, her ghost would appear. "And if I left, I have no doubt he'd take the opportunity to replace me with someone much more compliant."

So, he stayed because he cared for the town. His town.

I swallowed hard, deciding to change the subject. "How does a military man learn how to make pancakes like that?"

"My mom taught me. Flour and eggs are cheap." He paused. "We ate a lot of pancakes."

I was really bad at conversation topics.

I wasn't sure how to respond to that, so I took the easy way out. "My mom makes German pancakes."

His brow rose. I'd obviously piqued his interest.

"You've never had German pancakes. They're really puffy and—"

"If someone had learned to cook, maybe—"

I picked up the kitchen towel he'd set down on the counter and threw it at his head. He ducked, and it missed him entirely.

But the smile I got was well worth the effort.

I didn't think I'd ever seen Macon Green truly smile until that moment, and it was dazzling.

"You missed."

"I don't think I had a chance in hell," I admitted.

That scarred brow arched. He was obviously enjoying the banter. "You could sneak up on me in the dark, and you still wouldn't have a chance in hell."

"Someone obviously did," I said, pointing to the tiny line above his eye.

His fingers touched it, as if he'd forgotten it was there. "Bar fight," he explained. Now, it was my brow that arched. "That I broke up," he added with a genuine grin. "On the job."

I laughed. "Who knew keeping the peace in Ocracoke could be so dangerous? Any other battle scars?"

He didn't answer, but the heated stare he gave me said it all. *Wanna find out?*

I swallowed audibly.

"Do you want something to drink?" Macon asked, and I breathed a sigh of relief at the quick change of subject. "I, uh…don't keep any alcohol in the house, but I can offer you a soda or…" He took a breath, avoiding my gaze, making me wonder if he was embarrassed or… ashamed? He opened the refrigerator door open once again. "Well, that's about it."

I laughed, purposely ignoring his nervousness. I could see

it wasn't a subject he wanted to address. "Water is fine, thank you."

We continued to make small talk while he finished a few batches of pancakes and heated some syrup in the microwave. He plated a few onto two plates and pulled out some butter. We both helped ourselves to the syrup, and then I followed him to the couch.

I set my glass on the coffee table, noting the stack of books and the newspaper. There was little else as far as decor, which either meant he was a minimalist or his wife had seriously cleaned him out.

Having met her, I thought I knew the answer.

Taking my first bite, I couldn't help but moan a little. First of all, I was starving. It'd been a solid ten hours since I'd eaten, and secondly, it was delicious. "This is fucking good."

"Better than German pancakes?"

"Yes, but if you ever tell my mom, I will end you. She's terrifying."

He leaned back, angling his body toward mine. There was a safe distance between us, but I still felt exposed. Still felt the heat of his eyes on me.

"What about your dad?" he asked. "Are both your parents German?"

I nodded. "Yes. I'm first generation. They immigrated here so my dad could pursue his music career. He went to Juilliard for his graduate work."

"No shit?" He seemed genuinely impressed.

I grinned. "No shit."

"So, what does he play?" he asked.

I watched him bring that fork to his mouth, and my own went dry.

No one should look that hot while eating.

"He's a violinist," I answered, focusing back on my plate. "But he hasn't played professionally for years. He was diagnosed with MS when I was a kid."

"That must have been devastating."

"It was," I agreed. "But his progression has been fairly slow. He's been able to walk up until this year. He's wheelchair-bound now, but he hasn't been able to hold a violin without shaking in decades."

"So, all that work and he had to, what? Do something else?"

I nodded. "Yeah, he became a teacher. A really good one, too."

"Just like that?"

"I'm sure it wasn't just like that, but he adjusted. He's amazing."

"You sound like you are close with your family."

I winced, thinking about the brief text I'd sent them when I got here. "Usually."

"Usually?" His brow lifted.

"They're not entirely thrilled with me at the moment," I answered, pushing the leftover syrup around my plate with my fork.

He waited for me to elaborate.

Oh God. How much do I want to tell him? The whole truth—boyfriend and all? Or just the bare minimum?

"They don't understand why I'm here," I simply said.

That's truthful.

Exceptionally lacking, but truthful.

"Why are you down here?" he asked before adding, "I know I said it was none of my business, but I'm curious as to why you would uproot your life—I'm assuming that's what you did since your family seems upset with you—and then come here, to a house you haven't visited in five years?"

Oh God. I'm gonna have to tell him, aren't I?

You should have told him the second you bought those gala tickets.

"I have a boyfriend," I blurted out, the words tumbling out of my mouth as my gaze met his.

The look on his face was…unreadable. At first, he looked shocked, wounded even, but then his expression went blank, almost passive. "Okay." The word came out slowly, and he gave each syllable extra emphasis. "Not sure how that answers my question."

I opened my mouth to answer, but I was still stuck on his reaction. Did I upset him? Or was I just reading him wrong?

"What? Oh, um…he proposed. And I couldn't say yes."

"Why?" he asked.

Still unreadable. Still emotionless.

Is this what an interrogation is like?

"That's what I'm down here to figure out. I quit my job and—"

"You quit your job?" His eyes widened, and he set his plate on the coffee table. "Jesus."

Well, at least that got some sort of reaction.

"That's where I lost my parents, too," I said jokingly.

"So, when you said you have no idea how long you're staying…"

"I really have no idea," I said, finishing his train of thought. I set my plate down on the table as well and rose to my feet. "I've held on to that house for five years and never managed to step foot in it, not a single foot since Daniel was in that accident."

He looked away, and for the first time since I'd told him I had a boyfriend, I saw something in his expression. Pain maybe?

"The only thing I could think of when Curtis dropped to one knee was this house and the life I'd planned here. So, I quit my job, told my family good-bye, and came here to…" I paused. "I have no fucking clue."

"You're here to let go," he said very matter-of-factly.

"I…" Was I?

"You can't say yes to your boyfriend because you're still holding on to this house. You need to grieve, say your good-byes, and then walk away. For good."

Those last two words felt like a gut punch, and I took a deep breath.

"You mean, sell the house?" I gulped. That didn't sound right at all.

"You can't start a new life while holding on to the old one." He shrugged.

"No." I shook my head back and forth.

I couldn't.

I wouldn't.

I loved my house.

But I couldn't stay here and marry Curtis. I knew that.

"There are too many issues. I have freaking bees! I can't sell a house full of bees!" I said, throwing my hands up.

He smiled, but it wasn't the kind that reached his eyes. There was that shadow again. "Luckily, you have someone who can help you with that."

CHAPTER EIGHT

Macon

he's engaged?

Not engaged.

Almost engaged.

She's almost fucking engaged?

It shouldn't matter.

I shouldn't care.

But the second she had said the word *boyfriend*, my heart had launched into my throat, and I'd felt nauseous.

It was bad enough that she had a dead husband I had to feel guilty about, but now, there was a boyfriend, too?

Fuck my life.

I'd been awake most of the night, and when the first rays of sunlight finally drifted through the curtains, I decided just to give up and throw some running clothes on instead.

But even that proved fruitless, and by the end of a hard five-mile jaunt around the island, all I'd accomplished was getting a few pastries and some bagels for my overnight guest.

I tried to be quiet as I entered the house. It was still early, and judging by the way she'd answered the door the other day in that teeny-tiny T-shirt, half awake, I'd guess she was not a morning person. Dropping the food off on the kitchen island, I started some coffee and headed toward my bedroom, intent on grabbing a shower before she woke.

Instead, I nearly walked right into her as she stepped out of the bathroom.

In a towel.

Fresh out of the shower.

My eyes drew down the length of her body and back up again. I couldn't help it. There was so much skin.

And it was all so very wet.

But then that conversation from last night resurfaced.

Boyfriend.

Almost fiancé.

Fuck.

I took a step back and cleared my throat.

"Uh, there are bagels and pastries on the island. I made some coffee," I said in one breath. "I'm gonna go grab a shower."

And then I got the hell out of there.

I went to my bedroom and closed the door behind me, my back sagging against the hard wood. I let out a long puff of air as my eyes closed.

Marin Mendez was the biggest clusterfuck I'd ever encountered.

She was the last person I should be around and yet the only one I couldn't seem to walk away from. I hadn't looked at another woman since Kristy. Her betrayal had been so devastating that I was beginning to think that part of me had died. I hadn't felt a single spark...

Why did it have to be her?

Ever since I'd collided with her that night in her house, all I saw when I closed my eyes was her. All I thought about when my mind wandered was...

Her.

Heading toward the master bath, her half-naked body still etched in my mind, I turned on the water and grabbed a towel.

She can never be mine…

The water warmed up as I pulled my shirt over my head and dropped my shorts.

She has a boyfriend…

Thoughts swirled in my head as I stepped in the shower, and I pictured that soft, wet skin. What I wouldn't give to be able to reach forward and watch that towel slowly fall to the ground.

To bend forward and lick every last drop of water with my tongue.

I was so hard; I fucking ached.

My hand drifted down, gripping my cock, the vision of her so crystal clear in my mind. I groaned, bracing myself against the tiles.

I'd take her right there in the hallway, pushing her back against the wall as I explored every damn inch of her.

I worked myself up and down as I imagined the sound of her voice as she begged for more. I could almost hear all those breathy little moans against my ear.

"Fuck," I muttered, my movements becoming frantic.

She'd throw her head back, her tight body spasming around mine.

And then fantasy and reality melded as I came, my body shaking violently.

But then the world came back into focus, and reality returned.

A fantasy—that was all it would ever be.

It was the wake-up call I needed.

I finished my shower, and by the time I was dressed, I knew what I had to do.

This had to end. All of it.

I could not be around Marin Mendez any longer.

I walked out of my bedroom fifteen minutes later with a clear head.

And even clearer intentions.

"I have an early shift," I said as I entered the kitchen, ready to do what was necessary. "Do you need a lift back home?"

Those dark brown eyes met mine, and all those clear intentions of mine turned to a pile of dust.

Fuck.

I swallowed hard as my mind quickly recalled every detail of the damn porno fantasy I'd just had in the shower.

"Uh, no," she answered, smiling at me from where she sat at the island. "I can walk. I need the fresh air. Thanks though," she said. She gestured toward her plate. "And thanks for breakfast. And you know, everything else."

Does she have to be so damn nice?

I sort of shrugged, turning my head away to avoid those eyes on me. I didn't deserve her kindness. "It was nothing. And you should be all clear now—the house, I mean. No fumes. But make sure to have that stove checked out. A handyman should be able to do it. I'll give you a couple of names."

"Handyman?"

I tried to make myself busy so she wouldn't notice the tremor in my voice, grabbing a travel mug out of the cupboard. "Yeah, I realized my schedule is swamped over the next few weeks with the extra shifts and being on call. I'm not sure how much time I will have to do everything on that list, so I figured it'd be easier for you to just hire a professional. I'm not exactly reliable, you know? And I don't want you to have to wait around for me."

Silence filled the room.

"I understand if that messes up our deal," I added, waiting for her to respond. When she didn't, I went on, "I'm not much of a dancer anyway. You're welcome to the tickets though."

Say something…

Anything.

When she still didn't respond, I went for that fatal blow. It was unnecessary. The silence alone told me everything I needed to know.

Finished filling my coffee, I turned and offered a forced smile, casually leaning against the counter. "And, hey, maybe by then, you'll have sold the house, and your boyfriend can go with you."

She looked up at me, wide-eyed. Both shock and disappointment painted her beautiful face.

Was I an asshole?

Yes.

But at least I was an asshole who wouldn't be fucking up her life anymore.

Go home, I wanted to tell her.

Go home and be happy.

Far away from me.

Ever since we'd become a deputy short, I'd become accustomed to eating my lunch while hunched over my desk, working on a mountain of paperwork.

But today, I needed some fresh air.

I was used to being the bad guy in this town. When people needed someone to step in, they called me, and I did what they couldn't. I broke up parties that got out of hand, I arrested abusive husbands, and, yeah, I'd even taken my own father to the station once or twice.

I was used to being that guy, and usually, I didn't lose sleep over it. At the end of the day, I was okay with who I was because I was making a difference.

Or at least trying to.

But today, I did not like myself.

I did not like that sad, disappointed look I'd put on

Marin's face, or the fact that I'd simply walked out the door rather than apologize.

But there wasn't a damn thing I could do about it.

I was too close.

Dangerously close. If I hung around Marin any longer, I wasn't sure I'd be able to stomach the idea of watching her go back to that boyfriend of hers without putting up a fight.

And I did not deserve her.

The cool air blew across my face as I sat in my cruiser. The engine was off, and I'd already eaten the sad excuse of a sandwich I'd grabbed from the local market. I had parked in my usual spot—in the far corner along the water's edge. I had to crane my neck to get a proper view, but at least from this angle, I couldn't see that damn memorial.

The tourists were sparse, and the ferry schedule had adjusted accordingly. I enjoyed this time of the year for that very reason. It was the only time when the town truly felt ours.

As I was watching the last few cars load onto the ferry, I noticed one get out of line at the last minute.

Why do I recognize that car?

It parked in the middle of the parking lot, and the engine shut off. I squinted, trying to get a view of the driver.

And that was when I saw her.

Son of a bitch.

Marin was in the front seat with her car filled to the brim.

If I didn't know better, I'd say she was leaving.

Or at least, she was trying to.

She pushed the door open wide, and she stepped out. She took one foot to the left and then plopped down to the ground, her hands cradling her face.

Shit, is she crying?

Why is she rushing home?

I thought about that conversation we'd had about her dad and his declining health.

I was up and moving before I had time to think.

"Marin!" I shouted, stalking toward her. "What happened?"

She looked up at me, and her tears doubled.

"Oh, for fuck's sake! Of course it's you!"

I froze. "What?"

"Of course you would show up when I was trying to sneak away."

Sneak away?

I looked down at her sitting there on the dirty ground, her eyes red and puffy. And all I could think of was the fact that she'd almost left and I had no idea.

She'd almost left…

"So, no one is hurt or dying?"

"No, you idiot. I was running away," she huffed. "Again."

"So, just to clarify," I asked, looking down at her, "no one is hurt?"

She glared up at me.

I held my palms face up. "I get it."

I didn't, but if looks could kill…damn.

"I thought you were going to sell the house?" I asked, still so relieved she was here and not on that stupid ferry.

She shook her head. "No, *you* said I was going to sell the house. I never agreed. You made a whole plan, and I have to admit, it sounded fairly logical…" Her voice trailed off.

"But?" I asked.

"But then you bailed on me and left me with nothing more than a list of names."

"I told you—" I started.

"I know," she huffed again. "You're busy. I get it. I really do," she said with sincerity. "That's not the issue. Well, it is, but not the way you think."

I raised my eyebrow.

"I quit my job," she reminded me. "The amount of stuff that needs to be done—"

Understanding sank into me. "You can't afford it."

"No," she admitted, looking highly embarrassed. "And

whether or not I'm in the right headspace to sell the house now or in a few weeks or months, I do not have the funds to put it on the market. Daniel's life insurance policy paid off the house, and what I had left, I used for the maintenance fees, which was entirely a waste because the house is falling apart anyway. So, I'm just going to go back home, beg for my job back, and figure the rest out later."

"And your boyfriend?" I asked. Even saying the word made my lunch go sour in my stomach.

She let out a sigh, her lips quivering. "I don't know. I haven't even called him in over a week."

"Stay," I said, making her eyes bolt upward.

"What?"

I took a step forward and planted myself next to her on the ground. The car was still warm from the heat of the engine, and I pressed my back against the door.

"I can do the repairs."

"But you said—"

"I know what I said, but I'll make it work. You need to sell that house, Marin. It's like a lead weight. It's holding you back."

She paused and then asked, "Have you ever considered selling yours?"

"What? Why?" My eyes found hers.

She shrugged. "Just asking."

What is wrong with my house?

"I don't want to burden you," she said, looking out into the empty parking lot.

"Then, help," I suggested. "I'll give you simple things you can do while I'm at work, and that will become our new deal."

"Our new deal?"

"I don't need to go to the gala," I said. "I don't need to make my ex jealous."

I don't need the temptation, was what I really wanted to say.

I already liked the idea of her turning this car around far too much.

"Are you sure?" she asked, her swollen eyes looking up at me.

"I'm sure," I answered. "Besides, that is not why you came here. You need to stay focused."

"You're right. You're absolutely right."

I nodded my head in agreement.

I'd never wanted to be so wrong in my entire life.

CHAPTER NINE

Marin

spent the rest of the day unloading the car I had meticulously packed, repacked, and then packed again.

I had no idea how Elena had gotten all the crap in there.

When Macon had left me alone in his house that morning with a list of names I should call, I'd felt utterly helpless.

The thought of selling my house made my chest hurt.

But when Macon was around, I was able to put it off. It was something I'd deal with—later.

When he left, I felt utterly alone.

So, I packed up all my shit, and I decided to run back to the safety of home.

But the second I got to the ferry terminal, I couldn't do it.

Where was home anyway?

Going back to Richmond meant having to face my family.

And Curtis.

I couldn't bring myself to get on that boat. So, I pulled out of line with all my shit in the back of my car, and I parked.

I had no idea what I was going to do.

That was when Macon found me, slumped against the side of my car, cruising my way into a panic attack.

Thankfully, he'd arrived before it had a chance to go nuclear.

That would have been embarrassing.

What I told him was true. I could not afford those repairs without his free handywork, but I was also not sure I could go through it all by myself.

Without him.

Somehow, in the span of a week, Macon had become something meaningful to me.

I wasn't sure what, but I was glad it was him who had barged into my house that night, and despite what I'd said to him after he walked up to me in that parking lot, I had been more than relieved to see his face.

I'd nearly gotten everything put back where I'd had it when there was a soft knock on the door. When I got there, I found Macon on the other side, dressed in jeans and a long-sleeved shirt. He smelled clean, like he'd freshly showered, and he had that burning intensity about him that never seemed to ease.

"You don't have to knock," I said casually. "I don't really have any other visitors. And besides"—I grinned—"I have the best security system around." I moved the door back and forth, demonstrating the squeaking noise that had given away his not-so-stealthy entrance the night I arrived.

He shook his head, his brows furrowed. "We're gonna fix that." He then looked down at the lock and back up and me. "And as for your security system, lock the door."

"But it's Ocracoke," I answered with a shrug. No one ever locked their door.

Those hazel eyes met mine, and I shivered.

"Lock the damn door, Marin."

Bossy Macon is back.

"Okay," I said, biting my lip to keep from grinning.

"Have you eaten?" he asked, putting a large box of tools down near the front door.

"I had ramen at noon. Does that count?"

"Barely," he answered. "I was going to go grab takeout at Billy's. Do you want something?"

I perked up. "Oh, can I go with you? I wanted to say hi. I didn't get a chance the other day."

Billy was one of the few people I'd actually connected with during my short time on the island. He'd been kind to Daniel, letting him work for hours on the patio by the water.

"You know he lives next door, right?"

"Well, yeah, but I can't just go knock on his door."

He looked at me, his face going blank. "Why?"

I opened my mouth and then snapped it closed again. Finally, I answered, "Because…" I paused, seeing his eyes light up as he grinned. "Because that's weird. I haven't seen him in years."

He just shook his head back and forth. "You really didn't live here long, did you?"

I just rolled my eyes. "Obviously."

"Billy would love the company," he assured me. "But if you're uncomfortable just dropping in, I can bring you over sometime."

"Have you and Billy always been close?" I asked.

Macon had mentioned him a lot, even saying he'd told him about our situation.

The real one.

"We weren't as kids," he explained. "But we've become pretty close over the last few years."

I wanted to ask more, but before I could, he asked, "Did you still want to come?"

"Shouldn't we call ahead?"

"No," he answered. "We can order there. It will give you more time to catch up."

He waited as I put on my shoes and finally grabbed my purse. We walked to the front door, and he paused, waiting for me to lock the door. I resisted the urge to roll my eyes.

Soon, we were on our way to the harbor, and I was sitting in his truck, enjoying the view.

Both the one sitting next to me and the one out my window.

"Oh, hey, I'm sorry about the shower," I finally said, remembering our awkward encounter this morning.

His eyes shifted to mine for the slightest second before they returned to the road. "You're sorry for showering?"

"I didn't even ask."

"I don't recall saying you had to."

The truth was, I hadn't exactly planned on it. It wasn't like I had clean clothes to change into, but I couldn't sleep. I'd been up all night, tossing and turning, and when I heard him slip out of the house at dawn, I became even more restless. I sat up in bed and scrolled through social media on my phone.

And then I looked around that sparse guest bedroom, and my thoughts started to drift back to Macon.

It didn't take long to find him.

For a guy who was all about safety, his profile was not nearly as private as I would have thought.

Of course, there wasn't much to it either.

I scrolled, and I scrolled.

He hadn't posted any updates in years. He'd been tagged in a few things related to the town and such, but personally, the only thing he'd changed in more than five years was his profile picture.

When I finally got to a picture of him and his ex-wife, I felt my heart stutter.

I recognized her immediately. That blonde hair and bright white smile. She had her arms wrapped around him, and that was when it hit me.

White-hot jealousy.

It was so swift and sudden that I threw my phone on the bed like it was on fire.

I hadn't felt that kind of jealousy since—

I needed to clear my head. I needed to get up and out of that room. So, that was how I ended up sneaking across the hall while he was out, hoping the hot water would wash those thoughts right down the drain.

It didn't.

When I heard the front door open, I quickly shut the water off and tried to dash back into the guest room, undetected.

But I ran into Macon instead.

He was slick with sweat, those massive biceps on display, thanks to the loose-fitting tank he wore. My eyes were everywhere, and before I could say a word, he'd darted down the hallway and disappeared.

Since then, I'd done a very good job of convincing myself that what I had felt was anger toward his wife because of how she'd treated Macon—not jealousy.

No. Definitely not jealousy.

We pulled to the curb, and Macon put the car in park. The smell of salty sea air and fried food drifted into my nose the second I pushed open the door and met Macon to cross the street.

Although the autumn in the Outer Banks wasn't known for being chilly, I pulled my sweater tight around my chest as the breeze from the ocean hit my face.

"Are you cold?" Macon asked.

"A little," I admitted.

He doubled back almost instantly before I could even protest. I stood on the other side of the street while he quickly unlocked the door and reached behind the seat, pulling out a zip-up hoodie.

"The wind can get pretty brutal this time of year," he said, handing it to me.

"Thank you," I said, slipping it on.

A slight grin tugged at the corner of his lips as he watched it swallow me, the hem nearly reaching my knees. "Come on."

We walked side by side onto the patio, where a few people were braving the wind. Billy was nowhere to be seen, so Macon suggested I head inside.

"You don't want to come?" I asked.

He shook his head. "You go ahead," he said. "I need to check on a few things for work." He held up his phone, but I wondered if he was just using it as an excuse to give me some privacy.

"What about your order?" I asked.

"Just tell him I'll have the usual. He'll know what you mean."

I nodded my head, and we parted ways. He walked over to one of the tables to sit, and I went into the small dining room.

In comparison to the outdoor patio, the inside of Billy's was minimal. Most people only came inside when it was too cold or raining.

And today must have been one of those days.

A few locals sat at the tables near the windows, soaking up the sea view while eating French fries and fried fish.

I searched the place until my eyes fell on a familiar face.

"Billy," I said, smiling.

"I was wondering when you were gonna pay me a visit," he said. He set down a big tub of dishes and wiped his hands, walking the short distance to pull me into a tight bear hug. "I thought about stopping by, but I didn't want to overwhelm you. You've been missed."

"I don't think that's true," I said.

"It's absolutely true. You're an O'cocker now," he boasted with a wink. "You can't leave."

I winced. "That's what I'm here to do actually."

He looked wounded. "You're selling? But we just became neighbors."

"I don't know. Maybe," I answered quietly. I didn't need to be part of the gossip train. "I haven't quite decided yet."

"What's the holdup?" he asked before adding, "Not that it's any of my business."

"I'm surprised he didn't tell you," I said, motioning over my shoulder.

"Macon?" He snorted his name, shaking his head. "Why?"

"Well, I know he told you about the *other thing*," I said, putting a hushed emphasis on the last two words.

He lowered his voice. "All he said to me was, 'If you hear anything, it's not true.' Macon is a man of few words. But he also doesn't like to share other people's business."

That was…pleasantly surprising.

"I'm not sure what the holdup is exactly," I said with a shrug. "I guess the logical thing would be to sell the house and move on."

"But?"

"But I've never been much of a logical person," I admitted. "It was my dream to live here. It's hard to let go of it. Even without Daniel."

"Daniel was a good guy," he said with a sad smile. "He was the reason I stopped giving free refills."

I laughed. "He did love to sit down here and work."

"He always talked about you. Loved to brag about your paintings." He smiled. "I know you miss him."

"I do," I said softly.

Billy's eyes moved past me toward the patio. "He causing you any grief?"

I knew who he was looking at.

"He's been doing some of my repairs. He's a huge help."

"That sounds like him," he said in that tone that only a very close friend used. "He likes everyone to think he's a jerk."

"But you know better," I guessed.

"Oh, he can be a jerk." He laughed. "But he's a good guy. Better than most."

A sadness washed over his face, but as soon as it was there, it was gone again. "So, can I get you guys something, or did you just come by to say hello?"

"Oh, we definitely came for food." I laughed. "Macon already knows I can't cook. Like, at all."

He grinned. "I remember. Daniel told me horror stories."

It warmed my heart that other people in the town had fond memories of my husband and that he would hopefully be remembered, even after I left.

If I left.

He started jotting down my order, and just as I was starting to give him Macon's, those eyes of his shifted past me once more, but this time, he didn't like what he saw.

I turned and saw Macon standing, his back now facing me. But even from that angle, I could see every tense, rigid line of his body.

And as my gaze moved past him, I saw the reason.

Kristy.

She was positioned between two women, all dressed similarly. They could have been clones, but I was guessing they were her friends. A strained smile was plastered across her face as she motioned with her hands. Then, her expression turned heated, and I heard Macon raise his voice.

"Uh-oh," Billy said. "I'd better go do something."

"Why?" I asked. I turned my head toward him and saw the panic on his face.

"Because the last time she laid into him like that, he went on a three-day bender, and it took weeks to sort him out."

I looked back through the window, seeing how tense he was. Seeing the power she had to destroy him again and again.

It was time someone put her in her place.

"No," I said, feeling anger build inside me. "Let me."

God, what a bitch.

Her voice carried over the patio as I pushed the door open.

She was so focused on herself that she didn't even notice me walking over.

But when I slid that possessive hand around Macon's

waist, the look on his face was priceless. Her eyes went wide and then narrowed like a predator.

And I knew exactly who was her prey.

"I got our orders placed," I said sweetly, looking up at Macon like he and I were the only two people there. Like she didn't even register in our orbit. "Shouldn't be too long."

To his credit, his acting skills seemed to have drastically improved, and the moment our eyes connected, a slight grin tugged at the corner of his lip. He one-upped me by wrapping his arm around my shoulders and pulling me tight against his side.

Like he'd done it a thousand times.

Like I belonged there.

I made sure to look at him just a little too long. I bit my lip and smiled in a way that insinuated that I was thinking of some very inappropriate things.

It helped that I most definitely was.

I did this all while Kristy watched.

While she *stared*.

And then, just when it started to border on straight-up rude, I finally turned to her and said, "Oh, hi," and then I let out a little giggle.

Like a love-drunk schoolgirl.

"We were in the middle of a conversation," she said, her words clipped and full of rage.

"Oh?" I said in a passive tone that told her exactly how much I cared—which was not at all. "What about?"

She folded her arms across her chest, her eyes flickering over the hoodie I wore. She either recognized it or knew it was way too big to be mine.

Good.

"It's really not any of your concern."

"Well, seeing as you are speaking loud enough for the whole island to hear, I'd say it sounds like everyone's concern."

A few people nearby coughed, stifling a laugh. Even one

of her friends had to turn, pressing her lips together to keep her expression neutral.

She huffed. "I was merely asking if Macon had something of ours from"—her words faltered—"before. And if he did—"

"I told you," Macon's deep voice said next to me, "I don't have your damn vase."

"A vase?" I echoed, trying to look interested.

She merely looked at me. All this was about a fucking vase?

"What does it look like?" I asked in a sickly-sweet voice.

Her eyes narrowed once more. "It's crystal. Very expensive. Why?"

"Oh. Well then, never mind. Macon bought me flowers the other day—he's always doing stuff like that. Anyway, I found this vase in the cupboard, but it wasn't crystal."

"Are you sure?" she pressed.

"Yes. Very. Besides," I answered, acting embarrassed and leaving nothing to the imagination as to what was going on in my head, "we sort of broke it when we—never mind."

Her cheeks flamed, and she looked up at Macon. "If you find it—"

"Oh, you'll be the first to know," he answered, a hint of amusement to his tone. "Enjoy your girls' day out."

She started to storm off, and I could feel him begin to pull away.

"No," I said, gripping his waist. "Not yet."

I turned to face him, our arms still wrapped around each other. "Is she looking back?"

"No. Why?"

"She will," I said a second before I reached up and kissed him.

CHAPTER TEN

Macon

ire.

I was on fucking fire.

The moment her lips touched mine, I was officially going to hell.

I knew I didn't deserve her.

I knew she was in love with someone else.

But none of that stopped me from running my hands through her hair, pulling her close, and showing her what it would feel like to be mine.

Even for just a second.

I felt a brief moment of hesitation, a flash of surprise, as her body met mine, but then—

Then, she fucking melted, and I knew she wasn't pretending anymore.

Her nails delicately grazed my cheek, so tentative. So unsure. She gripped the collar of my shirt, curling her fingers around the fabric until they made a tight fist.

I gave myself a moment to savor it.

One single moment to remember the touch of her lips on mine, the taste of her on my tongue, and all the moments we'd never share...

And then I pulled away.

"Remind me to never get on your bad side," I said. My voice was rough and ragged, betraying the tidal wave of emotions that were pouring out of me.

"She deserved it," Marin replied, slightly breathless. "She's vile."

I looked out toward the street. Kristy was long gone. I had no idea if she'd turned around, like Marin had promised she would.

I honestly didn't care.

"So, I guess we're dating again?" I said low enough so that no one else could hear. My arm was still slung around her shoulders, and I couldn't help but grin when she laughed.

"Sorry," she said. "I couldn't help it."

"I'm gonna go get our food."

"Okay," she said, stepping back.

Why did I suddenly feel so empty?

I tried not to dwell on that thought too much as I walked toward the double doors leading into the restaurant. I saw Billy putting down two plates at a far table, smiling and talking to the guests. There was a bag of takeout on the counter. I reached out to grab it and then pivoted.

"Whoa," he said, already walking toward me. "Don't think you're gonna just walk out of here after that melodrama I just witnessed."

"Melodrama?" I rolled my eyes.

"I only saw Kristy's side of things, but, dude, she looked pissed." He leaned against the counter, wiping a hand on his dark apron.

"She always looks pissed when I'm around. That's nothing new."

He laughed a big-bellied laugh that made his smile so wide that his cheeks nearly swallowed up his entire face.

"That was some kiss." He lowered his voice. "Real? Not real? What's the deal?"

"Did she see?" I asked, setting the food on the counter as I leaned on my elbows.

He grinned. "Oh, yeah. If steam could shoot out of some-one's ears…"

"I don't know why the fuck she cares. She's the one who left."

"Sometimes unhappy people are like that."

My brows furrowed in confusion. "She's happy. She practically has it tattooed on her forehead."

He shrugged. "Seems a little forced. Don't you think?"

I tried to think back to the Kristy I had known. The Kristy I'd fallen in love with wasn't the woman who had stood in front of me today. They were two very different people.

"When did you get to be so wise?" I goaded him.

"Comes with the beard," he joked. "And stop changing the subject. You didn't answer my question. Real? Not real?"

I let out a sigh. "That's too complicated for me to answer right now. And my food is getting cold."

"Too complicated? What the hell does that mean?"

"It means," I said with a frustrated pause, "that she has a boyfriend."

And deserved a hell of a lot better than me.

"Oh," he said, the word coming out in one long breath.

"Yeah."

His eyes went past me to the patio, where Marin was, and then finally centered back on me. "I'm gonna give you advice that might sound ludicrous and kind of cutthroat. Especially from someone who's currently in a long-distance relationship with a person thousands of miles away."

"Oh, yeah? What's that?"

He shrugged again. "I don't see any boyfriend around here. Do you?"

Every time I tried walking away from this woman, I found myself right back at her damn door.

"I think I've changed my mind," I said, hoping out of my truck.

She let out a sigh, the sound heavy against my ears. "You already said yes."

"Yeah," I countered, grabbing the back of my neck with my palm as I looked at the long walkway. "But then I thought I'd gotten out of it since we weren't really doing the whole gala thing anymore and I kind of forgot about it."

"It's a dinner party. How bad can it be?" I could hear her walking, the sound of her heels clacking on the wooden floor as she closed the distance between us.

"If I punch him, I'm gonna tell my deputy it was your fault."

She laughed, and then the door flung open. I found her standing there, looking at me, as her phone dropped to her side. "Would you stop loitering in my driveway and just get inside?"

I ended the call and shoved my phone back in my pocket, taking a moment to look at her.

Her dress wasn't fancy by any means, but it was the first time I'd seen her in anything but jeans and leggings. It was black and simple with long sleeves and a soft, velvety fabric.

And so fucking short.

My mouth went dry.

She must have noticed my silent perusal because a faint smile crept across her face as she nervously shifted her weight to one hip. "Are those for me?"

I looked down at the flowers I'd agonized over for the good part of an hour. "Apparently, I buy them a lot," I answered.

"What can I say?" She laughed, holding her hands up at her sides. "You're a really good boyfriend."

"You're going to ruin my hard-earned reputation," I joked as I followed her into the house.

"Oh, right." She grinned, taking the flowers in her hands. I watched her admire them, and a faint blush fell across her cheeks. Was she thinking about that story she'd made up too? "Because if you don't have a long-standing feud with the town doctor, life isn't worth living?"

"Exactly," I mused.

"Was it Molly?" she casually asked as she opened a cupboard and pulled out a vase. She bit her bottom lip, trying to keep her expression neutral as her eyes lingered on the etched glass a bit too long.

Yeah, she was definitely thinking about it.

She finally glanced up. "Is that why you hate each other? Did you, like, try to steal her away? Or did he steal her from you?"

"What?" I scoffed, taking a seat at her island. "No. I was never with Molly."

"Oh, but you wanted to?" She turned her head and placed the vase on the counter, staring at it a bit too long. She unwrapped the flowers and began arranging them one at a time.

"Maybe. For a minute when I was young, but it wasn't anything serious. Not like—"

You.

I gulped, averting my eyes, and then swiftly changed the subject. "You ready?"

"Oh, um, yeah," she answered, glancing at the vase one last time. "I just need to grab my purse." She walked toward the living room but then double backed. "Oh, and the wine. Oh, I grabbed some soda, just in case—" Her words halted, and she looked at me with a mixture of embarrassment and guilt.

She'd bought the soda for me…

God, why did I have to be such a fuck up?

"I probably should have said something the other day at my house rather than making you guess. I'm sorry," I said, feeling quite awkward. "I haven't exactly been social since—"

"Don't apologize. And you don't owe me an explanation."

I scrubbed a hand down my face. I didn't like talking

about this, but I needed her to know. Maybe I wanted her to know I wasn't a good guy. Maybe I just wanted her to know me. Either way, she needed to hear it.

"I did not handle Kristy leaving well—the cheating and then the pregnancy." I winced, deciding to leave out that it had all happened at around the same time as the ferry explosion. "My dad was a drunk, and I soon realized I was walking down a very similar path. When I started hiding whiskey in my desk drawer, I knew something had to stop."

"I'm so sorry." Her expression showed no judgment. No pity. Just warmth.

"I'm not very proud of it," I answered, remembering all the times when I had been a kid that I begged my dad to stop. All the times I'd sworn I'd never be like him. And yet…

"Look at us, son." He had held up his drink in a grand salute. "Like two peas in a pod."

I stifled a shudder.

"So, you just quit?"

I swallowed the lump in my throat, remembering to ask a similar question about her father and his music career. "No, I've failed—more than once. But I've been sober for a while now. The running helps. I probably should go to meetings, but I just can't go in there and admit to everyone in the town…" I paused. "No one knows. Except for Billy."

And you.

And my father—but I kept that dark secret to myself.

Her eyes rounded in understanding, as she took a step forward but stopped. "Will you be okay? Tonight?"

I nodded. "Yeah, it doesn't bother me. I was never a social drinker anyway."

Just a lonely drunk.

She looked conflicted, her eyes still on me. "Okay, but one word, and that's all you have to say. One word that you're uncomfortable, and we're out of there."

My lip curled, and she obviously understood where my mind was going.

"With the alcohol. Not our host!"

Well, damn. So close.

<hr>

To Molly's credit, her food was so good that it almost made the tense atmosphere that settled around the dining room table worth it.

Almost.

In addition to Jake and Molly, Dean—Jake's best friend—and his wife, Cora, had been invited to tonight's little social gathering, probably to aid as a buffer between the two of us.

Not sure why anyone thought that would help.

After an equally tense hour of drinks, we'd all moved to the inn's large dining room, and Molly had brought out enough food for Thanksgiving and Christmas combined. Jake muttered something about her overdoing it, and she shushed him. And then the silence had settled.

So much silence.

I looked around the room, finding a large antique-looking clock above Jake's stupid head.

Jesus. We'd only been here for an hour.

Longest damn hour of my life.

I ate more potatoes and took a drink of soda, wondering just how long we had to stay after cleaning our plates for it not to be considered rude. Five minutes? Ten?

"Okay," Marin said, who was seated next to me, "this is crazy. I know I'm not from here, but what the hell?"

You could have heard a pin drop from a mile away as everyone's eyes darted around the room, waiting for someone to say something.

Finally, Cora snorted into her napkin. "I don't get it either, but then again, I'm originally from Texas."

Jake turned to me, and I stared at him, my eyes narrowing.

"Seriously? You guys are ridiculous." Marin placed a hand on top of mine, making me look down instantly. "Jake"—she turned to him—"Macon had a teensy-weensy crush on Molly, way back when you were kids, but he's over it now. So, are we good now?"

Jake's eyes went wild.

"What the hell, Macon?" He turned to me.

"Thanks, Marin," I said dryly, trying to sound bored as my heart beat wildly from that single touch of her hand. "I think that helped a ton."

Molly laughed, and then to my surprise, Dean joined in.

"I did, too," he said casually. "From about second to fifth grade, I think. Maybe sixth?"

Jake turned to his best friend, looking at him like he'd never seen him before. "What the fuck? You, too?"

Dean shrugged, and I tried not to stare as he placed his arms up on the table. A twinge of guilt turned my stomach as I saw his prosthetic. "She was the only girl in our grade, man. What did you expect?"

"I guess I expected you to tell me sometime over the last three decades."

"We were engaged." He grinned. "For four years! I figured that might have been a clue."

Dean's wife was just shaking her head back and forth, laughing.

No jealousy. No anger.

They were all crazy.

"I love this conversation." Molly laughed, making Jake groan. "I really do."

"Just be glad Macon didn't ask her to marry him, too," Dean joked. "You were gone a really long time."

Jake's gaze went to me and then back to Dean, until finally, he just scooped more potatoes onto his plate.

"Asshole," Jake muttered.

"I'm the asshole?" Dean scoffed. "You're the Neanderthal who can't handle the thought that someone had the hots for your wife—decades ago."

"That's because, decades ago," he said, looking at her

from across the table, "I already knew she was going to be my wife."

They stared at each other, and it was the kind of look that made other people in the room uncomfortable.

It was the kind of look Marin had given me when she walked up next to me yesterday at Billy's.

Like I was her world.

Like I was her other half.

Only for Jake and Molly, there was no acting involved.

"So, wait," Marin said, thankfully interrupting the eye-fucking that was going on next to me, "you only had four people in your entire class?"

"You lived in Ocracoke for how long, and you're only now figuring this out?" Dean laughed.

"It was only a few months actually," she corrected him. "And I guess I knew, in the back of my mind, but I never really thought about it. So, you"—she pointed to us—"just the four of you…this is literally your entire class?"

We all nodded.

"It's like a class reunion." Molly laughed before adding, "Wait, did we have one of those?"

"No," I answered, already seeing her eyes perk up. "And please don't make us."

The conversation seemed to just flow after that. Jake and I still kept a decent distance, talking mostly to others rather than each other, and by dessert…I didn't like him any less than I had when I came.

So, that was progress, right?

Marin laughed more in those few hours than I'd ever seen. She connected with Cora and Molly, and I knew, just to see that smile, I'd spend a thousand hours with Jake if it made her happy.

I hadn't forgotten the words Billy had said to me.

Did I want to give her a reason to stay? Yes.

I wanted to remind her of that kiss and the way it had felt, that exact second when she gave in and kissed me back, knowing she wasn't pretending anymore.

But I would not make her do something she would someday regret.

Nor did I want to chain her to a place or person that only reminded her of pain.

"You look happy," Jake said while Marin was in the kitchen with Molly and Cora. "You don't have that usual scowl plastered on your face." He made a motion with his hand, waving it in front of him.

My eyes narrowed.

"Oh, there it is." He took a sip from his wineglass. "Is she staying?"

Dean looked on, watching the two of us.

I let out an exasperated sigh. "I don't know."

"Do you want her to?" he asked, leaning back in his chair.

I lifted an eyebrow. "I didn't know you cared."

"Look, Macon. I don't know what went wrong with us," he said casually.

I let out a forced laugh. "You don't?" I looked at him and then Dean, shaking my head. I'd told Marin there was no real reason I hated Jake, but there was. There was a whole childhood's worth. "Seriously?"

He stared at me blankly.

"You heard Marin tonight. There were only four of us. Four." I emphasized the last word by holding four fingers in front of me. "And it was always the three of you and me. You all had each other, and I had—"

No one.

I watched his eyes fall to the table as he processed my words.

"We invited you to stuff," he said. "Early on. Parties and shit. My mom wanted the four of us to be best friends."

Dean interjected, "Mine, too."

"But she always told me that your dad would reply and

say you didn't want to. After a while, I started to take it personally."

And I'd treated him horribly because of it.

I thought back to all those times my dad had told me we weren't like them. That we didn't belong. But really, it was just an excuse for his hate.

"What a fucking asshole," I said, staring at my half-empty glass of Coke.

"Guess we owe each other a lot of birthday presents," Dean said, cutting the tension.

"I heard Macon needs a new vase," Jake quipped, holding his wineglass in the air as a personal salute.

Of course someone had heard us that day on the patio.

"This town is ridiculous."

The sound of feminine laughter filled our ears, and I couldn't help but grin.

"You want a bit of advice, Macon?" Jake said, his tone sincere. "Don't let her go without making sure she knows."

He didn't have to say what. I knew what he meant.

Before I had the chance to respond, the woman came back in, and my eyes found her. Every time I convinced myself I could do this—just help her with the house and walk away— I'd find myself staring into those brown eyes, and I'd waver.

No. Not waver. I'd fucking stumble.

"You ready to go?" she asked, her fingers touching my shoulder.

If we only had a few minutes left of this charade, I wasn't going to waste it. I reached up, clasping my hand over hers, savoring the feel of it.

"Yeah. You?"

She nodded.

I rose from my seat but kept her hand in mine. She shifted her fingers, intertwining them with mine, like she had that first day on the patio at Billy's.

"Oh, hey, Macon. I have a few extra vases if you need one," Molly teased, walking up next to her husband.

I rolled my eyes. "You, too? Seriously?"

"Who do you think told me?" Jake said.

Molly shrugged. "Best gossip I've heard all year. Did she really try to slap you?"

"What? No," Marin exclaimed, an amused expression on her face. "Although I'm sure she wanted to."

"Who knew Macon was such a romantic?" Jake said, slipping an arm around his wife.

Molly looked up at him, her hand sliding around his waist. "You know, I wouldn't mind some flowers."

"Can we break a vase?" he asked, a wicked gleam in his eye.

"And that's our cue to go," Dean groaned, tugging on Cora's hand. "Bye!"

Marin laughed, and we said our farewells also, thanking Molly for the food. Jake and I gave each other a nod, and the women hugged, promising to get together soon.

"Was it as bad as you'd thought it was going to be?" she asked as we walked down the walkway toward my truck. She still hadn't let go of my hand, and I wasn't going to relinquish it.

"No," I admitted, thinking back to my conversation with Jake and Dean. "I think some bridges were mended."

"Really?" She looked up at me with hope.

"I still think he's a prick, but I don't hate him," I said before adding, "Much."

She smiled as I begrudgingly let go of her hand, so she could get into the truck. I wondered if it would be the last time I held it.

When I slid in next to her and started the engine, I turned. "Did you have fun?"

She nodded, a bright energy about her. "Yes. Molly and Cora are really nice. It makes me sad that I didn't get the time to know them—before."

"How did you end up here?" I asked, knowing she and

Daniel had barely just arrived when he died. "I mean, what was the plan?"

"It was my dream," she explained. "Daniel was just nice enough to support it. But it came at a price."

"What do you mean?" I put the car in gear and pulled out of the driveway.

"I quit my job—"

"Seems to be a habit of yours." I smiled.

She gave me a wry grin. "That time, I had a plan. I was a graphic artist," she explained. "Still am, or was, until a few weeks ago. But I hate it."

"Why?"

"Because I went to school to paint."

"You went to art school?" I asked, realizing how much I didn't know about her.

"Yes," she answered. "I wanted to be a painter from a very young age. But my mom—being the practical woman she is—was worried that it wouldn't be a stable job, so I minored in graphic design to appease her. It was supposed to be a fallback, but the moment I got out of college, I got scared."

"You never tried?"

She shook her head. "I got a job as a graphic artist, took my comfortable salary and benefits, and that was that."

"So, how did you end up here?"

"I was miserable," she said. "Daniel knew it. My parents knew it. Everyone could see it, but me. One night, after coming home from a particularly bad day at the office, Daniel asked what my ultimate dream would be, and after a bit of persuading, I finally told him. I wanted to live on the beach and paint. And so, that's what we did."

"And he was on board with that?"

"Yeah," she said, her voice soft but filled with warmth. "He applied for a promotion that would get us the salary we needed, but the travel that it required was brutal."

We were at a Stop sign, and I looked over at her. "Did you ever get a chance to paint while you were here?"

"Yes," she answered, her tone changing abruptly. "But I never got a chance to do anything with it. Most of it is hidden away in closets. I feel like I let Daniel down in that way. He sacrificed everything so we could move down here, and I gave up."

We drove down the empty street, as the autumn breeze filled the air.

"I doubt he'd see it like that," I said, pulling into her driveway. I turned to her, noticing the way the moonlight danced along her skin. "You could still do it, you know?"

"What?"

"Paint," I said. "Sell your work, live the dream you wanted."

She looked at me and tilted her head, a teasing smile tugging at the corner of her lips. "I thought you said I needed to sell and move on."

"And I thought you said you hadn't decided."

The words hung in the air, and I couldn't help but stare at her.

God, she is gorgeous.

And I knew at that moment, I'd never be able to walk away.

No matter how many times I kept trying, I'd always end up back here, trying to figure out a way to make her mine.

A tiny movement in the corner of my eye jerked my head toward her house.

"Did you leave the lights on?" I asked.

"No," she answered, still looking at me. Then, she turned and saw the warm glow from her bedroom and kitchen.

"Did you lock the door?"

"I—" she stammered, her eyes going wide. "I don't remember."

"Dammit," I cursed. "Does anyone have a key?"

"No," she answered. "Just me."

I pushed the door open, and she followed.

"Stay here," I said, turning to face her.

When she took another step forward, I took her hand, pulling it to my chest. "Please."

She swallowed, fear painting her features as I strode off.

I stepped lightly over the threshold, that damn door squeaking as I closed it. I looked around but saw no one. The movement I'd seen in the truck was in one of the bedrooms, so that was where I headed.

If someone was in her bedroom…waiting for her…

I took a deep breath, letting all those years of training kick in.

Calm and steady…

One step, then another. I silently moved down the hall-way. Nearly every light was on. Not exactly the smartest intruder.

A shadow. Someone was indeed in her bedroom.

I instantly saw red.

I tried to stuff all my emotions back down. I turned toward the door and looked inside. A man sat on the bed.

On her fucking bed.

His eyes met mine and widened.

"What the hell?" he said a second before I pulled him to his feet, slamming him against the wall.

"Who the fuck are you?" my voice boomed.

"Curtis?" a soft voice said behind me. "What are you doing here?"

So far, I was not a fan of Curtis.

Of course, he could hold the title of Nicest Guy on the Fucking Planet, and I'd still hate him.

Solely based on the other title he held.

Marin's boyfriend.

Almost fiancé.

I let out a ragged sigh.

Fuck my life.

I'd stepped out of the room shortly after Marin entered and I let Curtis's feet touch the ground again. But not before an introduction was made.

"Who is he?" Curtis asked, sending an accusatory glance my way.

"He's a friend," Marin answered angrily. "And a cop. We thought someone broke in, for God's sake!"

I gave Marin one last glance. "I'll let you two have a moment."

I'd been sitting on a chair in the living room ever since.

A friend.

I'd never hated a word in the English language more.

"You said you'd give me time!" Marin's voice echoed through the hallway.

"It's been two weeks, and no one has heard from you, Marin!"

My fists tightened. I kind of wanted to hit the guy just for yelling at her.

"That's not true. I talked to Elena the other day. And I texted my parents when I got here."

Silence.

"So, it's just me that you're not talking to?"

She didn't answer.

"I just wanted to make sure you were okay," he said, his voice softer, but the thin walls kept no secrets. I could still hear every word.

"Did you even bother checking with my parents before you drove all the way down here?"

"I missed you," he said in a tone so familiar that it made me nauseous.

Because he was familiar.

He knew everything about her.

He knew her laugh, her favorite food, the way she looked when she slept.

And I was just…

The friend.

"I can't do this right now," she finally said.

"Just let me stay the night, and we'll talk in the morning."

Stay here? With her?

So very nauseous.

"I can't," she said, her voice barely a whisper. "I can't have you stay here. Not in this house…" The pain in her words echoed down the hallway. "I'm sorry."

"Why won't you talk about it? You've never told me anything about your life before—"

"I can't. I don't know why," she said.

Those words must have stung because Curtis's voice changed, sharpened. "Where am I supposed to go, Marin? It's nearly ten at night."

Fucking asshole should have thought of that before he drove down here.

Just when I was about to get up to intervene, Marin came down the hallway, her face red and her eyes swollen.

She looked up at me and stopped. A moment passed. And then another. I saw her lip quiver as she tried not to cry.

It didn't work.

"I'm guessing you heard that," she said.

I tried to give her a half-hearted smile. "The walls in this house are pretty thin," I said. "You do not want to know what I heard during those childhood sleepovers."

She sniffled out a laugh before rubbing under her wet eyes. "I don't know what to do. I can't call Molly because—" She looked up at me, biting her lip.

Because Molly thought we were dating.

And this was her real boyfriend, who needed a room.

"I have a place he can stay," I said gently. "One of my rentals."

"You have rentals?" Her voice was so quiet.

"I'm decent at investing," I explained. "And I like to fix stuff."

Those tears were fucking killing me.

"Are you sure?" she asked.

Was I sure I wanted to offer up my empty rental as an alternative for him sleeping anywhere near her?

Hell yes.

I merely nodded.

"Okay." There was no energy to her answer. None of the spark and the vibrancy she'd had only minutes ago in the car when she was talking about her art and life on the island with Daniel.

How easily the words had come.

Why couldn't she talk about him with Curtis?

Was it because I was the friend and he was the lover?

Or I was part of her past and he was her future?

Whatever the reason, I was just glad I was able to do this one thing for her. To give her a reprieve for the night.

But I couldn't stop the morning from coming.

She'd have to make a decision eventually.

CHAPTER ELEVEN

Marin

My brain hurt.

My heart hurt worse.

And on top of all that, I was so damn angry.

Macon had given Curtis the key code and directions to his rental thirty minutes ago, and soon after, I'd watched both men quietly walk into the night.

I'd been staring at my bedroom ceiling ever since.

I had no idea what to do.

No idea what to say to Curtis in the morning. No idea if I should ask him to stay or make him leave.

When I'd watched Macon march into my house, I'd been paralyzed by fear.

What if someone was in there? What if he got hurt?

What if I never saw him again?

So, I threw caution to the wind and chased after him.

Without thought. Without reason.

I just jumped out of the truck and bolted toward the door. After I got in, I tiptoed down the hallway and froze when I heard yelling. I raced into the room, and that was when I saw him—pinned against the wall like a rag doll.

I should have been happy to see him, right?

Relieved?

But the moment I saw Curtis, I felt like I was back in my apartment, looking down at him on one knee.

And all I had wanted to do was run.

I needed to stop staring at this damn ceiling.

I picked up the phone and called the one person I needed the most.

"What the actual hell? Do you know how late it is?" Elena said, her voice groggy and hoarse.

"You know"—a smile was already spreading across my face—"there was a time in our lives when the evening didn't even start until ten or eleven."

She yawned so loudly in my ear that I had to pull the phone away. "Yeah, I remember. I also remember being a lot hotter and a lot younger back then."

"You're still hot."

"Tell that to the men on my dating app."

My eyes widened. "Dating app? Did you and Chad—"

"Yep."

"Was it bad?"

I was the worst friend on the planet. I should have called sooner. I'd told Curtis we'd been talking, but in truth, this was the first time I'd checked in since I had gotten here.

"No." She yawned again, this time a bit quieter. "It wasn't even a big deal really. I just brought it up, and he seemed—"

"What?"

"Relieved."

Lines creased my forehead. How was she so calm about this? They'd been together longer than Curtis and me.

"And that doesn't upset you? That your boyfriend seemed relieved to be rid of you?"

She laughed. "It would have if the feeling hadn't been mutual. We were both relieved, honestly." She paused, and I could hear her shuffling around her apartment. "Like I said before, we were better as friends, and we both deserve a hell of a lot more."

I thought about that and then finally asked, "How do you

know? I mean, did you always know and just ignore it? Or was it like an epiphany that just fell from the sky one day?"

"Why?" she asked.

I let out a sigh. "Curtis showed up."

"Wait. Like, there? At your house in North Carolina?"

"Yep."

"Are you serious?"

"Yes, and I told him you and I have been talking since I got here so—"

She snorted. "You overestimate my relationship with Curtis if you think we speak when you're not around."

Oh, I hadn't really thought of that. Aside from the whole surprise-party debacle, I didn't think he'd interacted with my family much either.

"I was just so mad, you know?" I huffed. "He was just here—in *my* house—and he was upset because I hadn't been in contact with anyone—"

"How did he even know that?"

"He didn't!" I threw an angry hand in the air even though no one was around to see it. "He was just upset I hadn't contacted *him* even though he'd told me to take all the time I needed."

"Apparently, not *all* the time." I could hear her eyes rolling all the way in Richmond.

"No," I agreed.

"So, wait," she said. "Where is he now?"

I could hear her snacking on something. She'd fully committed to not going back to sleep anytime soon.

I should feel bad about that, but I didn't.

I needed my best friend right now.

"He's at Macon's rental. Or one of them."

"Macon?"

"Oh, right." It had been a while since I'd talked to her. It had been two weeks, but Macon's name fell from my lips like something so familiar. Like he belonged. I shoved that thought away for a later time. "He's a friend," I explained. "A cop actually. Deputy? Anyway, he's been helping me with a few things around the house."

She made a gasping sort of noise. "Hot Cop?"

My brows wrinkled as I turned on my side on the bed. "What?"

"That's what you used to call him when you lived there—Hot Cop."

"I did not!" I definitely would have remembered that.

She laughed. "You did. You used to see him at the—"

Suddenly, a memory came rushing back.

Long walks, short lines, stolen glances.

"The coffee shop." My hand went to my mouth in disbelief.

I had liked to go for walks early in the morning on the days when Daniel was out of town. I would sometimes stop at the coffee shop on my way back, and I'd always see Macon there, buying coffee before his shift. And then one day—

"He even bought me a cup of coffee when I forgot my wallet."

"And you threatened me that if I ever told Daniel you called him Hot Cop, you'd kill me."

A faint smile spread across my lips. Yeah, I'd said that.

"How could I have forgotten that?"

"Memories are funny like that, Marin," she said. "I think sometimes, we push down things that are painful."

"My life with Daniel wasn't painful." It had been beautiful.

"No, but his death was—"

My throat suddenly felt thick.

"It's getting a lot easier," I said softly. "At first, I just wanted to cry. All the damn time."

"And now?"

"And now, I—" I thought about my conversation with Macon in the car. "It kind of feels like home. I think I could be happy here. But when Curtis showed up, I suddenly felt guilty." I swallowed back the lump in my throat. "Like I should be grieving more."

And moving on.

"You've been grieving for five years, Marin."

"I know," I said. "I just always thought coming back here would be awful—like walking around a horrible nightmare. But if anything, I feel like I've just awoken from one."

"Did you just call Curtis a nightmare?" she joked in an attempt to lighten the mood.

But it made me realize something.

"I've been living two separate lives. Before Daniel and after Daniel. Curtis always asks me about my life before, and I always avoided telling him."

"Why?"

"Because if I tell him, then he becomes a part of it. Part of me. Right now, I'm in this safe little bubble." I let out a breath. "I can tell myself I've moved on, without ever letting him in. But in reality—"

"You haven't moved on, because you don't love him."

I let out a long sigh. "Yeah."

I knew I loved him—in a way. But I also knew I was not in love with him.

"Do you think you'll ever be able to love him? To let him be part of your life?"

"I—" I thought about how I had felt when I saw him standing in my bedroom. That instantaneous need to run. "I wish I could. But no, I don't think so," I confessed, feeling like the worst kind of person. "What if this is all I'm ever able to give, Elena? Like, what if I'm just emotionally stunted and this is as good as it's gonna get?"

"Or," she offered up. "Maybe this is all you're able to give to Curtis. Have you thought about that?"

"I don't think Curtis is the problem," I sighed. "I definitely think it's me. I'm broken."

"Why would you say that?"

I'd never told her this because I was worried she would

judge me. Or that it would cross a line since she was my sister-in-law.

"Well, aside from the inability to talk or share anything of myself. I've also never let him sleep over," I admitted. "Two years of dating, and he's never once slept in my bed—."

"Oh, sweetie." Her voice was soft and full of compassion. "That's…" She paused. "That's okay."

"No, it's not. Like I said, it's me." A wave of guilt swept over me. "He's perfect and patient, and I feel like I'm stringing him along."

"I doubt that's how he sees it," she countered.

"And…" I hesitated.

"And what?" she asked. "I can tell you're stalling, even over the phone."

"I haven't…" I let out a frustrated groan. "I mean, when we…I just that I can't—. Maybe that part of me died with Daniel."

There was silence on the other end of the line. So much so that I pulled the phone away and checked to make sure she was still there.

"Are you saying that you haven't orgasmed? In two years?"

"Well, technically, five. But yes."

"Are you fucking kidding me?" She seemed angry.

"Are you mad? At me?"

"What? No! Maybe a little that you didn't tell me. I could have bought you a vibrator or given you some tips or something."

"Oh my God."

"But, no," she said. "I'm mad at Curtis. Two years? I mean, shit. Chad and I didn't ever have fireworks, but even we managed to get each other off."

Well, okay.

"We don't—" I huffed. "We don't have sex that often. I think it was just another one of those things Curtis figured we'd work out later." But relationships didn't work like that. You couldn't tally up your problems like a to-do list.

"No wonder you panicked when he proposed. God, Marin, why didn't you tell me all this before?"

"I was embarrassed."

"There is nothing to be embarrassed about," she insisted. "You lost your husband. Did you really expect it to be that easy?"

I didn't know how to respond to that. I'd fallen in love with the first man I'd ever dated. I hadn't really known what to expect. I never thought I'd have to do this.

She let out a huff. "Have you ever considered that you and Curtis simply aren't compatible—in that way? That maybe there's just no physical spark?"

I rolled my eyes. "Sometimes," I answered. "I guess I just tried to tell myself there was more to a relationship than that."

"Well, sure," she agreed. "But, don't you want more? I mean, I used to share an apartment with you. I know that kind of relationship you and Daniel had and it was not boring. I have nightmares because of the things I heard."

I snorted. "You do not."

"I do, too. You guys were loud. So damn loud. You try sleeping while your brother is moaning your best friend's name down the hall. Fucking gross."

I closed my eyes, remembering lazy Sundays in bed, when there had been nothing to do but live in each other's arms.

"God, I miss him," I said softly.

"Yeah," she said. "Me, too. Look," she said. "I can't tell you what to do when it comes to Curtis—only you know what to do. But it sounds to me like you've already made up your mind. I think part of you already knew the second you decided to go back to Ocracoke."

I pressed my lips together, trying to keep my emotions in check.

"So, maybe it's a good thing he showed up. You can finally give him an answer."

"I don't think it'll be the answer he's hoping for." My nerves twisted in a knot.

"No," she agreed. "But it's the one he deserves. You're not the only one who needs to move on."

And she was right. He might not see it now, but he deserved someone who would scream yes from the rooftop the second he dropped to one knee.

And that wasn't me.

We started to say our good-byes, and I heard that telltale yawn of hers. I started to settle back on the bed, and I knew I couldn't let her go just quite yet.

Because if I was confessing things tonight…

"I kissed Hot Cop!" The words tumbled out of my mouth so quickly that I wasn't sure she understood.

There was an audible silence.

"What?" It was almost a gasp, high pitched and shrill at the end. "We've been on the phone for how long, and you're just telling me this *now*?"

I laughed, loving her all the more in that moment.

And then I proceeded to tell her everything that had happened since I'd arrived in Ocracoke.

And I did mean everything.

I told her about showing up to the gala ticketing event and pissing off Macon's ex. Our deal. The kiss.

"So, it was just for show then?"

"Um…" I bit my lip. "It was supposed to be."

"What does that mean?"

I let out a big, long breath. "I kissed him to make his ex jealous, and then…" I paused, remembering the exact moment. His sudden surprise. The jolt of electricity I'd felt between us. The sensational heat as I felt as his fingers dug through my hair and he pulled me close.

And that body…

Every inch was just as hard as I'd imagined it would be.

"He kissed me back."

He had *really* kissed me back.

"And?" she asked, completely engrossed now and not at all tired.

"It was so fucking hot."

It was the first time I'd admitted it. To myself. To anyone else.

He'd kissed me back, and I had known right then and there that neither of us was pretending.

"Hmm, interesting."

"Interesting?" I echoed her, sitting up. "That's all you have to say?"

"Well, it's just…I'm gonna make an observation, okay?"

I rolled my eyes. This was what happened when you had a lawyer for a best friend. "Okay."

"You've been depriving me of sleep for a while now, talking about all the ways in which you and Curtis are all wrong for each other."

"Uh-huh."

"And then you went on to say how broken you are and how you'll basically never love again."

"Right…"

"Well, it seems like, in the short time you've been in Ocracoke, you've managed to find someone who proves all those theories incorrect, wouldn't you say?"

My eyes widened.

Macon was easy to talk to, and to open up to.

And when it came to…*that*.

I cleared my throat.

"So, perhaps it's not that you're broken or unable to open yourself up to another. Maybe you were just looking in the wrong place."

"But that's…" Crazy? Ludicrous? "I haven't even broken up with Curtis. I can't just suddenly start dating Macon."

There was a brief pause before she said, "Seems to me like you kind of already are."

I tried pushing Elena's words to the back of my mind the following morning as I walked over to Macon's rental.

I couldn't think about Macon until I got through this morning.

Then…

Well, then I had no idea.

My stomach did a flip-flop as I thought about it.

Could I really just jump from one man to the next?

I'd only dated two people in my entire life.

Two.

Daniel had been my first and only boyfriend until Curtis.

In the back of my mind, I never really thought about a future with Curtis. I guessed maybe that should have been a clue. Every time he brought it up, I'd get that same feeling of panic rise in my chest that consumed me the night of his proposal.

Was I even ready to entertain the idea of another relationship?

I hadn't even broached the idea that Macon might not want to—

Those thoughts had been swirling in my head since the moment I had woken up. And the longer I was awake, the more and more they spiraled out of control. After a lengthy shower and three cups of coffee, I had finally worked up the courage to text Curtis to let him know I would be coming over to talk.

His one-worded reply told me he probably already assumed the worst.

I took my time walking there, a poor attempt to enjoy the fresh ocean air and the brisk autumn weather. It didn't have anything to do with the fact that I was stalling.

Not at all.

Eventually, I found myself standing in front of a small one-story yellow house. The grass had recently been mowed, and the landscaping had that same simple and clean aesthetic Macon had chosen for his own home.

There was a sign by the front door that said, *Welcome to Ochre Bay*.

He'd named his rental. Why did I find that ridiculously cute?

I suddenly wanted to know what the rest of them were called and what they looked like.

Focus, Marin.

I took a long, deep breath and tried to pull myself together, placing a hand in my coat pocket as I stepped forward.

Just then, the door opened, and Curtis stepped out.

He was freshly showered, his brown hair wet and brushed back. He held a coffee cup in his hand, and from the look on his face, I could tell he hadn't slept well.

That made two of us.

"Hi," he managed to say.

"Hi."

I walked forward and met him the rest of the way, and he stepped to the side, allowing me to enter. I took a second to look around, noticing how different the interior looked compared to Macon's house.

It was bright and welcoming with fresh paint, new appliances, and updated furnishings—such a stark contrast to the mismatched furniture that littered Macon's living room.

It was like he'd given up in his own home after she left.

Or he hadn't even tried.

"It was nice of your friend to offer his place for me," Curtis said, pulling my attention back toward him. "You'll have to thank him for me."

"Um…" I flinched, remembering the conversation I'd had with Elena. "I will."

He eyed me, taking another sip of his coffee. "Do you want a cup?"

"Oh, no," I said. "I've already had several. Thank you though."

Silence filled the space.

Finally, I took a seat on the sofa, and he followed. He continued to watch me with those tired eyes.

He let out a ragged breath. "I think I know why you're here."

"Oh?" I tried to will my emotions to behave.

Keep it together.

"Come on, Marin." He tilted his head to the side and gave a sad smile. "It shouldn't be this hard to say yes to a marriage proposal."

My lip quivered and a tear trailed down my cheek. "I'm so sorry, Curtis. You have no idea."

He set his coffee cup down and slid closer, taking my hand in his. "It's okay. I knew coming down here would probably not end well for me."

"You did?"

He nodded, a heavy weight of sadness clouding his features. "Like I said, it shouldn't be this hard."

I knew he wasn't just talking about the proposal.

He meant all of it.

My relationship with Daniel had been far from perfect. There were times when we argued or disagreed, but the easy part? The absolutely effortless part?

My love for him.

That was something I never had to question.

The day he had dropped to one knee, there was no hesitation.

No second-guessing.

I reached into my coat pocket and pulled out the velvet box. The one he'd given me before I left for Ocracoke.

I placed it on the coffee table.

"I wish I could have said yes," I said softly.

"Me, too."

"You're an amazing person, Curtis. Truly. I wish I could have been that person—your person."

"I wish I could have been that person for you, too." His voice was thick. "I don't regret it though. I will always be glad I was the one who was in the elevator all those times. I'm so glad I met you."

"Me, too." And I meant it.

He might have not been the right person, but in a way, he'd been the right person at that moment. He'd been a big part of my life for the last two years, and even though I knew I didn't love him, I'd still miss him.

He pulled me into his arms, and we held each other for a long time.

For the last time.

Finally, I got up to leave, and I knew he would follow shortly after. There was nothing keeping him here anymore.

"How long will you stay?" he asked, standing at the threshold.

"I'm still not sure," I answered.

He leaned against the doorframe as I took a step onto the porch. "I hope you find what you're looking for."

I gave him one last look, memorizing the color of his eyes and the gentle slope of his jaw. "I'm working on it."

And then I walked away. For good.

CHAPTER TWELVE

Macon

Growing up, I used to make up stories. My mom had always told me I had a vivid imagination. But in reality, I just liked to see her smile.

It was a rarity in our fucked-up house.

But after she died, my imagination had kind of died with her.

Today, however?

It seemed to have miraculously resurrected, and it was running rampant.

After I'd left Marin's house last night, I hadn't been able to stop thinking—about her.

About him.

About her and him...together.

Ever since she'd told me she had a boyfriend/almost fiancé, I obviously knew he existed, but like Billy had said, he wasn't here. It was an easy detail to ignore. Especially when our "deal" had us acting like he didn't.

But here he was. In my town. In my fucking rental.

I thought back to that moment I'd walked into her bedroom. The moment I pulled him off that bed and shoved him against the wall.

He was different than I'd thought he'd be.

I didn't know what I had expected, but I guessed I never imagined Marin's boyfriend would be so…ordinary. It wasn't that he was bad-looking. He just seemed so very typical, with his lean frame and clean-cut hair.

Shit, when was the last time I got a haircut?

I sat in my cruiser in one of the parking lots by the marina, looked down at my watch, and groaned. It had been twelve hours since I'd left her house.

It was nearly noon. Surely, she'd gone over to see him by now. Or maybe she'd forgiven him for coming unannounced and decided to invite him over after all.

She could be giving him a tour of the town right this very second, walking through the streets, showing him all the shops and restaurants.

Or maybe they decided to stay in …

Nope. That wasn't an image I wanted to explore. Not even a little.

I scrubbed a hand down my face, feeling the day's worth of stubble I hadn't bothered to shave. I needed to eat, and every muscle in my body ached like a bitch.

My run this morning had been…excessive.

The extra miles and then the weight training after helped me deal with the stress, but by the time I got home, I barely had enough time to shower and get dressed.

Breakfast had been the last thing on my mind, and now, I was starving.

I started up the engine and pulled onto the road. The urge to drive by my rental and check to see if Curtis was there was strong. But I'd never stalked a renter before, and I certainly wasn't gonna start now. So, I headed to the local coffee shop instead.

The parking lot was relatively empty, which wasn't surprising for this time of day. They'd only recently started carrying sandwiches and things in an attempt to expand the business beyond the morning crowd. I was just glad to have somewhere else to grab a quick sandwich.

The options in Ocracoke were limited, which meant things got boring real fast.

The moment I stepped into the small shop, my breath stopped.

She was looking up at the menu, wearing black jeans and a green sweater I'd seen on her before. Her dark hair was pulled to the side in one of those loose braids I loved.

I glanced from one side of the shop to the other.

She was alone.

I took a step forward, feeling determined.

She turned, and her eyes met mine. A sudden but brief moment of surprise crossed her features, and then a shy smile spread across her face.

Hope blossomed in my chest.

God, I was a glutton for punishment.

Her eyes followed me as I casually took a place behind her in line, my arms clasped in front of me. Anyone could have mistaken us for strangers if it wasn't for the mischievous grin plastered across my dumb face.

She bit her bottom lip to keep from smirking and then turned to face forward. A moment passed. And then another.

Finally, she whipped her head back around.

"Did you forget your wallet again?"

Those big brown eyes widened as a hand flew up to cover that perfect pink mouth. "Oh my God! You do remember?"

My grin widened. "Of course I do," I answered. "Who would forget buying a beautiful woman coffee?" *The fuck do you think you are? Cassanova?*

"And do you do that often?" she asked, not seeming to be fazed by my really lame attempt at flirting.

Janet, the owner, was merely standing behind the counter, watching. I guessed she, like the rest of the town, thought we were dating and was just amused by our antics.

"Buy beautiful women coffee?"

I slowly shook my head back and forth. "Just that one

time." It was the truth, which was why it stuck out in my mind so vividly.

That, and she was damn hot.

"Then, maybe I should return the favor."

God, her smile.

"Can I buy you lunch? Do you have time?"

For you? I have all the fucking time in the world.

I looked at my watch. I had thirty minutes, max. "Yeah, I have time."

We gave Janet our orders, and when it came time to pay, I tried to pull out my wallet.

Her hand fell on top of mine, stopping me. "I'm paying, remember?"

I wanted to remind her that she didn't have a job. That she was living on a limited income.

But I had a feeling she'd had enough of people telling her what to do. So, I simply nodded and let her plunk her debit card down.

There was some cozy seating in the small coffee shop, but it all felt a little cramped, especially with Janet now watching and listening to everything we said like we were her own personal soap opera. After getting our food, I asked Marin if she'd be interested in eating outside.

Her eyes darted over to Janet and then back at me, and she laughed under her breath. "That would be great."

We left the coffee shop and crossed the street. I showed her to an old bench that faced the water. Thankfully, the breeze was fairly calm today, and the afternoon sun made the chilly temperature manageable.

Still, I asked, "Are you cold?"

"No," she answered, her head leaning back to bask in the warmth of the sun. "It's actually pretty perfect."

I ignored everything else and just looked at her. "Yeah, it is."

Sunrays scattered across the water as I unwrapped my

sandwich. She did the same, her body angled toward me as she leaned against the weathered wood.

"So, are you going to ask me about Curtis?" She stared up at me through those thick lashes, waiting.

"No." I wanted to, but I wasn't going to.

"Why?"

" 'Cause it's not my place, Marin. If you want to tell me, you will. But otherwise, I'm just going to enjoy this lunch I got from a beautiful woman."

A shy smile spread across her face.

She ate a bit more, staring at the water as the waves gently lapped at the shore. Finally, she looked up at me. "We broke up."

I froze.

"You did?" I cleared my throat, hoping she didn't notice the slightly elevated tone in my voice.

"I should have known, you know?" Her voice was assuredly calm. No tears. No sadness. "I mean, who has a panic attack when their boyfriend drops to one knee?"

"You had a panic attack?"

She'd left that part out in the previous story.

"Yeah." She awkwardly bit her bottom lip, her sandwich all but forgotten on the bench. "In front of my entire family and a bunch of friends."

"That sounds…" *Awful*. I kind of understood why she might have wanted to flee to another state now.

"Embarrassing?"

"I was going to say stressful, but, yeah, I'm sure it was that, too."

"I mean, that should have been a giant red flag right there, but I thought maybe there was just something wrong with me."

"There's nothing wrong with you," I said sincerely.

She didn't look like she agreed.

"So, where is Curtis now?" I asked, looking out toward the water.

"Um, I don't know," she answered. "We said our good-byes a few hours ago. I'm assuming he left after that."

Her gaze met mine and held.

How did I respond to that?

I'm sorry? 'Cause I wasn't.

Not really.

I was sorry if she was in pain. But I wasn't sorry Curtis was gone. It was selfish, but I just didn't care.

Not anymore.

I probably *should* care. The fact that her husband's name was carved on that memorial just a few miles down the road should be enough to make me stop this whole damn thing.

But, I couldn't.

I was sick of denying my feelings for her, and she was only going to be here for so long.

"Do you want to go on a trip with me?" I suddenly said.

"What?" The word came out more like a laugh.

"To the mainland," I elaborated, realizing that must have sounded crazy, out of context. "I told you a while ago that we needed parts."

Her face fell. "Oh, right. The house."

"I don't care what you do with the house," I told her. That was a lie. I cared. A little too much. "But you need to get those repairs. You can't live in a house with that much shit going on."

She pondered that statement for a moment before looking back at me.

"So, I guess if you're still fixing my house, that means our deal remains"—she pressed her lips together, looking up at me—"intact."

Guess I need to buy a suit.

My face broke out into a wide grin. "I guess so." But then I added, "But only on one condition."

Confusion painted her face. "What?"

"You give me the rest of that sandwich," I said, pointing

down the entire other half of her sandwich she hadn't touched. "I'm fucking starving."

That damn smile made a triumphant return. "Deal."

A few days had passed until my next day off, and between work and being on call, I barely had time to see Marin. Halloween came and went in that time, and I managed to stop by and work on a few things house-related, but there had been little time for much else. I had enjoyed the pictures she'd sent me of her cute cat ears though as she passed out candy to her neighbors.

I liked chaotic days at work—I thrived on them usually. But right now, it was just annoying the shit out of me.

I had no idea how long Marin planned on staying in Ocracoke.

It could be a few weeks or a couple of months.

All I knew was that my time with her was limited, and I wanted to spend every damn second with her, which was why my crazy work schedule was seriously stressing me out.

But even with all that stress, I was managing it. And that was something I hadn't been able to say in a long time. My morning runs were enjoyable—not the grueling marathons I usually put myself through when shit hit the fan.

Rolling into my day off, I had been in such a good mood, that Sheriff Hayes couldn't even bring me down. But, two unplanned visits in a month—what was this guy up to?

When I'd tried to ask him, he'd just changed the subject and tried to shove baby photos in my face.

I'd simply smiled and then told him to have a nice day.

Pretty sure I scared the shit out of him.

I'd woken up this morning, feeling eager and somewhat anxious at the same time. I knew it'd only been a handful of days since Curtis had left, but I felt like my time with Marin was finite.

And I wanted to make the most of it.

We decided on an early start that morning. Or I guessed I did.

She had mostly groaned a yes at the idea.

I picked her up around eight, and after I made sure she'd locked the door—she didn't need any more unwanted house guests—we headed out. The sun was bright, and the weather was unseasonably warm for early November. I tried not to stare as I pulled out of her driveway and headed down the road, but it was damn difficult. She was wearing a dress again, and one glance at those bare legs had me almost going headfirst into a ditch.

"Have you eaten?" I asked, giving her a quick glance. "Do you want to grab coffee?"

A tiny smirk formed at the corner of her mouth. "I'm afraid to use any appliance in my house after the pilot light issue, so, no, I haven't eaten. And, yes—the answer is always yes when it comes to coffee."

"Well, let's get you coffee."

A few more blocks down the road, I pulled into the familiar parking lot. There were a few more cars this morning, but I managed to find a spot, and we both hopped out. As we got to the door, I pulled it open, letting Marin go ahead. As she slipped passed me, I placed a hand on her waist and followed behind her.

Her lips parted in surprise as she looked up at me.

What? I mouthed, feigning innocence.

We were "dating" after all. I could see the amusement in her eyes as her lips turned upward. When she leaned in, giving her silent approval, I almost threw my fist in the air like I was the fucking king of the world.

But I didn't. 'Cause I wasn't an idiot.

"Morning, Captain Green," Janet said as we walked up to the counter.

"Morning," I answered, noticing the way her eyes

lingered on Marin and then to the possessive hand that was wrapped around her.

"This is Marin," I said, realizing what she was waiting for. "She lived in Ocracoke for a short time a few years ago."

Janet nodded. "Yes, I remember. You used to come in here often."

Marin nodded. "On my morning walks, yes."

I didn't know how many times we'd run into each other here, never saying more than a friendly hello.

Well, she said a lot of hellos. I gave a lot of manly nods.

The first time I'd ever said a word to her was the day I stepped up to pay for her coffee. It was also the last.

Until that night in her house a couple of weeks ago.

Janet gave Marin a warm smile and took our orders. This time, Marin let me pay.

I suggested we go sit while we waited, and she agreed, pulling me over to a cluster of couches and chairs in the corner. It was about as far away as we could get, but I still caught Janet's stare from across the room.

That old woman must have fucking eagle eyes.

"Do you think she knows about the vase?" Marin asked, making my eyes fly up to hers.

"What?" I choked out.

She laughed, amused by my reaction as her voice lowered. "Molly told me how gossip works around here."

"She would know," I muttered.

"Why?" She furrowed her brows, misinterpreting my words.

I sat up a bit. "No, I didn't mean it like that. It's just that Molly's life has been fuel for a lot of the gossip in the past. The thing with Dean and Jake—that kind of stuff doesn't happen much around here."

I ignored the fact that my own life had contributed to quite a lot of gossip over the years, thanks to Kristy.

"They seem pretty okay with it." She shrugged.

"I know. It's fucking weird." I didn't understand how they

all sat around the table and laughed about it, especially when Jake had nearly lost his shit over the mere fact that I'd once had a crush on his wife.

A crush.

His best friend had slept with her. Whatever.

She snorted. "I think it's nice."

"Really?" I challenged. "You don't think you'd be jealous to see Curtis with someone new?"

Her expression changed, and I suddenly regretted my words. Shit, it was too soon.

"No, actually," she answered with a tilt of her head. "Curtis and I were always good at being friends. But not so great at anything else." She paused for a minute, as if collecting her thoughts. "My best friend, Elena, just broke up with her boyfriend, too, and I think it was the way she phrased it that put it all in perspective for me."

"And what was that?"

"She said they both felt relieved," she explained. "And as hurt as I think Curtis expected to be, I think, ultimately, he felt a bit of that at the end."

"Relieved?" That was an unexpected answer.

She nodded. "Yeah. I think maybe that's why he came down here. He knew one of us needed to take that final step, and he knew I hated the idea of hurting him."

Maybe I didn't hate Curtis so much after all.

"And you feel relieved, too?" There was that hope again.

"Yeah, I do," she answered softly. "I knew we weren't meant to be. It just took me a while to admit it to myself. And to him."

We both stared at each other.

The chime on the door dinged, announcing a new customer, and breaking the spell. I looked up and instantly froze.

My father had just walked in.

Marin must have noticed the change in me because her

eyes followed mine. She might not have known who the piece of trash was, but she obviously knew I did.

"Are you okay?" she asked.

"No," I answered, resting a protective hand on her knee.

I wanted to throw her over my shoulder and get her as far away from him as possible.

But this island was only so big, and he was bound to show up sometime.

He looked pretty haggard, but I'd seen him much worse. His clothes were wrinkled and stained.

At least when my brother and I had been little, he'd tried to hide it.

It took him a moment to notice us. He never was very sharp this early in the morning. But when his head turned, he saw Marin first.

His gaze swept up her legs, lingering on those bare thighs for far too long.

I wanted to break his damn nose.

And then finally, he looked up, and that was when he saw me, and the asshole fucking smiled.

"Haven't seen you in a while," he said, stepping away from the counter.

"Not long enough," I answered.

I saw Janet out of the corner of my eye with our order, but she instinctively stopped, placing it on the counter, and then backed away.

"Heard you got a new girlfriend." His eyes roamed, and this time, he took even longer. "Pretty."

My hand on her leg curled into a fist. Marin silently watched our exchange, obviously confused. But it didn't stop her from placing her own hand on top of mine, unclenching my fingers to rest on her leg once more.

I took a deep breath. I wouldn't take his bait.

"Why are you here?"

It wasn't like him to be out this early. He was like a vampire—allergic to the sun and human emotions.

"Nothing beats a good cup of coffee," he answered, and then he gave Marin a wink. "Especially after you've had a few too many."

A few too many. Fuck me.

He didn't know how to *not* have a few too many.

"You know how it is, right, *son*?"

I felt Marin stiffen next to me as all the puzzle pieces settled in place for her.

A memory flashed in my mind. A late-night visit. His ass on my couch, smiling like a Cheshire cat as a bottle of whiskey sat on the table between us.

"Not so high and mighty now, are ya? It'd be a shame for the town to learn of your little... problem."

I swallowed down a lump in my throat.

"Don't call me that."

Only my father could make a term of endearment sound demeaning.

"Would you rather have me call you Captain Green?" he sneered.

"Well, since the only time I ever see you lately is in an official capacity...seems pretty fucking appropriate."

He stepped forward, and that was when I really got a whiff of it—the alcohol and sweat from his clothing.

How many times had he come home like that?

How many times had I sworn I'd never be like him?

How quickly I'd broken that promise...

"Not the only time," he reminded me with a wicked grin.

"Is this your way of saying you miss me?"

"You've always had quite the mouth on you, haven't you?" He shook his head back and forth, a cruel smile playing across his lips.

"Learned from the best," I fired back, hating that Marin had to be here to witness this.

"No, that's all your mama, boy." He made a noise, kind of like a whistle. "The mouth on her."

I was up in a flash. "No." My voice was low. Menacing.

"Not her. You can drag my name through the mud, but not hers."

His eyes were dancing with mischief, and I knew I'd reacted exactly as he'd hoped.

I felt Marin's hand slide into mine. It was warm and grounding. I turned to her and looked into those chocolate-brown eyes. I expected fear or regret, but all I saw was understanding, and that…well, that was something I wasn't sure I deserved.

Before I could turn back to my father, she surprised the shit out of me and beat me to it. Her determined gaze could have knocked over a bulldozer.

"I'd say it was nice to meet you, Mr. Green," she said, her voice brimming with confidence, "but, well, my mother taught me it's rude to lie. So, if you'll excuse us, our coffee is getting cold."

My jaw would have hit the floor if I wasn't waiting for my father's heated reaction.

Not letting me down for a second, he went for a final blow. "You letting your woman fight your battles for you now?"

I wasn't going to give him the satisfaction of getting another rise out of me. "See, that's the thing, *Dad*," I said, the word so grating on my tongue that it sounded dirty. "You're not even worth the fight."

Marin snorted, and a slow grin spread across my face. "Enjoy that coffee. Oh, do everyone a favor and take a fucking shower."

My hand slipped around her waist again, and we headed for the counter. I grabbed the brown paper bag, and Marin carried the coffee. I knew his eyes were on us, watching as we made our exit, but I didn't give him another glance.

He wasn't worth it.

Or at least, that's what I tried to tell myself.

CHAPTER THIRTEEN

Marin

We'd managed to make it to Macon's truck without any further incidents with his father.

But since we'd gotten in, he'd gone unnaturally still.

I bit the corner of my lip, worrying.

I'd always had an inkling his family life was bad. He hadn't told me much, but what he had said wasn't good.

But this…

God, my whole damn heart hurt for him.

"Macon." My voice was barely a whisper.

I was afraid to startle him, but he finally turned.

"Do you want to go somewhere?" he asked, those hazel eyes blazing with emotion.

I simply nodded. Anywhere sounded better than here.

He started the engine and pulled out of the parking lot. We drove a bit, passing familiar landmarks and street signs until I finally had an inkling of where we were going.

"Springer's Point?" I guessed.

"I like the trees," he said, referring to the ancient live oak trees that were known to line the trail and the beach.

It also happened to be the beach where the infamous

pirate Blackbeard had been killed, but I doubted that was relevant right now.

He parked at a nearby church since there was no actual parking at the trail site. He turned off the engine and looked out at the empty lot.

"I'm sorry," he finally said, his brows so tightly scrunched together that it looked painful.

"You're apologizing? Why?"

"I'm sorry you had to see that." He took a deep breath. "See him."

I turned and scooted closer. For once, I wasn't hating the bulkiness of a truck. "You are not responsible for your father's actions."

"No, but I could have controlled my response to him," he said. "He always knows exactly what to say to get a reaction out of me."

"Your mom?"

He nodded as his hands rested on the steering wheel. "Things were always bad. My dad never made our lives easy, but when my mom died"—he blew out a long breath—"it just got worse."

"How old were you?" I asked. I always had a feeling she was gone, but until now, he'd never confirmed it.

"Twelve," he said. "Car accident."

"Here?"

The speed limit was, like, twenty-five.

He shook his head. "No. Up near Corolla on the interstate. My dad said she was visiting friends, but I think she was leaving—or trying to."

My eyes widened in shock. *His mother tried to leave her own kids?* "You think she would do that?"

"I think my dad made life bad enough that I could understand her wanting to get away—even if that meant leaving us behind."

"Why do you think your dad would lie to you about something like that?"

"Well, besides the obvious reason, he's a dick." He gave me a sad smile that didn't reach his eyes. "I don't think he wanted to admit to us or to anyone that she would leave him."

"But you knew?"

He nodded. "She didn't have friends. He's made a lot of enemies on this island throughout the years. He doesn't pay his debts, he cheats and steals. It made me hateful, and bitter and our family suffered the consequences." The pain in his eyes was immeasurable. "She would have had nowhere to go. But I also remember noticing a lot of things missing around the house. The few pictures she had of us, a few things she had from her childhood—things like that."

I couldn't stand seeing him so broken any longer. I closed the distance and took his hand. His thumb brushed over mine. Slowly, deliberately.

"Do you think she would have come for you? After she left?" I asked, still so shocked she would leave. But then I had no idea what their life had been like.

"No," he answered, but then quickly followed it up with, "I don't know. Maybe eventually. But I guess we'll never know."

No, I guessed he wouldn't. And what a thing to wonder for the rest of your life.

"Do you want to go for a walk?" I asked.

"What about the ferry?" His eyes met mine, brimming with concern.

"We can catch a later one," I suggested, realizing just how at ease I was with our travel plans.

I'd thought I'd be nervous about the prospect of getting on that ferry again, but I was actually kind of excited to explore the rest of the Outer Banks with him.

And wasn't that a testament to growth and healing?

"Sure," he said. "But you need to do me a favor and eat first." He motioned with his head toward the paper bag that held our breakfast—which was getting colder by the minute. "God only knows when you'll eat a proper meal again."

I laughed. "With you around? Probably sooner than later."

I did as I had been told and ate my turkey bacon and egg sandwich while he ate his. We chitchatted about some of the repairs we'd done over the last week since I'd actually helped, and he mentioned some of the things he needed to grab while we were on the mainland.

Finally, we finished and headed out. We both took our coffee, which wasn't nearly as hot as I'd liked. As we headed toward the trail, I grabbed his hand, weaving my fingers with his. He looked down, a hint of surprise spreading across that handsome face of his.

"There's no one around," he said, giving me an out on our deal.

"I know," I said, pulling him forward. As he caught up, I met his gaze, and because I was a coward, I added, "Just in case."

We settled into a rhythm, walking hand in hand down the trail toward the beach. For a while, there was just the sounds of nature—the birds and the rustling of the trees.

I took a sip of my coffee, letting the warmth coat my throat and my belly. Finally, I asked, "You mentioned a brother?"

He nodded. "Zander. He's four years younger than me. I don't think he ever forgave me for enlisting after high school and leaving him all alone. He left Ocracoke the second he turned eighteen—didn't even wait until graduation. He hasn't been back since."

"Do you know where he is?"

He shrugged. "I found him once in California. He was working on a road crew with a band. Seemed pretty happy." He looked out toward the trees and then took a long sip of coffee. "Wanted nothing to do with me though."

"I'm so sorry," I said, realizing how often I said that when it came to his life.

"I get it," he said. "I can't imagine life was easy for him after I left. I abandoned him. I'd hate me, too."

"You were eighteen, and he was your brother, not your kid."

"You gonna always stick up for me like that?" He looked at me with a sort of shy grin.

"Well, someone has to," I said adamantly.

He tended to put the weight of the world on his shoulders. Someone had to remind him he wasn't responsible for all of it.

"What about your siblings? I'm guessing they don't hate you like mine does?"

I shook my head back and forth at his dark sense of humor. "No, they don't, but I'm sure they've disliked me over the years. It's not easy being the oldest."

"No, it's not," he agreed.

Feeling like we'd had enough of the heavy talk, I took advantage of the trash can we were about to pass, chucking my empty coffee cup inside.

Looking at Macon, I let go of his hand a second before I exclaimed, "Beat you to the beach!"

I saw his surprised expression as I tore off into a run ahead of him.

"You know I'm a runner and ex-military, right?" he hollered after me, obviously giving me a head start while he got rid of his coffee cup.

"I ran track in high school!" I yelled, wondering where he was. But I couldn't look back. The trail was too rough, and I was wearing heeled boots. "And I run on the treadmill." I didn't say how infrequently it was. He didn't need to know that.

I barely heard him. His movements were so quick and stealthy that by the time I realized he'd gained on me, his arms were wrapped around my waist and hauling me off the ground. He spun me around, my back against his hard chest as the sound of my laughter filled the silence around us.

He set me down, and I turned to face him, both of us still breathless.

"I think I won," I said, looking out at the water just ahead.

"I gave you a considerable head start," he countered. "We'll call it a tie."

Only then did I realize just how close we were. So close I could feel his chest rise and fall. I could see the tiny flecks of gold in his eyes and feel the heat of his body tightly pressed against mine. He cupped my cheek, that intense hazel gaze searching mine.

Was he asking for permission? If so, he had it.

Was he worried about the deal? If anyone would see? I didn't care. There could be a hundred people on this beach or none. I still wanted him to kiss me more than my next breath.

But he didn't.

Instead, he took a step back, his hand dropping to the side. "We should get back," he said, his voice rough and raw. "We'll miss the next ferry."

His eyes lingered over mine for a second, then two, before he turned back around and started back toward the truck.

I guessed I was supposed to follow.

I contemplated the idea of warning him, just to be on the safe side.

But ever since we had left Springer's Point, he'd seemed to be lost in his thoughts.

I didn't want to make things worse by telling him there was a small chance I could lose my shit the second we got on that ferry.

I'd managed to ride the ferry here without having a panic attack…

Sobbing didn't count.

It didn't.

Also, that was two weeks ago.

Basically a lifetime ago.

I thought back to that moment I had stood in front of my apartment building and said good-bye to Elena.

It really did feel like a lifetime ago.

I'd dreaded returning to Ocracoke for five years—dreaded the idea of walking into that little island house and seeing Daniel's things and having all our memories play out in my mind. But I no longer feared the ghosts that lingered within those walls.

For the first time since I'd lost Daniel, I felt like I was finally moving forward rather than standing still.

I still missed him. God, I missed him. But I knew he'd want this for me.

He'd want me to be happy.

And I think I was. Or I was getting there.

As we headed down Highway 12, away from town, I felt confident. Excited even. I was looking forward to our day away, and I was sure that once we got farther from Ocracoke, I could coax Macon out of whatever funk his father had put him in.

I glanced toward the water, looking out beyond the waves, wondering what the day would bring. The ocean glinted and winked at me as I turned my head toward the other side, and that was when my eyes collided with the ferry memorial.

I'd never taken the time to actually stop and look at it. I never had the courage. But I knew it was there. I'd been invited to come down and see its dedication ceremony.

But I'd declined.

Seeing it felt too raw. Too real.

I'd managed to ignore its existence since I'd been here. But today, I knew I'd see it. I'd prepared myself.

So, why did my throat feel like it was going to close and there wasn't enough oxygen in the truck the moment I looked at it?

Macon's large figure loomed in the background.

Just then, he turned and looked at me. He smiled.

My pulse started to race.

"Are you okay?" The concern in his voice was sudden and palpable.

"What?" I answered, rubbing the spot over my breasts where my heart throbbed. "Oh, yeah. Fine."

He focused back on the road, but I caught his gaze once more as we turned into the ferry terminal.

And there it was. The monstrous boat. I closed my eyes, and all I saw was fire. So much fire.

Oh God.

I tried focusing on something. Anything solid. But everything was moving and swaying. So much noise.

Too much.

It's too much.

My breath became rough and ragged, as I struggled for control.

Macon drove onto the ferry, the sound of the truck going onto the boat causing me to let out a quick gasp. His eyes darted over to mine and then back toward the person who was directing traffic as he moved forward and quickly parked.

"You're not fine," he insisted.

My eyes welled with tears, but I tried to hold it in. But then I looked up, and all I could see was the boat and him.

"Shit," I heard Macon utter as the panic took over.

My breaths started coming out too quick, too fast, and my lungs burned.

"Marin," he said. "Marin, look at me." His voice was calm, but commanding.

I turned, my vision blurry from tears. How had he become so important? So fast? My breaths shortened as the sound of plastic crinkled in my ear.

"Hold out your hand," he instructed. "Do you see what I'm placing in your palm?"

I tried to look down. My head felt dizzy. So dizzy.

Is that candy?

"Put it in your mouth," he ordered. "If you don't, I will."

I didn't have the mental capacity to ask why. I just trusted him. I shoved whatever it was in my mouth and immediately felt overwhelmed.

My eyes burned, and my lips puckered. My staccato breath faltered as I gasped, sucking in a breath to acclimate to the pungent, sour taste in my mouth.

I looked over at him, and his steady gaze was locked on mine. My heart rate slowed.

"It's a Warhead," he explained. "It's so sour that it shocks your system, and since your brain can only handle so much, you're trading one emergency for another."

That's actually quite genius.

"You stopped my panic attack with a Warhead?" I asked as the sour sensation began to dissipate. My voice sounded hoarse and strained. "How did you even—"

"Not the first panic attack I've dealt with," he said, not bothering to elaborate. I was sure he'd seen all sorts of stuff in his line of work. "And when you mentioned the proposal the other day, I threw a few in the truck. Ice works, too, but these are definitely more convenient."

I didn't know how to respond to that kind of attention and care.

I kind of wanted to fling myself across the seat and kiss him.

But my mouth was currently occupied, and my body was so tired that I felt like a wet noodle.

And there was that whole thing with him almost kissing me and then walking away.

I wasn't sure I could handle rejection on top of this right now.

Or ever.

"I have breathing exercises I do," I tried to explain, needing him to know I wasn't completely incapable. "But I just couldn't focus."

"You don't have to explain yourself, Marin. I get it."

But I didn't.

I'd felt good about the ferry. Confident actually. And then it was like someone had flipped a switch, and I'd gone from happy and fine to…this.

I looked over at Macon, and suddenly, I remembered exactly when the panic had started—when I looked at *him*. The memorial had been hard to look at, but the second I turned towards Macon…

"I'm gonna go get some coffee," he said, pushing the door open to hop out. "Do you want some?"

My mind still in a daze, I nodded. "Sure."

I watched him walk away, still trying to come to terms with my new reality.

My panic attack wasn't about my past.

It was all about my future.

CHAPTER FOURTEEN

Macon

"You're so quiet," Marin said as we drove down the long stretch of highway.

She'd been admiring the view and trying to catch a glimpse of lighthouses and the weathered houses on our way up the coast, but she was right.

I was being quiet.

"Sorry," I said lamely. "Just focused on driving."

I'd been reticent for most of the day. Ever since we'd left Springer's Point, I'd been so stuck in my head that I didn't know what to say or how to say it. This was not how I'd thought the day would go—how I'd thought any of this would go.

We'd docked in Hatteras hours ago, and since then, we'd made our way to a few stores, grabbing everything from air filters to plywood, and now, we were headed to a late lunch.

And up until now, I'd said maybe three sentences.

"Can you pull off?" she asked, pointing toward a scenic turnout. "Just ahead over there. I want to see if I can get a picture of the lighthouse for my mom."

"Sure," I answered.

Oh, look. One more. I'm Mr. Fucking Chatterbox.

I pulled the truck to a stop and turned the engine off. Stepping out, I decided to meet her on the other side and take a moment to enjoy the last bit of warm weather the season was giving us. I held back, leaning against the truck, and watched as she pulled out her phone, aiming it toward the water. But then she abruptly stopped and turned back toward me.

"What is going on?" she asked bluntly, the picture forgotten as she tucked her phone back in her purse.

"What do you mean?" I deflected.

She gave me a stern look, crossing her arms over her chest. "You are never this quiet. Is it me? Is it because of what happened on the ferry?"

"No," I tried to assure her, but then her expression changed like she'd been physically wounded. "Shit."

I looked away, feeling frustrated. I shoved my hands in my hair and groaned before turning back around.

"You should go home," I finally said.

"You want to go home?" she asked, her brow furrowing in confusion. "Already?"

"No, that's not what I meant." I let out a huff, hating every word that was coming out of my mouth. "*You* should go back home. Back to Richmond."

Her eyes widened and then rounded in disbelief. "Why? Why would you say that?"

I looked out toward the water, knowing this was my one shot to be the good guy. My one chance to do right by her and, judging by her reaction to the ferry today, she clearly wasn't ready for this anyway. "Because I can't pretend with you, Marin," I confessed, the words coming out faster than I could think. "I don't know how. And it doesn't seem to matter to me that you're still grieving or you just broke up with someone; I can't seem to walk away. Believe me, I've tried. And you deserve better than the wayward son of a drunk."

Her breath caught, her body frozen as she looked at me. "Is that why you didn't kiss me?"

"What?" That was not the reaction I had expected.

"At the beach today. You were going to kiss me, but you didn't."

God, how I'd wanted to.

It would have been so easy.

But ever since she'd arrived, it's like I'd been balancing all my emotions on a scale. On one side was the immense guilt I carried. On the other—the happiness I felt when I was around her, the passion, the immense fear that she'd one day leave if she discovered the truth.

Somewhere along the way, I started caring more about her than that guilt.

Or at least, I thought I had.

"I didn't want to start something you'd end up regretting." I finally said. That scale had tipped back in a major way today. The guilt I felt was palpable, and I knew I should just come clean.

She took a tentative step forward. "But what if I want to? Start something, that is?"

My eyes flew to hers, everything else forgotten. "Don't say it if you don't mean it, Marin." She opened her mouth to respond, but I cut her off, taking a step forward so that we were face-to-face, nearly touching. "I was willing to let you go because I thought you weren't ready, but—"

Her breath caught because she knew the words I was holding back—that I'd make her mine in every sense of the word.

"Do you want to know why I panicked on the ferry today?" she asked, her brown irises looking up at mine.

"I know why," I said, already starting to take a step back.

She caught my hand, holding me in place.

"You don't," she countered. "And I didn't at first either. You see, I'd been excited to board the ferry today. I thought I'd be able to handle it—it's why I didn't even mention it to you. Coming to Ocracoke was exactly what I think I needed to heal, to finally be at peace."

She looked up at me, so confident. So self-assured. No matter what happened or where she ended up, I was glad her trip to Ocracoke had given her that.

"But," she continued, "the moment my eyes collided with the memorial, I started to feel uneasy. The panic didn't kick in until I looked at you."

"What?" My breath hitched.

"All I could think of was, *What if it happens again? What if I lose someone else? What if I lose...you?*"

If my heart could stop beating, it would have. Right then, right there on the side of Highway 12.

"I know it was irrational," she went on. "I know it's stupid."

"It's not stupid."

I cupped her cheek, unable to stop myself. She leaned in, her eyes fluttering closed for a brief second before she looked up at me once more.

"It was never fake," she said. "Not for me. Not for a second."

I'd known since the moment she had kissed me on that patio that something real existed between us. But I hadn't realized until those words came from her lips just how much I needed her to acknowledge it.

I needed to know she'd chosen me.

That she'd chosen us.

My hand found those silky curls, and I savored the feel of them between my fingers as I bent down, touching my lips to hers. I was tentative at first. This wasn't our first kiss, but it was our first real kiss, and I wanted her to feel cherished, so I took my time. My mouth brushed against hers, a sweet caress as we explored each other.

She rose to her tippy-toes, her arms wrapping around my neck, and her fingers dug into my hair. I tilted my head, parting her lips with my tongue, and our kiss turned heated.

All common sense went out the window as my hands

snaked around her waist. I lifted her off the ground and pivoted us around, pushing her against the back of the truck. She let out a little gasp of surprise as I devoured her, going far beyond what was appropriate for public view.

But I didn't care.

At that moment, there was only her and me.

I was on fire again; that same inferno swept over me as I tried to control my need to consume her.

My hand slid down her thigh, finding all that bare skin where her dress ended. My fingers pressed into her, grabbing the back of her knee. I wanted her wrapped around me.

I wanted—

A car whizzed by, and the horn blared in my ears. Teenagers whistled and hollered as they drove by us.

I released Marin's leg, letting it fall back to the ground. I was breathless, my forehead resting against hers as I realized just how completely out of control I'd been. If it hadn't been for the sound of the horn—

"I think we might need a new deal," I said. It took effort to speak as I fought the need to kiss her again.

"Why?" Her eyes met mine.

"Because if we don't set some rules or boundaries, I am going to end up doing something stupid, like taking you into my truck and fucking you right here on the side of the road, and I think we both know you wouldn't have any objections."

She bit down on that bottom lip, still swollen and red. A shy smile spread across her face.

I could see the way she was looking at the truck, and I knew she was picturing it in her head.

Just like that fucking vase.

I let out a groan, and she laughed.

"Not helping, Marin."

"I want to date you—" I started to say.

"We are dating," she interjected, a flirty smile spreading across her face.

"You know what I mean," I said, squeezing her waist, which only made that smile spread wider. "I want to date you for real. I want to take you out to dinner. I want to hold your hand and kiss you when no one else is looking. I want to take my time with you, Marin."

I wanted to know she was choosing me, over and over.

Not just today.

I needed to know I wasn't a rash decision. A rebound or a fling.

I wanted to give her a reason to stay.

I wanted… to earn her.

"I can agree to that. But on one condition." She pressed her lips together, staring up at me with all sorts of mischief in her eyes.

"Anything," I answered.

"Don't take too much time, okay?"

This woman was going to be the death of me.

It had only been two days since our ferry excursion, and already, I was convinced I was the dumbest man on the planet.

I had to have been out of my goddamn mind when I told Marin I wanted to take things slow.

Now, less than forty-eight hours later, I was so fucking horny that no amount of jacking off could stifle it.

Marin and I hadn't even seen each other much in that time, but when we had, it had taken me every ounce of restraint to not toss caution to the wind and take her.

Everywhere.

Anywhere.

Over and over again.

"You okay, man?" Billy asked as we all sat around his dining room table that evening.

Eli was in town, and Billy had invited us over for dinner.

Marin was beyond thrilled to meet his boyfriend, and incredibly honored to know she was part of a very exclusive club.

I was glad Billy had finally found someone, but I wished he trusted the people in town enough to share it.

"What?" I answered him, my eyes focused on Marin across the table.

She was talking to Eli about places she'd visited in New York, and she suddenly laughed at something he'd said. She turned and caught me staring and blushed.

"Oh, yeah. I'm fine. Why?"

Billy looked over to where my eyes were locked. "Man, you've got it bad."

I opened my mouth to deny it, glancing over, but I didn't even bother. "Yeah, I really do."

"Do you think she'll stay?" he asked. It was the question on everyone's mind, it seemed.

"I'm gonna give her every reason to," I vowed, unable to think of a future without her in it.

"I'm happy for you," he said. "After all the shit you went through, God knows you deserve it."

His words made me flinch. *Because I didn't. Not really.* "Thanks," I managed to say as I finished off my third Coke.

Billy took a sip of red wine, some fancy-ass shit Eli had brought, as his eyes swept over mine in a way I recognized all too well.

He was such a mother hen.

I'm fine, I mouthed, rolling my eyes.

I got up and headed toward the kitchen to grab another soda.

Billy had always been my biggest champion. He was the only person who had stuck with me through everything, even when I didn't deserve it.

He never wavered.

He was a class act, and I owed him more than friendship. He'd pulled me back from the depths of hell more than once, and for that, I owed him my life.

I returned a moment later, settling myself next to Marin, as Billy answered the door and paid for the pizza. This evening was a much more relaxed affair compared to the dinner party Molly had organized. We ate around the table while music played, and everyone got to know each other.

"So, what do you do, Marin?" Eli asked as we all sat around, mostly finished with our food.

I'd met the man several times over the last year, and he seemed to ooze style from his very pores, from his designer clothes to his perfectly styled hair. He owned a small but well-known restaurant in New York, although Billy had yet to visit.

I thought it was a bit of a sore subject.

Kind of like the one Eli had just brought up.

I could feel Marin instantly tense next to me, and her cheeks reddened. Was she embarrassed?

"Um, at the moment, I'm not sure," she answered honestly. "I've done graphic design for most of my life, but I went to art school, and I'd love to get back into my craft."

Billy chuckled, placing a hand on Eli's shoulder. "Oh, you've got his attention now. Eli is obsessed with art."

Eli merely rolled his eyes. "Not obsessed. Just a very enthusiastic patron," he said with a wink. "What type of art do you do?"

"Oh, um, I paint. Landscapes mostly. That's why I moved down here initially. I wanted to open a gallery or, at the very least, sell my work to some of the local shops."

"Really?" Eli leaned in, his interest piqued. "And you painted locally?"

"Why?" Billy teased. "Thinking of bringing a piece of Ocracoke home with you, dear?"

"I always bring a piece of Ocracoke home with me." He set down his napkin and placed a dramatic hand on his heart. "Right here."

Billy laughed, but the way he and Eli looked at each other

was anything but humorous, and I turned away, all too aware I was intruding on a very personal moment.

"Well, I'd love to see some of it—that is, if you're willing to share it?" Eli asked, his attention fixed back on Marin.

She hadn't even shown her work to me. I wasn't even sure she'd pulled any of it out of storage, let alone looked at it since she'd arrived in Ocracoke.

I wasn't sure how it would affect her if she did.

I looked over at her, fearful this all might be too much, too soon. I could see her mulling it over as her hand fiddled with the stem of her wineglass. She looked over the heads of the two men in front of her, toward the window that faced her house, like she was staring right at the place where those canvases were.

Finally, she nodded, her lip turning upward. "Sure, let's go."

My eyes widened. "You want to go now?"

Eli and Billy seemed on board, sliding the chairs back to follow her as she immediately rose from the table.

She merely shrugged, the determination written all over her face. "If I don't do it now, I'll lose my nerve. And Eli leaves tomorrow, right?"

"I do," he simply acknowledged.

"Well, okay then," I said, meeting her gaze. "Let's go."

We left everything behind—the dishes, the pizza boxes, our drinks—and all four of us traipsed across the grass to Marin's house. I gave her a quiet nod of appreciation when she pulled out her key and unlocked the front door.

The loud, annoying creak announced our entrance, reminding me of yet another thing I hadn't fixed. The light flicked on, and everyone took a glance around.

She'd made small changes, but overall, things remained mostly the same. Her appliances now all worked, although I doubted she used them much, still relying on takeout and her trusty microwave. The bee situation had also been taken care of, and thankfully, their hive hadn't been in the house, just near enough that they could get in through a hole near the roof, which was now fixed.

Her keys and purse were placed on the kitchen island as she turned to look at everyone. "Everything is in the guest bedroom," she said, a hint of nervousness in her voice.

We headed down the hall with her leading the way. I followed close behind and watched as she turned the corner. The lights came on, and I looked around. The bed was made, and the dresser was neat and clean.

No paintings anywhere.

"Need any help, Marin?" I asked.

"Oh…" She hesitated, clearly flustered. "Over here."

She headed toward the small closet, sliding it open. A brief memory of a younger me slipping in there during a game of hide-and-seek came to mind.

"Most of them are in here. This is where I kept most of my supplies and stuff. I had plans to turn this room into a studio, but during those first few months, my family and friends kept coming down to visit, which is why it's set up like this."

And why it remains…

Although she spoke about her late husband with ease, I still couldn't shake the guilt that clung to me.

The fact that this room had stood frozen in time because he'd died.

Because their dream had been so tragically interrupted.

Could I ever make it up to her?

I stepped forward to help as she buried herself in the closet, moving an easel and a few blank canvases until, finally, she got to several that were leaning against the wall.

"Oh, here they are." She grabbed the smallest one, pulled it out, and placed it on the bed with little finesse. She didn't even bother looking at it before she went back for another.

As soon as I saw it, my breath caught.

Oh, holy fuck.

I'd lived in Ocracoke for most of my life, and I'd never seen anyone capture the island's raw beauty like Marin. The way the light glinted off the water and the movement of the trees.

"Jesus." The curse flew from my mouth, and Marin turned swiftly around.

She found all three of us frozen in front of the bed.

"What?" she said, looking down at it and then back at us. "Is it bad? I have more if you hate that one." She nervously started biting her bottom lip.

"Good God, Marin," Eli said. "This should not be in a closet. It's a crime against humanity."

I looked up at her. I'd always assumed she was a good painter—I didn't know why; I'd just had a feeling. Maybe it was the way she talked about it—the enthusiasm, the passion. But this…this was beyond my comprehension.

"I don't know shit about art, but this is…Eli's right; this should be shared."

She pulled out several more, and they were all just as amazing, if not more so. She'd accomplished a lot in a short amount of time, and I loved watching her eyes come alive as she talked about her technique and style with Eli.

She was in her element, and it was hot as hell.

"I know Billy was joking," Eli said as we all headed toward the front of the house. Eli and Billy stopped just shy of the front door. "But I would love to buy one if you are ever interested."

"Charge him a fortune for it," Billy said with a sly wink as he slid his arm around his waist. "He's got it to spare."

"I'll think about it." She laughed.

Eli gave Marin his number, and we bid them good night after they both assured us they'd take care of the cleanup from dinner.

I honestly thought they just wanted some alone time before Eli left tomorrow.

Shutting the door after they left, I turned around to find Marin staring at me, the hunger in her gaze telling me exactly what she had in mind.

My eyes traveled the length of her body, and I took a step forward before I froze.

"I should go," I said, my voice already betraying the need pulsing in my veins.

"Why?" she asked.

"Because right now, the only thing I can think about is taking you back to that bedroom so I can spread you out among all those canvases and do all sorts of dirty things to you," I confessed. "But this is your house, and I know how sacred it is."

Her breath caught.

It seemed I had no filter when I was around her.

Absolutely none.

She looked at me and took a tentative step forward. "When Curtis was here, it felt wrong," she explained. "It doesn't feel that way when you're here. It never has."

"Why?" I asked, trying to understand how I could be any different.

"I don't know." She shrugged. "When you're here, it just feels…"

"What?" I asked, already knowing the answer, but needing to hear it all the same.

"Right." She answered. "It feels right."

I moved, pulling her to me, and our lips met in a passionate, frenzied kiss. The last two days of sweet and playful caresses felt like one long, drawn out session of foreplay, and I was about to combust.

Sweeping my hands under her ass, I hauled her off the ground, wrapping her long legs around my torso as I made for the guest bedroom. She moaned into my mouth as her arms snaked around my shoulders again, and her nails dug into my hair.

My cock strained against my jeans, already hard, dying to break free, but tonight was all about her.

We made it down the hallway, and I turned and pressed her into the doorframe. The lights were still on in the guest bedroom, and she pulled back just enough to look in and see the canvases spread across the room. Her legs slid down my body one at a time before she turned, and I found a very hesitant expression staring back at me.

"There's something I need to tell you."

CHAPTER FIFTEEN

Marin

The words died in my throat.

Just tell him, Marin.

It's just a precaution. Just a warning.

Wouldn't want to bruise that male ego.

I swallowed hard. "I don't even know how to say this," I said, walking into the room and taking a seat on the bed.

I moved a few canvases so there was a space for him to sit next to me. I still couldn't comprehend their reaction to my paintings.

But that was something to ponder later.

I blew out a long breath, grateful he was giving me time to gather my thoughts. And my confidence. "I didn't start dating Curtis until three years after Daniel died. Before that, there was no one."

He nodded. "Okay," he said, trying to make sense of what I was telling him. And then some sort of realization spread across his face. "Are you trying to ask if I'm clean? Because I haven't slept with anyone in years. Not since…"

I gulped. I wasn't going to ask. Hadn't planned to, but now that I knew, I wasn't sure if I was relieved there had been no one else, or perhaps a little sad that he'd been so lonely for so long.

"That's not..." I paused, feeling frustrated with myself. "No, that's not it. But since you brought it up, I'm on the pill in case you were wondering." I brought my hands together in an awkward motion as he studied me.

I thought about telling him the length of time it'd been since Curtis and I had been intimate, but I felt like I was killing the mood pretty decently already.

No need to do any more damage.

"Maybe because Curtis and I were more like friends, or maybe there's something wrong with me, but I haven't..." I let out a huff that sounded more like a groan.

He pondered over my words for a moment until at last, I looked up at him. "I haven't had an orgasm in five years."

It could have been a few seconds before he responded, but it felt like a millennium. Every second that went by was agony as I waited for him to respond.

Finally, I gathered the courage to meet his gaze. Macon looked at me as a wolfish grin spread across his face.

"Five years, huh?" He gently pressed me into the bed, his large body looming over me. "That's a lot of time to make up for. Guess we'd better get started."

My stomach flip-flopped as he bent down and kissed me. Slowly. Deliberately. I felt his teeth gently tug at my bottom lip, causing chills to ripple down my spine.

"Believe me, Marin, there's nothing wrong with you, and I'm going to prove it. I'm going to make you come so hard that you'll see stars," he whispered in my ear. No hesitance. Not an ounce of insecurity—as if he could summon my orgasm from his sheer will alone. "And then, when you're so unbelievably spent that you feel like you can't even move, we're gonna do it all over again."

My eyes widened as I felt something flutter deep in my belly.

Oh...*oh.*

Maybe he could, in fact, summon it.

His mouth crashed over mine as his body pressed me

deep into the bed. I molded into all those hard lines, that muscle and warmth. I felt his hands everywhere, in my hair, gliding over the front of my blouse.

And then he was gone.

I looked up to see him at the foot of the bed, kneeling in front of me. Leaning up on my elbows, I watched as he carefully removed my boots, undoing the laces as I met that intense gaze. A tiny smirk tugged at the corner of his lips. It was arrogant and smug, as if he knew exactly what he was capable of.

And God, I couldn't wait to find out.

My socks went next. He was slow and methodical, as if he had all the time in the world, trailing his fingers over the inside of my ankle before he rose to his knees.

He was dressed in simple jeans and a long-sleeved green shirt. The color made his eyes look more green than hazel, and I couldn't help but stare.

"I've fantasized what it would be like to strip you bare," he said, his voice rough. He gently pressed me back down against the bed, and his hand slid under my blouse. "I never thought I'd be so lucky."

He cupped my breast through my bra, and I let out a gasp, quivering as his fingers skimmed the delicate skin. I felt myself grow wet between my thighs.

A grin played across his face, like he already knew.

His hand came away, lingering on my hip. "Unbutton your shirt, Marin. I need to see you."

I obeyed his command as my hands rose to the blouse. I watched as he followed each button as the fabric gave way and parted, finally falling on either side of my ribs.

"My fantasies didn't do you justice."

I wouldn't mind hearing about these fantasies—in detail.

He took his time again, trailing his fingers over my bare skin. He scattered kisses over my collarbone and down between the valley of my breasts, and then he found the front clasp of my bra. His eyes lifted to mine, and that wicked smile returned. With a twist of his fingers, my breasts were free, and his mouth closed over my nipple.

"Oh my God!" I yelled as his tongue swirled around my hard peek.

I tried to squeeze my thighs shut, but Macon's large body kept my legs spread, and I could only lay there, pinned to the bed as he chuckled, knowing exactly what his touch did to me.

"See, the thing is," he said, his hot breath against my bare skin as his lips kissed a path down my stomach. "I haven't even started yet."

Who knew Macon Green was such a freak in the sheets?

I bit my lip, trying not to grin as I watched him work the button of my jeans. My belly clenched as nerves hit me. It had been a long time since I'd done anything other than just plain old sex.

His hands stilled. "You're looking at me like a deer in headlights, Marin. Tell me what's going on in that head of yours."

"You don't have to…" I knew not every man liked to.

He looked at me with an incredulous stare. "I don't know whether I should love or hate Curtis at this moment."

"Why?" I asked, watching as he slowly started to slide my jeans off my hips.

"Because I can't quite decide if I'm more upset that he let you go two years without giving you pleasure or if I'm just so damn glad I get to be the one to do it instead."

My jeans hit the floor, and his gaze settled on mine.

"Believe me when I say this, Marin: Watching you come, knowing it was me who did it—whether it's on my fingers, my face, or my cock—it will always be an honor."

Oh. My. God.

His hand slid up to the waistband of my panties, and I thought for sure he'd nudge them down, but instead, he just continued that slow pace he'd set, like he was memorizing my body with his touch. It was torture.

And I knew he was doing it on purpose.

His fingers slowly moved down my thigh, tracing my knee and then working their way back up toward my center. My breath caught as he brushed the lace that covered the most intimate parts of me.

"This doesn't even feel like a challenge." He smirked, cupping me through the fabric. I gasped, needing more. "I think you like this."

I nodded, unable to form words.

I wasn't even sure I knew my own name anymore.

I'd seen so many different versions of Macon. I'd seen him scared, bossy, anxious, and indifferent.

But I'd never seen him like this.

All doubts and insecurities had been left at the door, and in here, he was commanding. He was self-assured; he oozed sex like it was his whole damn job.

In the bedroom, Macon was a god.

And I would gladly be his willing sacrifice.

"Take off your shirt," I told him, feeling a bit bold. "It's only fair." I looked around, as if to prove my point.

I was lying on the bed with my bra and shirt spread open, my breasts bare and my jeans on the floor, while he was still fully clothed.

I was dying to see him.

All of him.

He obliged, leaning back to reach over his shoulder. His shirt came off in one fluid movement, and he threw it on the floor.

My eyes went everywhere, all at once. Chiseled and cut just like I knew he'd be. God, I wanted to run my hands all over that lean muscle. I wanted to trace every line with my tongue.

"My fantasies didn't do you justice," I said, echoing the words he'd said about me.

His control seemed to slip a little, and his mouth slammed

down on mine, kissing me deeply. A moan escaped from my lips as I felt our bodies touch.

Skin to skin.

It was my undoing.

I pulled him onto the bed, and he shoved one side of my shirt and my bra off my shoulder. I shook it off, doing the same with the other side, and he tore it free and threw it. His hand found the back of my knee, pulling my thigh and wrapping it around his body.

I bucked my hip against him, and he groaned.

With my leg still wrapped around him, he pulled up to a sitting position. "Straddle me," he demanded. "I want to feel you everywhere."

I did, and I immediately felt how much he wanted me, even through his thick jeans. His hands ran down my sides, until one slid around my front. That wicked grin returned as his fingers found the waistband of my panties. They slipped under, touching the slick folds underneath.

I gasped as a part of me came alive for the first time in five years.

"Lift up," he instructed. His voice was low, rough.

I did as he'd told me to, so consumed by need and the will of his fingers that I'd do just about anything he asked at that moment.

And he fucking knew it.

He let out a quiet laugh, his forehead meeting mine as two digits went deeper and his thumb lazily circled my clit.

"Oh shit," I uttered.

He slid them out, rubbing that tight bundle of nerves. I felt that familiar flutter, and I gasped.

My hips rolled as I felt those digits slide back in, curling forward. He let out a groan, his eyelids drooping as his head tilted back.

Like he was barely holding it together.

It was all the confidence I needed.

I felt beautiful in his arms.

"That's it, Marin," Macon said. His voice came out ragged as that intense gaze swept over me like I was the most captivating sight on the planet. "Just like that."

Our movements became frantic as he fucked me with his fingers, rubbing my clit as I rolled my hips. His head bent, and his mouth closed over one of my nipples, sucking and grazing it with his teeth.

"Oh God," I said as my belly tightened and my core clenched. "I think I'm gonna—"

"I know," he said against my chest, a smug sound of satisfaction. "Ready to see some stars?"

He flicked my clit.

Once, twice.

And then I shattered, screaming out my orgasm as my body quaked and the earth fell away. It was divine, and yeah, I'm pretty sure I went into the stratosphere. It was something I'd thought I'd never experience again.

And I didn't feel broken anymore.

I sagged against Macon, my body more relaxed than I could remember. I felt his fingers retreat as he leaned back and met my stare.

And then he did something truly wicked.

He placed those glistening fingers in his mouth, and he licked them clean.

"Now," he said, giving me that signature smirk, "time for round two."

Oh shit.

"I've been trying to call you for days," I said the moment she answered. I'd just finished breakfast, and I was about to go for a walk when my phone rang. "What the hell?"

"Well, it's nice to talk to you, too." Elena snickered as I settled into the plush gray chair in my living room. "I know. I got all five of your voice mails. I've just been—" She made a noise that was halfway between a groan and a scream. "Work. Work is fucking crazy right now and I don't think I've ever been so close to just quitting and running away to a little island."

"Do it!" I exclaimed. "We could be roomies again!"

I looked around the room and tried to imagine Elena here. It felt like too small of a space for her larger-than-life personality.

"Believe me, after the last week, I've seriously considered it. But I highly doubt that tiny-ass town needs a criminal attorney."

"No," I agreed. Her law degree would be wasted here. There was very little crime here—something I was thankful for. "But I'm sure they wouldn't mind a super-sexy resident novelist."

Silence filled the line. She'd always said she could fill a bookstore with all the stories she had in her head.

She'd heard some weird shit in her line of work.

"That's cute," she finally replied. "But I am not you, Marin. I know you hold on to that memory of me saying I wanted to write a book, but that was all it was—a fleeting memory. Nothing. And besides, that was clearly before I discovered the real reason for living." She paused for dramatic effect. "Money. And all the stuff I can buy with it."

I rolled my eyes. "So, now, all those girlish dreams are, what? Bullshit? You're just gonna work yourself to death so you can buy another Birkin bag?"

"Yes," she answered firmly, but there was a hint of amusement in her tone. "Because I'm fucking worth it. And maybe one of these days, I'll take my Birkin bag to Rome or Venice. Or put it in the passenger seat of a nice Porsche."

"You're—"

"Amazing? Yes, I know."

I fought the need to roll my eyes again. I knew I'd never change her mind. She'd worked hard to get where she was, and she wouldn't stop.

Even if it made her miserable.

"So, tell me about Hot Cop," she said, segueing the conversation away from her.

I instantly blushed, remembering last night.

He'd made good on his promise, not only breaking my five-year dry spell, but doing it over and over again.

He was a magician.

"I'll take the deafening silence as a good thing," she said.

"So, so good," I finally answered with a wide, toothy grin, pulling Macon's warm hoodie closer to my body. It smelled like him, woodsy and clean. I dug my face into it and inhaled like a freaking crazy person.

"So, back to being a member of the Big O club?"

"Oh my God," I answered.

I was always amazed by how brazenly unfiltered she was when it came to sex. Like it was as natural as breathing. And Elena never believed in depriving herself of… fresh air.

"Are you giving me a play-by-play or scolding me? I can't tell," she joked.

"Elena!" I yelled at her through the phone, but then gave in because I really, really needed to talk about it. All of it. "Okay, yes. *It* was amazing. He is amazing. I didn't think I would ever be able to…" My words trailed off.

"Oh, sweetheart, I told you it had nothing to do with you. That sometimes, sex—"

"We haven't even had sex yet," I confessed, "He just…" My cheeks blushed.

Talking about sex with Elena was still very strange. It used to be strictly off-limits. I had been married to her brother, and she did not want to know. Maybe that was why I'd found it so hard to tell her about Curtis.

"You haven't?" She sounded surprised, but in a good way. "Huh. Well, I think I like Hot Cop a little more now."

"He has a name. You know that, right?"

"Yes, but Hot Cop has such a nice ring to it, don't you think?" She laughed. "Plus, you started it."

My eyes wandered around the living room and then toward the door, and I remembered the way Macon had tried to leave last night.

"When you're here, it just feels… right."

"Do you think I should feel guilty? For moving on so quickly after Curtis?" It was a question that had been on my mind a lot lately. I'd told my parents and my siblings about my breakup, but I hadn't told them about Macon.

She took a moment before she replied. The rain started to fall, and I listened to the slow, steady *tap, tap, tap* against the window.

"I don't think there is any rule book, Marin," she finally said. "If there were, who the fuck cares? Would you walk away from the possibility of something amazing just because you're worried about hurting a few feelings?"

"No," I answered before I amended, "At least, I don't think so."

"You shouldn't. Would it have been easier on everyone if you and Macon had stumbled into each other months from now? Sure. But you didn't. You met now. And you of all people should know that life is tragically short and you never know when it's going to end." Her voice grew thick, and I felt mine do the same.

She never showed much emotion. She was always tough as nails.

"It's so fast though," I said. "What I feel for him, it feels so—"

Intense. Overwhelming.

Fucking terrifying.

"There you go, trying to put rules on something that isn't supposed to make sense," she pressed. "Love is complicated and messy. But don't walk away from a good thing because you're scared. Run toward it, with open arms, and grab it by the fucking balls. Hell, I would."

I let out a choked laugh, feeling my eyes brimming with tears.

Love.

Is that what this was?

My mind didn't want to think about that right now.

"You said his name," I said, offering up a dumb joke as a reply. Because otherwise, I was going to cry.

"Oh, for fuck's sake." I could hear the eye roll hundreds of miles away.

But I understood the assignment.

Be happy.

And don't let anyone tell me otherwise.

By the time I got off the phone with Elena, it was nearly noon.

Time to go.

I'd been pleasantly surprised when Molly had messaged me a few days earlier and asked me to lunch.

More than pleasantly surprised. I had nearly squealed with excitement.

I had always hoped to make friends when Daniel and I moved here, but establishing myself in a brand-new place turned out to be more intimidating than I'd imagined. Dreams and fantasies were easy. Real life? That was something entirely different, and I'd quickly discovered how hard living away from home could be.

But this felt like my second chance.

And I was going to do it right this time.

I dressed warmly, knowing we'd probably eat outside. With dark jeans and a thick sweater, I pulled my boots on and stepped out into autumn weather. The early morning rain had cleared, and now, the clouds lingered, and there was a distinct chill in the air.

I took my time walking to the marina, stopping to pet a sweet dog and chat with a neighbor. I passed the coffee shop and the little bench, and as I crossed the street to the marina, it dawned on me how much Ocracoke felt like home.

There were times when I'd once felt alone here, but the island itself always felt safe. Like visiting an old friend rather than meeting a new acquaintance.

By the time I got to Billy's, my muscles were achingly warm, and I'd managed to work up quite an appetite. The scent of french fries and seafood hit my nose the moment I stepped on the patio. My mouth watered instantly. Billy should bottle that smell and sell it.

I noticed Molly right away. Her blonde hair blew in the breeze as she rested a hand on her little baby bump. She smiled and waved, having claimed a table near the water.

I waved back and headed her way. That was when I noticed she wasn't alone.

"Hey," I greeted Molly as I approached.

I'd met her sister only briefly, but even then, I had been struck by their similarities. Both blonde and beautiful, but where Molly's style was simple and understated, Millie was anything but.

She looked like she should be sitting at a coffee shop in Paris or walking in a runway show.

"Hi!" Molly replied, turning to her. "This is my sister, Millie. I hope you don't mind if she joins us. I know you said you wanted to meet more people on the island."

"No," I answered. "Of course I don't mind. That's sweet of you."

"We met briefly at the ticket event, right? You came to my table," Millie said.

"Yes." I nodded. "You have a lot of great stuff. That candle saved my life. I did not know how funky a house could smell after five years of being closed up."

She laughed, and even that was beautiful. "You should stop by. That was just the tip of the iceberg. I have a ton of stuff."

"She's even working on her own line of clothing," Molly bragged, giving her sister a proud grin.

"It's far from complete, but someday. Eventually." She

looked wistfully toward the street, in the direction I assumed her shop was in.

"Do you sell any art? Like by local artists?" I asked, feeling my anxiety kick up a notch.

She shook her head, and my heart plummeted.

"No, it's not really in line with my brand. But my husband does."

"Oh?" I tried not to seem too excited. I didn't want to come off too eager.

Because I definitely was.

"He used to just sell his own work in his gallery, but the demand has gotten out of control, so he's scaling back and opening the space up to other artists."

The puzzle pieces started to fit together.

"Your husband created the memorial," I said, my throat feeling suddenly thick.

She nodded with a sort of reverence in her tone as she said, "He did."

"I was asked to come to the installation, but…" I paused, and both women looked at me with compassionate stares. "I couldn't make it."

"Have you seen it? Since you came back?"

I nodded my head. "Just from afar."

"You should go," Millie encouraged. "It has a calming sort of feel to it. Peaceful, you know?"

I wasn't sure how peaceful I could feel, staring at my husband's name engraved on a memorial, but I moved on. "And he does all of it without sight?"

She nodded. "He wasn't trained that way, but when his sight became compromised, he had to learn everything all over again."

There was no sadness in the way she spoke. No sense of loss. Only pride.

"How is the island life treating you?" Molly asked.

"Great," I answered confidently. "Ocracoke has been good for me. Better than I could have expected."

"This place is magic, I swear," Millie said.

"If I had heard you say that ten years ago, I would have fallen out of this damn chair and died of shock." Molly laughed.

Millie made a gesture of annoyance toward her sister. "Ten years ago, I was a very different person."

"And there was no hot British stone carver for you to stare at."

"I do love to watch him work." She grinned, letting out a dreamy sigh. "He is so ripped; it should be illegal."

I laughed, doing a double take when a waitress showed up at our table. I'd almost forgotten other people worked here. The young woman took our orders, and I was relieved when I wasn't the only one to order fries and a burger.

"Are you still going to the gala?" Millie asked after the waitress dropped off our drinks.

I leaned back in my chair. "Yes."

"With Macon?"

I nodded.

"Macon Green?" she clarified.

Was there a different Macon I wasn't aware of?

"Yep."

She just stared at me.

Molly looked at Millie and shrugged. "I told you."

I looked at the sisters, a silent conversation going on between them.

"What?" I finally asked.

"Well..." Millie's mouth opened, but it was like the words couldn't form.

Molly's eyes narrowed. "I told you not to."

"Yeah, but I've got to know," she pressed.

"Oh my God. What?" I asked, now genuinely amused.

What were they arguing about? It kind of made me miss my own sister in a way.

"It's just that he's such a—"

I laughed. "Jerk?" I offered.

Her body sagged in the chair like I'd just confirmed exactly what she needed to hear. "Yes, exactly. And Molly says that you're so—"

"Nice?" I guessed.

Her eyes lit up. "Yes!"

Molly snorted, and my laughter doubled until Millie joined in.

"Is he paying you? Like, are you doing him a favor? 'Cause then maybe I'd understand."

My eyes widened 'cause that hit a little too close to home.

"No," I answered, shaking my head back and forth, still amused. "I'm very much a willing participant."

"What are you willingly participating in?"

That voice.

I'd always loved the sound of Macon's voice.

But now, after hearing him last night…so demanding, so sure of himself.

It was like a damn aphrodisiac.

I started to turn, but he was already there. I felt his hands brush my shoulders a second before he bent over and his lips met mine.

My hand found its way to his chin, pulling him closer, wanting more.

But we had an audience, and one of us had to remember that.

It clearly wasn't me.

He pulled back, and I saw that cocky smile a second before he rose to his full height again. I turned around, and he was looking at me expectantly. Right, he'd asked me a question.

"You," I answered, making his eyebrow rise. "I'm a willing participant. With you."

He looked even more confused. It was kind of adorable.

"I asked if you were paying her," Millie said dryly.

He gave her an incredulous stare. "I'm gonna pretend you didn't say that."

Millie just laughed. "Blink twice if you need help, Marin." She did just that, exaggerating the motion. One blink, then two as she leaned back in her chair, looking smug.

I shook my head in amusement and turned my attention to Macon. "Are you on your lunch break?" I hadn't expected to run into him here.

He nodded. "Not really a lunch break though. I ordered ahead. I have to get back to the station."

"Busy day?" I asked as he stared at me intently. It gave me shivers.

"Yeah." It came out like a sigh.

"Dinner tonight?"

He nodded again as his eyes briefly went to my collar-bone, where he was lazily running his thumb over the tiny sliver of bare skin.

A ripple of pleasure ran down my spine.

Did he know what that was doing to me?

The corner of his mouth curved upward.

Of course he did.

"We'll have to order, or I'll need to grab some stuff. I haven't been to the grocery store in a week or more."

"Why, Macon?" I asked, quirking my brow. "Distracted?"

"Mmm," was all he said, leaning down to kiss me once more.

When he walked away, I'd all but forgotten Molly and Millie were even there.

When I finally peeled my eyes away from him, I found both women just staring.

"Well, damn," Millie said.

"That was…" Molly stuttered.

"What?" I asked, my eyes going wide. Was it something I'd said? "What?"

"I'm a happily married woman, with a sinfully sexy husband, but I've got to say…" Molly started.

"That was hot as fuck," Millie finished, leaning back in her chair. She used her paper napkin to fan herself. "The way he looks at you."

My cheeks instantly reddened.

"I felt like I was a voyeur, watching someone's foreplay." Millie laughed, and then she looked at me. "It's like you tamed a wild beast."

My brow shot up at those words. "I didn't tame him. He didn't need to be."

"Okay, maybe a bad choice of words," Molly interjected. "I think what Millie is trying to say is that Macon has always been, like we said, a bit rough around the edges. I guess we're kind of wondering how you softened those edges. 'Cause that was not the Macon we're used to."

"He's not an ogre."

"We never said he was," Molly said.

Millie made a sound like she wasn't too sure, and I caught her sister giving her a stern look.

"What?" She shrugged. "You do remember how he was when Jake came back? I wasn't here, but I haven't forgotten what you told me."

I winced. *Do I even want to know?*

"What was he like?" I asked, because despite my fear, I did want to know.

"He was mean. Cruel even." It was Molly who spoke. "He went out of his way to humiliate Jake when we got back together, knowing it might hurt Dean and his family. And, well, you know they've never gotten along."

I could hear the hurt in her voice, and I didn't doubt her words. I knew there were things Macon had done that were unkind.

But I also knew there was no such thing as a saint.

"I'm sorry that happened to you," I said with sincerity. "I really am, and I know that doesn't make up for it, but have you ever stopped and thought about what was going on in Macon's life at that time?"

The two women knew as well as I did exactly what Macon

had been going through then—the entire town couldn't stop talking about it.

"I'm not saying his actions are excusable, and I'm definitely not apologizing on his behalf, but I just want you to ask yourself if it were you…could you maybe understand why he would lash out? Especially given the fact that he was pretty much alone."

Molly's eyes drifted to inside of the restaurant, where Macon had entered just moments earlier to place his order. She swallowed hard. "I wasn't exactly nice to him, either. I was kind of petty."

It was easy to forget that emotional pain wasn't so cut and dry. And sometimes, those who lashed out and hurt us the most were just trying to ask us for the simplest thing of all —help.

"I didn't change him," I said. "He's still the same person he's always been. He's just in less pain."

Saying those words out loud made me realize just how much I needed to hear them. Not for Macon, but for myself.

Three weeks ago, when I had driven onto that ferry, I had been no different than I was today.

But I no longer carried the pain and the guilt I'd brought with me.

And what a difference it made.

"But if you ever tell him I told you that, I'll deny it," I joked. "He likes everyone to think he's a mean brute."

A ruckus of female laughter filled the patio.

Macon stepped out just then, one hand on the door, one wrapped around his takeout. His gaze found me. So many dark promises and wicked possibilities in a single glance. His mouth curved into a crooked grin.

I felt a zing go straight to my core, and my thighs pressed together, so tightly that I thought my knees would crack.

He let out a silent laugh.

Asshole.

"I feel like I'm seeing Macon Green in a whole new way

today, and I've gotta say," Millie said as I turned back around, "it's kind of making my head spin. Like, seriously, did he just eye-fuck you from across the patio?"

It was a good thing I hadn't decided to take a sip of my water 'cause I would have spit it all over the table.

"Millie!" Molly scolded her, but I could see the amusement on both of their faces.

And I could not hide the rush of embarrassment that spread across my face.

"I'd say I missed that part—the very start of a relationship where everything is sex all day, every day, but..." She shrugged, grinning from ear to ear.

"She's gonna say they're still in that stage. Literally nothing's changed."

"Nope." She laughed. "I mean, can you blame me? Have you seen my husband?"

The dynamic between Millie and Molly reminded me of Elena and me. Millie had this razor-sharp quality to her like Elena while Molly was more reserved, like me.

"My best friend reminded me that I used to refer to him as Hot Cop when I lived here. I had totally forgotten. I think I'd buried a lot of my memories from Ocracoke."

"It's understandable. You went through a lot," Molly said. "But I'm glad you came back. I know it probably wasn't an easy decision. Did Macon help you decide?"

"What?" I looked at her in confusion.

"You said you were talking for a while. I was just wondering if he was the one who helped encourage you to come back."

My mind was racing at the speed of light, trying to catch up to her. Racing back in time to that moment on the patio.

"We've kept in touch a bit here and there since I moved back to Richmond, and when I got in the other night..."

"Oh, um..." I stumbled over my words. "A little, I guess. He's been incredibly supportive."

Not a lie. He had been incredibly supportive.

They both seemed happy enough with that answer, and I was saved from any more questions when our waitress arrived with our food, and the topic was changed.

"So, Marin, have you picked out a dress for the gala?"

Suddenly, my eyes went wide.

The gala. That was in a week.

The *black-tie* gala.

"Shit." I looked down at my jeans and sweater, knowing my closet was filled with their matching brothers and sisters.

Millie was looking me up and down. "I can help you," she said. "I used to be a buyer for a fashion label, and it came with a lot of perks—most of which I had to sell to buy my store, but I did manage to keep a few things."

"I couldn't—"

"Oh, please," Molly said. "You'll be doing her a favor. She loves dressing people up. It's like a grown-up version of playing dolls for her."

"It is," Millie said. "I can't lie."

I let out a sigh of relief. "That would be a really big help."

"Great! We can head over to my house after lunch if you have time? I have the store covered for the rest of the afternoon."

"That would be great," I said as I tried to gather up the courage to ask my next question. "And while we're there, do you think I could talk to your husband? I have some paintings I think he might like to add to his gallery."

A surprised expression crept across her face. "Absolutely."

I'm doing it, Daniel. I'm really doing it.

CHAPTER SIXTEEN

Macon

'd been staring at her text for the better part of an hour. I had just walked in the door when I got the alert on my phone. Since then, I had taken a shower and changed.

Now, I was just standing in my kitchen, staring at those seven words she'd sent, trying to make a decision.

MARIN

My house at 6. Pack a bag.

My initial response was an obvious one.
Hell yes.

But then I remembered it had only been three days since we'd stood on the side of that road and I'd made that very stupid deal.

That doesn't sound like taking it slow.

MARIN

That's presumptuous of you. I slept over at
your house, and nothing happened.

I thought back to that moment when I'd run headfirst into her after she took a shower.

So naked. So wet.

Did I ever tell you how much I wanted to rip that towel off and just take you right there in the hallway?

MARIN

You know my house has a shower. Two actually.

Not helping.

MARIN

I just want to wake up next to you. Plus, I have good news.

Well, damn. How could I say no to that?

What news?

MARIN

Come over and find out.

I'll see you in fifteen.

She sent back a happy emoji that makes me both roll my eyes and grin like a fucking idiot.

I headed for my bedroom and began throwing shit into a duffel bag, wondering what could have possibly put her in such a good mood.

I was in the truck and headed to her house in less than ten minutes. The days were growing shorter now as the holidays approached, and although it was still early, the sun had already sunk into the horizon.

The headlights illuminated my arrival as I turned into the driveway. I saw Marin step out before I even turned off the ignition. Her hair glistened under the glow of the lights as she moved, those brown eyes finding mine like a tractor beam.

I wondered for a brief moment if there would ever be a time when she wouldn't take my breath away. If I would ever look at her and not feel the air being sucked from my lungs because it was just so unbelievably hard to believe that she was real.

And that she'd chosen me.

I hoped to fuck not.

"You're staring," she said, meeting me halfway.

"How can I not?" I murmured, placing a tender kiss on her lips. "Look at you."

And I did just that. I took a step back, my hands in hers, and I took my fill. My eyes roamed over the soft swell of her breasts to the curve of her hips and those endlessly long legs. She was perfection. To me, she was utter perfection.

"You brought a bag?" she asked, her cheeks already red from my relentless perusal.

"Yes." I motioned to the truck. I'd wanted to see her so badly that I left it behind. "Are you going to tell me what your good news is?"

"Soon," she teased. "Leave your bag there. We're going for a walk."

"What?" I looked around, the stars already high in the sky. "Now?"

She nodded, a bright smile on her face. "Yep. I believe the request was"—she used her fingers to make air quotes—" 'I want to hold your hand and kiss you when no one else is looking.' " She made a dramatic show of grabbing said hand. "So, let's go."

"All right," I conceded, chuckling under my breath. We headed down the driveway, hand in hand, the breeze blowing gently as the crickets chirped in the distance. "Where are we going?"

"Out to dinner," she answered with a very nonchalant shrug.

I stopped and turned to her as things started to click in place. The bag, the walk, dinner. Did she actually have any good news, or was that just a ploy to get me to spend the night? 'Cause she really didn't need to try that hard. My sense of resolve on the subject was paper thin. "Are you trying to check off all the things on that list? At once?" I asked, remembering everything I'd said that day on the side of the road.

"I want to take you out to dinner. I want to hold your hand and kiss you when no one else is looking."

She tried to look innocent, but the blush that crept up her neck called her bluff so quickly that she might as well have *liar* tattooed on her forehead.

I took a step closer, our noses practically touching. I could feel her breath as she sharply inhaled. "Are you trying to seduce me, Marin?"

She looked up through those thick lashes as she bit down on that bottom lip.

"Is it working?" she asked.

Fuck yes, my cock answered.

The corner of my lip twitched. "Let's go to dinner."

Dinner was…

Well, it was torture.

But she wanted to seduce me, so I was playing along.

So, we'd walked under the moonlight. We held hands while no one was watching. We kissed—even though we'd already thoroughly checked that one off the list.

We had gone to a small restaurant in town that neither of us had been to. It was relatively new. The chef was a transplant from Charleston who had bought the dying restaurant from a local who'd needed to retire. What they'd transformed it into was something truly special. Intimate. Expensive, of course, but amazing nonetheless.

We dined on pasta and seafood, and all the while, I watched Marin as her mouth purposely lingered over her fork just a moment longer than necessary. Her tongue darted out, licking her lips with slow, meaningful purpose.

"You are evil," I said, giving her a pointed stare.

Her brow rose as her hand reached across the table. She stroked the skin just about my collarbone. "Am I?"

I grinned, remembering that moment on the patio at lunch. Such an innocent caress, but I had known what it did to her. I could feel her breath hitch and the way she sort of melted into her seat.

"Do you want dessert?" I asked after our plates were cleared.

"I absolutely do not want dessert." She pressed her lips together, stifling a laugh. She did not want to stay here a minute longer. "Do you?"

"Oh, I do," I answered, leaning forward so my voice was low enough that only she could hear. "But not here."

Her cheeks flamed red again.

The blessed waiter brought our check shortly after that, and we were on our way a bit quicker than was probably considered polite. The blocks between the restaurant and Marin's house, once short, now felt endless as the anticipation grew.

I considered throwing her over my shoulder like a caveman and making a run for it, but we were already the source of too much gossip in this town.

I didn't need to cause more.

So, we walked hand in hand again. We talked. We kissed under the stars, and I found myself looking down at our intertwined fingers.

I remembered the first day she'd slid that hand in mine. She was a fucking force of nature, putting the sheriff and Kristy in their place without even batting an eyelash. I hadn't known what to make of her.

I still didn't.

How did I reconcile this gift I'd been given? How did I look at her and not drop to my knees in fucking gratitude every damn day? I had known the moment I held her hand that day on the patio that I didn't deserve her.

Not her kindness or her friendship.

And not a single thing that followed. I still didn't. But I'd spend every damn day trying to make myself worthy.

Because there was one thing I was certain of.

I loved her.

Maybe I always had.

Since the moment she had stepped onto the patio.

Since we had collided in her dark house.

Or even years before, when I had helped out a beautiful woman in a coffee shop.

When we finally reached the house, I went to my truck and grabbed my bag.

Turning back to her, I saw her waiting and asked, "Are you sure?"

I didn't want regrets. I didn't want this to be a rash decision based on need. It was why I'd asked for time in the first place.

Because I knew when I went into that house, there would be no going back.

"I took my time with Curtis," she said. "I took so much time that I forgot the point of it all." She stepped into my embrace, her hand cupping my chin. "Don't make me wait any longer."

My lips spread into a smile under her palm. "It's been three days," I reminded her.

Honestly, we had lasted longer than I'd thought we would. I was surprised we hadn't caved on the way back to the ferry.

"You can learn a lot in three days," she said. "About a person, a town, yourself. Do you know Aiden Fisher?"

"I—what?" *Did I hear her right?* "Yes?"

She laughed, obviously amused by my confusion. "Did you know he opened his gallery to feature other artists? But they have to be local. That's the requirement."

My brain was trying to keep up. Finally, it did. A hundred emotions hit me all at once. She'd said she had good news.

"Local? You're selling your art?"

She smiled, and it was so genuine, filled with a contented happiness that made my heart ache.

"Yes, and I'm already quite in demand. I already sold one to Eli before he left this afternoon and another to Molly for the inn."

"You're staying?"

She nodded, her head bobbing up and down with so much excitement that I thought she'd pull a damn muscle.

I wanted to tell her I loved her.

I wanted to tell her I'd devote my life to making her happy.

I wanted to tell her a hundred things and more.

Instead, I just wrapped my hands around her ass and hoisted her up. She made a little squeak, laughing as her arms wrapped around my neck. The stupid duffel fell off my shoulder, and I grabbed it, shifting her to one arm.

"Well, if that isn't hot, I don't know what is," she said, her eyes fixated on the fact that I was now holding her with one hand.

"I've carried groceries heavier than you," I said, giving her backside a squeeze just to hear that squeal once more.

"You say the sweetest things." She laughed, clutching my shoulders. Her hair was wild and loose, those dark brown curls tumbling down her back.

"I can't believe you're staying," I said, still in shock. I had hoped. I'd dreamed, but I'd never actually thought…

"I can't believe you thought I'd leave." Her expression changed, going from playful to serious, as her hands grasped my chin.

"You left your home, your family."

"I left an apartment, not a home," she countered. "And, yes, my family is there, but it's their home. This…" she glanced toward the bright yellow door. "This is mine. This is where I belong. I *am* home, Macon."

"Well, let's go home then."

It was a short distance to the door, and after a few

awkward moments of Marin trying to shuffle through her purse while simultaneously being held, we managed to get in.

I dropped the bag to the ground immediately.

The moment the door was shut, I had her shoved against the nearest wall, my hands under her shirt and our tongues moving in tandem.

She let out a little gasp as I cupped her breast through her bra.

Any more of that, and we wouldn't make it any farther into the house.

"Which room?" I asked. I didn't want to make assumptions.

Her room was a sanctuary—a private place. I didn't want to ruin any memories that might linger there.

She looked up at me with those swollen lips and a heated gaze. "Master," she said as if it were the most obvious answer in the world. "I'm not making love to you in the guest bedroom like some dirty little secret, Macon. I want to wake up with you in my bed."

I swallowed down a dozen emotions, kissing her forehead for the briefest moment.

With her legs still wrapped around my waist, I carried her through the living room and down the hall, not bothering to turn on the lights. Somewhere along the way, she dropped her purse and shrugged off her jacket.

Turning into the room, I found the lights and let Marin slip down to the floor. I took a moment to look around, finding crisp white bedding and matching curtains. There were tons of pillows piled on top of the bed in shades of blue that all coordinated with paintings that lined the walls.

"You must have just hung these," I said, recognizing several from the night before.

She nodded. "I wanted the room to look"—she paused—"different."

She wanted it to be hers.

"Your paintings, Marin." My eyes swept the room. "They're incredible. *You're* incredible."

When I finally turned back to her, I realized she hadn't been following my tour of the room; she was just watching me.

"You make me feel incredible."

I took a step forward, pulling her into my embrace. "I can make you feel all kinds of things," I promised. "You just have to tell me what you want."

I felt a shiver run down her spine.

"What do you want, Marin?"

Her eyes met mine, that sweet blush painting her cheeks. "Everything," she answered. "I want to feel everything."

Good answer.

Our lips met in a frenzied kiss as my fingers swept through her hair. Her arms wrapped around my neck as I pushed her backward until her knees hit the edge of the bed.

"I need you naked." My voice was rough, and heavy with need.

"You first," she said, her brow lifting in challenge.

Oh, I liked this side of Marin—that wild side of her that had been dormant for so long. The side of her that now only belonged to me.

"All right," I agreed.

She sat on the bed, sliding back until her head hit all those pillows resting against the headboard. She leaned back on her elbows and waited.

"Comfortable?"

She made a point to take one leg and throw it over the other. "Very." And then she added, "Proceed."

"Trying to make me feel bashful?" I asked as I pulled my shirt up and over my head.

Her gaze moved downward, over my pecs and down toward the deep V of my hips.

"There's not a bashful bone in your body."

Her teeth bit down on her bottom lip as my hands reached for my belt buckle. "No, I'm just making things even."

"Even?" I pulled the leather back, undoing the loop on my belt.

She watched every movement intently.

"You had me very naked last night. And you were not. Seems only fair," she said with a shrug.

"I was shirtless," I reminded her as I slowly unbuttoned my jeans.

A gleam of mischief sparkled in her eyes. She leaned forward, grabbed the hem of her sweater, and pulled upward. In two seconds, it was on the floor as she peered back at me, looking victorious.

"Completely shirtless," I said, pointing to the lace bra that still remained.

She met my challenge and reached around her rib cage, unsnapping the hook. I watched in goddamn wonder as the straps fell off her shoulders. *So damn gorgeous.*

"You're distracted." She laughed.

"Of course I am."

"Strip, Macon. I want to see those clothes on the floor." Her brow lifted.

Well, if I wasn't already hard as a fucking rock, I would be now.

"Yes, ma'am."

Her laugh echoed around the room as I unzipped my jeans and let them fall to the floor. I stepped out of them and looked up. Marin was staring at me like a ravenous bear, and the second my hands went to my boxer briefs, she was up and at the edge of the bed.

At first, I thought maybe she was having second thoughts. Maybe I'd misread that expression on her face.

But then she stepped forward, and her fingers closed over mine. I could smell the fruity aroma of her shampoo. I could feel the heat of her body as I gripped her waist. Her hands slid under the thin fabric, over my ass and my hips. I pushed the boxers down, giving her more access, and I chuckled when I heard a gasp fall from her lips.

"We can take it slow," I assured her as she took a long, brazen stare at my cock. "Now, I believe I've held up my end of the bargain."

"Oh, you definitely have."

She stepped back, her hands reaching for her jeans. She made quick work of the button. The sound of the zipper was music to my ears, and she let out a little laugh as she wiggled out of them, revealing tiny black panties I wanted to rip with my teeth. Instead, she slowly slid them down to the floor, and I fought the need to just bury myself in her right there on the fucking floor.

"On the bed," I instructed, clearing my throat. "Just the edge."

She did as I asked, and I sank to my knees in front of her.

Like I was kneeling before a goddess.

And it was time to worship.

"Spread those thighs for me, Marin. I want to see all of you."

Although she was getting bolder in the bedroom, that blush returned, a shy smile tugging at the corner of her lips. She was slow at first, just the tiniest wiggle of her feet as her legs inched further apart, but when she saw my heated gaze, she gave in.

"That's it," I said.

I kissed her inner thigh, moving inward. She shuddered as my hair brushed the sensitive skin there.

Last night, her first orgasm had been with my fingers. The second, on my tongue.

I'd been dreaming of both ever since.

Now, I just had to decide which one I wanted to do first. I looked up at her. So full of anticipation. So eager.

Mmm, both.

Definitely both.

I bent forward and buried myself in her heat. She tasted

like honey. Sweet, decadent, and fucking addictive. She let out a moan as I dragged my tongue over her clit, her thighs falling to the sides as I slid a finger into those slick folds.

"Oh shit!" The curse echoed off the walls.

I chuckled, and even that made her jolt, her body writhing as I licked and sucked. Her hips moved, rocking against me.

I added another digit, and she gasped. Her fingers dug into my hair, holding me captive as she sought her release.

And damn if that wasn't the hottest thing I'd ever seen.

"I want to hear you scream, Marin," I said right before I sank my tongue down on her clit and sucked, sending her over the edge. She let out a cry so loud that she could have leveled a building.

Her legs were still shaking when I wrapped an arm around her waist, pulling her all the way onto the bed.

"How do you do that?" she asked, her words coming out staggered and breathless.

"Do what?" I leaned into her, running a hand down her side.

"That," she said, her brows lifting like it was obvious. "It's just so effortless. Is it—are you always…"

Now, it was my time to raise an eyebrow.

"What are you trying to ask me? If I'm just good at sex? Because, sure, the answer is yes." I gave a lazy grin. I had been far from a saint before I married Kristy. "But as you know, it can be different, depending on who you're with."

"Is it different with me?" she asked, a touch of nervousness in her tone.

"Very," I answered, leaning down to kiss away all that anxiety. "It's the best I've ever had."

Her eyes widened. "But we haven't even had sex yet."

I grinned, moving to gently spread my weight on top of her. "Oh, I know."

As I settled between her thighs, that overwhelming need to tell her I loved her swept over me. To not only claim her with my body, but also with my soul.

But fear was a fickle thing.

I'd been in the military, in more scary situations than I could count.

Yet telling the woman I loved those three little words seemed more terrifying than anything I'd encountered before.

I looked down at her, hoping she understood.

If I couldn't yet say it with words, I would show her with my actions.

I bent down, placing a slow and tender kiss on her lips. As I tilted my head, her tongue met mine, and our passion reignited. A hand ghosted down her side, over her thigh, tugging it around my torso. I could feel her wet and ready underneath me.

"I need you," she pleaded. "Please, Macon."

I nudged her legs apart, nestling between her thighs. "You don't ever have to beg," I promised her as I moved my hips, sinking in inch by inch.

It was the best kind of torture.

"Are you okay?" I asked, giving her time to adjust.

Her hands slid around my ribcage. "Yes, more."

She rolled those fucking hips, and I nearly lost my goddamn mind.

I sank into all that wet, tight heat. "Fuck," I groaned. "You're gonna make me look bad with moves like that."

She did it again, wrapping her legs around my torso. "Come on, Captain Green." She grinned. "Show me what you've got."

I've created a monster.

I pulled out, nearly to the tip, and then gave a deep thrust. This time, she was the one who cursed as I moved again, hitting just the right place.

"How the fuck?" Her eyes nearly rolled back in her head.

I knew a few tricks.

But I didn't want to spend the whole time showing off. We had plenty of time for that. Right now, I had other plans.

I scooped my hands under her, pulling her upward. "Straddle me," I instructed. "Like last night."

She repositioned her legs so that they were on either side of me. With our bodies still joined, I didn't have to tell her what to do.

This was what I wanted.

I wanted to see her in command.

She needed to know I wasn't magic. That she could take control—of her body, us—and bring herself to orgasm just as easily as I could.

I watched as she ground her hips, her head falling back as I scattered kisses along her neck and down between the valley of her breasts. The sound of her breath in my ear and the little whimpers of pleasure drove me fucking crazy. I knew she was close.

"This is all you," I murmured. "Your pleasure, your power. Now, take it."

Her movements became frantic as she rode my cock hard. Her fingers fisted my hair as she pulled me into a fierce kiss. She moaned in my mouth loudly as her orgasm swept over her, and I swallowed the sound as she shattered in my arms.

A sight to behold.

I didn't even wait, flipping her back on the bed as her body still spasmed around me. I was a man undone. Every ounce of control had snapped as I watched her chase that release, knowing how broken she'd felt without it.

"So fucking beautiful," I said, burying myself deep. Once again, they weren't the words I wanted to say. "And mine."

She rolled those hips again. "If I'm yours, I get to call you mine."

A wide grin spread across my face. "Are we making more deals?"

I hit that spot again, and she let out another gasp. She nodded.

"That is one deal you never have to worry about, Marin. I've been yours since the moment you stepped off that ferry."

I let go, thrusting fast and hard, as our mouths met in a passionate kiss that mimicked our lovemaking. My name sprang free from her lips as I felt her climax again, those tight walls clamping down around my cock like a vise.

I came hard.

I let out a guttural groan as the room tilted and my body melted into hers.

Nothing should feel that good.

Nothing.

I met her gaze, kissing her forehead, her cheek, her lips.

A wry smile spread across her face. "So, round two?"

God, I really had created a monster.

CHAPTER SEVENTEEN

Marin

was blissfully, wonderfully, achingly sore.

I'd been up for a while now, just watching him sleep. Sunbeams filtered in through the gauzy curtains. It brought out the natural highlights in his sandy-brown hair and the stubble on his chin. I wanted to run my fingers over it, trace the curve of his jaw, the tiny white line that scarred his eyebrow. It was well past eight, and I loved watching the easy rise and fall of his chest, knowing he slept so easily.

I wanted him to sleep this peacefully every day.

"Are you going to stare at me like that all day?"

The sound of his voice made me jump, especially since he'd spoken with his eyes still closed. A slow smile crept across his face a second before I saw his hands reach around my waist. His catlike reflexes had me pinned beneath him in seconds.

Those hazel irises were now staring down at me, and a smug grin replaced the smile. "Can't sneak up on me, remember?"

"You weren't awake the whole time," I challenged him.

There was no way he'd pretended to be asleep for that long.

"Mmm," was his only response. Macon's version of a concession.

"Are you sore?" he asked, his voice rough and breathy as his gaze began to wander.

Heat pooled between my thighs.

"Yes," I answered softly.

"Too sore?" His body was above me, his weight gently hovering over me. A hand slid down my waist.

"If I was?" I asked, wondering what he would do with that wandering hand.

"Then, I'd suggest a shower," he said. "With me, of course."

"Obviously." I played along.

"I'd need to wash you, paying special attention to all those sore spots," he went on, his hand drifting lower.

"That's very kind of you." I gasped as his fingers ghosted over the sensitive skin between my thighs.

"Marin."

"Mmm?" I managed to say.

"Too sore?" he asked again.

"No," I finally answered.

"Thank fuck." He was off the bed in a second.

He grabbed my hand, and I came willingly, sliding to the end of the bed. The moment I stood, the world tilted, and I was upside down.

"Where are we going?" I laughed as he hauled me over his shoulder.

"Shower, of course."

"I told you I wasn't that sore," I reminded him.

"I know. But now, we get to do all those things in the shower, *and* I can fuck you."

"You're insatiable," I told him.

"Only with you, Marin," he declared. "Only with you."

He didn't set me down until we were in the master bath. It wasn't big by any means, but it had been updated with bright white tiles and a large shower.

"This looks different," he said, placing me on the counter.

It was cold, but I liked sitting there, watching him move around in my space. He turned the faucet, adjusted the temperature, and grabbed towels, all while completely nude and not in the least bit shy about it.

"What in the world were you doing in the master bath of your friend's house?"

"Hide-and-seek, obviously," he said with a grin. It made him look young and happy, and I suddenly wished I could see pictures of him as a boy.

But then I remembered the kind of childhood he'd had, and I reconsidered.

Would he look sad in them? Lonely?

"How did you manage to have a friend here?" I asked. "Did your dad like the family?"

He grunted, "No, definitely not. He just wasn't around at the time. Fishing boat gig, I believe. Anyway, our moms met at a school function. It was good. Normal, you know? They just didn't stay long."

"You felt safe," I said, realizing just how crazy life could be, "in my house."

"Yeah," he answered, stepping forward to kiss my lips. "I guess I did. I actually thought about buying it when it went on the market, but then my life fell apart."

My eyes widened. "And I bought it instead."

"Can't say I'm sad about it," he said. "About the way things turned out." And then he must have realized what he'd said because he started to backtrack. "I'm sorry. That's not—"

I shushed him with a kiss. "I know," I said. "We can't change the way things happened. But we can still be grateful for each other."

"I don't know if I'll ever stop being grateful for you," he said.

"How grateful?" The words left my lips like a challenge, and he was more than willing to accept.

He held out a hand toward me, pinning me with those intense hazel eyes of his. I met him halfway, our fingers touching as he tugged me toward the shower. The water was hot, and the steam floated around us like warm clouds.

We took turns washing each other's hair and body. He had to kneel for me to reach his hair. The position gave him other ideas, and suddenly, the shampoo was forgotten. His head was buried between my legs, and I was writhing and moaning his name. When I came back to earth, he made good on his promise to pay extra attention to my most intimate areas, and as he ventured lower, I felt that fire build in my belly once more.

The soap dropped, and I felt him press me against the tiles.

"Are you sure you're not too sore?" he asked again.

I nodded. He could have fucked me raw, and I'd still be here, nodding my head up and down with just as much enthusiasm.

I felt his hands cup my ass, and as one slid down my leg, I did the one thing I'd been dying to do since I'd undressed him the night before.

He was heavy and hard against my stomach.

He let out a curse the moment my hand wrapped around him. "You gotta give me a warning. That right there could end me."

I let out a laugh, running my hand up and down his cock. He groaned, and I felt a little drunk on the power I had over him. His hands went around my waist, lifting me, and I guided him inside me. The moment our bodies connected, he didn't hesitate. With a single thrust, he filled me completely.

I'd forgotten how good this could feel.

How right it could feel.

Water poured down on us as his mouth met mine. His pace was surprisingly slow, a contrast to the frenzied start. He took his time, as if he meant to pull every moan and ounce of pleasure from me before we were done.

"I want to hear my name on your lips again, Marin," he said. "I want this whole fucking island to hear you and know you're mine."

His pace quickened then, the sound of skin on skin driving me wild as I felt him reach down and place his thumb right on that delicate bundle of nerves.

I moaned, over and over, feeling that rushing sensation deep in my core. I met his thrusts, grinding my hips against him, and I felt myself fall, tumbling over that cliff. I screamed his name, and somehow, I knew…it would be the only name to ever fall from my lips again.

I left Macon in the bedroom to dress while I headed to the kitchen.

I was still wrapped in my towel, my hair a wet mess of curls, but I was starving and needed to check the food situation, which I feared was dismal.

I really should start acting like an adult.

No one my age should be so incompetent when it came to feeding themselves.

I walked into the kitchen and opened the fridge, which I knew was a fruitless endeavor. I hadn't put anything but leftovers in there since I had arrived in Ocracoke.

So, unless Macon was interested in leftover French fries from Billy's…

I went to the pantry next.

"No luck?" He stepped behind me, dressed in clean jeans and a dark blue hoodie that molded to his body perfectly.

"I have ramen," I answered.

He made a face that resembled something akin to disgust.

I laughed. "Do you want to go to the coffee shop?"

"That would be great." It was his day off, which meant I had him for the entire day. "Maybe we can run to the market afterward and grab food. Real food."

"Mmm." I grinned, stepping closer to plant a sweet kiss on his lips. "I have been craving pancakes."

"And I've been craving maple syrup," he replied right before his hand slid under the towel to the apex of my thighs. "Right here."

"Like I said"—I laughed—"insatiable."

"That's because you drive me fucking crazy." He kissed me quickly and deeply before abruptly pulling away. "Go put some clothes on or else we're never getting out of here today."

That didn't sound like the worst idea, but I guessed we would need food at some point.

I started to walk away, but then I paused because it just dawned on me. "No run today?"

He shrugged. "I think I'm okay today."

My eyes lingered on him, and he obviously noticed the concern.

"It's fine, really," he urged. "I run a lot when I'm stressed. I've been actually just enjoying it lately, like I used to."

"So, you're not going to get all soft on me?" I joked, making his smile reach all the way up to his eyes.

"I will never be soft around you," he quirked an eyebrow.

I turned back toward the island and grabbed a kitchen towel to throw at his head again, and like before, it sailed over his head as he expertly dodged it. He stepped closer, enclosing me in his arms as he pressed me into the granite behind me.

"You really need to get dressed," he practically growled. "Seeing you in this towel...in this kitchen...it gives me all sorts of ideas."

"Like what?" I goaded him.

"Like breaking a fucking vase." He grinned. "For real this time."

"Oh, well, you'd have to buy me new flowers first." I laughed. "If you want to make the fantasy accurate, that is."

"We can use our imagination."

But before I could answer, the doorbell rang.

He groaned, and I laughed once more, looking down at my very indecent appearance.

"Can you answer it? It's probably just Molly, coming for her painting. I only brought a few of the small ones over to show her after I met with Aiden. I had the rest on my phone and she chose the large one I did of Silver Lake Harbor."

"Molly bought your painting, sight unseen?" he asked.

I only nodded.

"Marin, that's amazing."

"Really? You don't think she's just being nice?"

He shook his head. "No, she doesn't just put anything up in that inn. It's her family legacy. I think you should consider that a huge compliment."

I felt both embarrassed and proud at the same time. "Well, go answer the door so I can get paid," I suggested.

He slapped my butt before I could get away and was rewarded with a giddy yelp.

I heard him chuckle as I fled down the hallway.

Just as I rounded the corner to the bedroom, the sound of that creaky door opened, and I heard a very familiar voice.

But it wasn't Molly.

It was my mother.

Oh shit.

I threw on a pair of shorts and a shirt as quickly as humanly possible, but I highly doubted it took a rocket scientist to figure out what Macon and I had been up to.

Early morning, wet hair, and mismatched clothing.

Why, yes, Mom and Dad…we did just have sex. Come on in, won't you?

"Hi, Mama," I said, racing out of the bedroom, haphazardly trying to fix my hair. "Hi, Papa."

"*Liebling*," my dad said. No hello. No hug. Just *liebling*.

God, I felt like I was sixteen all over again, coming in late from curfew.

Macon cleared his throat and then awkwardly said, "I think I'm going to give you three some alone time."

When his eyes found mine, I felt my heart plummet.

He tried to hide it, but I saw it. The flash of hurt in his eyes.

Just last night, I'd told him he wasn't some dirty secret, and here were my parents, not twelve hours later, showing up at my doorstep, completely unaware of his existence.

Like I was ashamed of him and everything that had happened between us.

I'd told my parents about my breakup with Curtis, but I'd left out the most important detail—that I'd met someone else.

Someone incredible and kind. Someone I'd fallen in love with.

The realization hit me with a jolt.

Oh God, I really did love him.

And I'd failed him because, like Elena had said, I was scared of others' reactions.

I took a step forward and then another. Finally, I met his gaze and placed a light kiss on his cheek. My parents looked on with a healthy dose of suspicion.

"I'll call you in a bit."

He gave a brief nod, and then I watched him walk out, resisting the urge to follow him. I swallowed the lump in my throat, knowing I would make things right.

Turning back to my parents, who were unusually quiet, I took a deep breath and prepared to put them in their place. "Is this a habit now? Showing up at my door, unannounced?"

They seemed a bit taken aback, but you know what? So was I. There was such a thing as a phone.

And I was an adult.

Maybe one who didn't cook or visit the grocery store nearly enough, but I still didn't deserve to be treated like a child.

"We were worried," my dad said as my mother took the opportunity to make herself at home.

I didn't hold that against her. As mad as I was at them, I never faulted her for taking care of my dad. She wheeled him over to a spot near the living room couch, making sure he was comfortable before taking a seat next to him. I sat down across from them, tucking my feet under me as I leaned back in the chair.

"How are you even here?" I asked, knowing the ferry schedule and my dad's illness.

There was no way they had driven all night and taken the first ferry in. That would have been way too much stress on both of them.

"We drove down yesterday and stayed at an inn in town."

They had stayed at Molly's. It was the only inn I knew of. Ocracoke had hotels, B-and-Bs, and tons of rentals, but Molly's place was unique.

"And you didn't think about just calling me?" *Like a rational person.*

"You've barely spoken to us since you left. And when you broke things off with Curtis…" My mom paused before moving on altogether. "It's been weeks. How much longer will this go on?"

How much longer will this tantrum of yours last? That's what she wanted to say.

My dad, who was usually my biggest supporter—in life and even against my own mother—remained silent. I took a deep breath and looked out the window toward the driveway. It was empty now, Macon's truck long gone.

"You didn't even like Curtis," I said. It was petty, but I was angry.

"Yes, we did," my dad shot back a bit too quickly.

I tilted my head and raised an eyebrow.

Finally, he threw up his hands, looking exasperated. "We would have loved him." He paused. "If you did." Seriously, did everyone know? They didn't think to clue me in? "We've seen you in love, *liebling*, and that…that was affection at best. Curtis is a nice man, maybe a bit shy for my taste."

"Everyone is a bit shy for your taste, Papa." I rolled my eyes.

"True." He chuckled. "But if he was your chosen, I would have loved him as I loved…" His voice cut off, and I nodded.

I wasn't the only one who had struggled with Daniel's death.

My parents had loved him like one of their own.

And they had grieved him just the same.

"When are you coming home?" my mom asked, getting back to the point.

My father was passionate in everything he did. My mother, the epitome of pragmatism.

I am home.

"I'm not," I stated.

The woman's eyes grew so wide that I thought they might just fall right out.

"What do you mean, you're not coming home? You can't possibly think you can stay. This was a nice dream when you had Daniel, but now—"

My face hardened. "You don't think I can do it by myself?"

"That's not…" She straightened slightly. "It's just not the same, and you know it. Daniel supported you before. You don't even have a job."

It felt like a slap in the face.

Did she really believe I was so reckless?

"I know that," I spit. "But I don't need one. I don't have a mortgage anymore," I reminded her, just in case she had forgotten. "And I've already secured a spot in a local gallery to showcase my paintings."

"That's wonderful, *liebling*." My dad's face lit up.

There he was.

My champion and eternal cheerleader.

The man who'd left his homeland to chase his own

dreams. And even though it hadn't turned out the way he'd hoped, he'd never deterred me from doing the same.

"Thanks, Papa." My face beamed.

Unfortunately, that pragmatic side of my mother, the one who'd seen the fruits of my father's labor fail, was still rearing its ugly head. "And you think that will sustain you?"

"Well, I made three thousand dollars yesterday, so, yes, Mama, I think I can make it work."

Without a mortgage and some serious budgeting, I could live on that money for a while if I had to, and she knew it.

"Is this about the man that was here?" she finally asked.

I had been waiting for her to throw this question out. I knew she'd been dying to ask about the mystery man since he'd walked out.

"Margarete." There was a warning tone in my father's voice.

Don't go there, it said.

She did anyway.

"Don't ruin your future for a fling, Marin."

I knew when she started calling me by my given name that things were bad.

I rose to my feet.

"Macon is not a fling." I seethed. "And let me remind you that you came to my house, unannounced and uninvited, so I'm sorry if you walked in on something you might consider inappropriate, Mother. Next time, perhaps"—I let out a huff —"call first."

I turned away, my arms tightly wrapped around my chest. I was angry and upset.

At them.

At myself.

If I had just been honest from the start, none of this would have happened.

My dad was the one who finally cut the silence. His voice was timid, but reassuring. "Tell us about your fellow, *liebling*."

I let out a ragged sigh of relief. He was offering a bridge. A way to make amends. As I turned back around, I found his kind eyes, and my own became wet with unshed tears.

"He bought me coffee once," I began with a sniffle and a laugh. It was random but a fact I found so innately important to our story. "When I forgot my wallet."

My dad motioned to the chair, silently asking me to sit, and I did so, needing the comfort he was offering more than I realized.

"He's a local deputy, a captain actually."

"That sounds like a very demanding job," my dad said as he gave me an encouraging smile.

My mother, however, remained stoic and silent.

"It is," I replied. "But he manages. He runs a lot. It helps."

I didn't tell them it also helped with other demons. That was Macon's tale, not mine.

"He came back to a hometown he hated, hoping to make a difference, but it cost him a lot." I looked out toward the window again, remembering the haunted look on his face that first day on the patio.

And the overwhelming urge I'd had to erase it.

"He's thoughtful, surprisingly funny, and smart—"

"And you love him." The words came from my mother. They were matter-of-fact, and yet, for the first time since she had arrived, I could feel the slightest warmth in her voice.

"Yes," I answered without the slightest hesitation, "I do."

"Is this why you're staying?" she asked as her guard slightly lowered. "Because of him?"

"No, I'm staying for myself," I stated. "When I came down here, I had no idea why I was doing this—only that I needed to. At first, I thought maybe I was supposed to say good-bye —sell the house and walk away from something I'd been holding on to for far too long."

"What made you change your mind?"

"I did," I answered with a smile. "I thought I was coming down here for Daniel. To say goodbye or heal? But the longer I was here, the more I realized this place had never been really ours. In the few short months we had lived here, I was mostly alone, and that wasn't his fault—he worked his ass off to make this dream possible for me. But during that time, I had fallen in love with this island." I remembered all those walks. All those solo expeditions around the island. "And coming back here, I remembered the love I had for this place. The connection. This is home for me."

"And how does Macon fit?"

Hearing Macon's name on my mom's lips made me smile. Not just because her accent made it slightly comical, but because it also made him real.

It made us real.

"He is a bonus. A really lovely bonus."

"Do you think we can meet him?" my mom asked before adding, "Formally? With proper attire?"

She gave me a pointed stare as her eyes wandered over my wrinkled clothes and messy hair.

I let out a laugh, my eyes still watery. "Absolutely."

CHAPTER EIGHTEEN

Macon

I needed to run.

There were too many thoughts, too many emotions in my head. The moment I got home, I headed straight for my bedroom, threw on a pair of jogging pants, and bolted out the door.

The instant my feet hit the pavement and my breath accelerated, I pushed harder.

I needed the distance today. I needed the burn and the ache.

I needed—

Fuck.

I didn't know what the hell I needed.

The moment I had pulled that creaky-ass door open, I had known it was Marin's parents staring back at me.

If her dad's wheelchair hadn't given it away, the resemblance would have. She had her mother's dark chestnut hair and her father's mesmerizing eyes.

They looked at me and then looked at the numbers on the door.

Yep, right address.

For a split second, I hoped there would be a spark of recognition as those familiar set of brown eyes lit up, and her dad would say, "Oh, you must be Macon! We've heard so much about you."

Instead, I was looked upon with suspicion and a healthy dose of judgment—both of which I was used to. I'd endured much of the same from Kristy's parents for the majority of our marriage.

I understood why Marin wouldn't have told them about me. She'd just broken off a long-term relationship, and when you explained it to someone, it did sound crazy.

Except I knew we were anything but.

I'd just thought she did, too.

By the time I made it out to Highway 12 and back, my body ached, my chest burned, and I was starving.

It was late enough in the morning that I thought a quick trip to the coffee shop was doable. I had zero food in my house, and if I had to walk my tired ass back there, I was at least gonna do it with a fucking bear claw in my mouth.

I was nearly back to Silver Lake Harbor and standing on the side of the road, waiting to cross. A car passed by as I stared at the ground, trying to catch my breath.

"I thought you didn't need to go for a run today."

I nearly jumped out of my own damn skin.

"Jesus, Marin. Fucking scared the shit out of me." I looked up to see her stopped in the middle of the road in front of me. I had been so lost in thought that I hadn't even noticed her car slow down in front of me. "I changed my mind," I answered her. "Needed to get out of the house."

"Did I just sneak up on you?" She started to grin but then stopped herself, as if she felt bad for it somehow. "Where are you headed?"

I motioned across the street to the coffee shop.

"I'll meet you over there?"

"Sure."

I jogged over to the other side, and even that made my calf muscles burn. By the time I made it to the parking lot, her engine was off, and she was stepping out to meet me.

She'd changed into a different pair of jeans and a dark orange sweater that brought out the dark chestnut in her hair.

I felt the dark clouds in my mind begin to ease.

"You look tired," she said, her eyes taking me in. "And sweaty."

My brow lifted. "Want a hug?" I held out my arms and took a giant step forward.

"No!" She laughed, darting away from me.

I caught her hand and pulled her toward me, making sure to keep enough of a distance.

I didn't blame her. I wouldn't want to touch me right now either.

"You can kiss me though," she offered with a shy smile and suddenly everything felt right in the world again.

"Already planning on it."

I angled my head, parting her lips with my tongue. She opened willingly and let me in with a little whimper.

"I fucking love that sound."

She grinned like a Cheshire cat. "Let's go inside before we do something stupid and give the sheriff a reason to arrest you on your day off."

I merely grunted, "I'd love to see him try."

She looked at me, her eyes giving a great big roll as we wandered inside. There were a few people at the tables and sofas, but thankfully, no one was in line.

Janet gave us a friendly greeting and took our orders much quicker today. Her interest in our torrid love affair was clearly waning.

Thank God.

"I take it, you need to head back," I said after she placed an order for three.

"Yes, but I have a few minutes. I was going to call you anyway."

We headed over to one of the tables this time, doing Janet a favor as I tried to avoid anything upholstered.

"How did it go?" I asked as we both took a seat. "Your parents, I mean."

"Good," she replied before amending her answer, "Well, mostly."

"I can't imagine they were thrilled to walk in on you practically naked." I grinned.

She swatted at my arm and then grimaced, making me laugh. She wiped her palm on my shirt. "Okay, one"—she held up a finger—"I was not naked, not when they saw me. And two"—she added another digit—"as I told them, I'm a damn adult."

"So, things did get heated." I winced, feeling guilty she had fought with her parents over me. I didn't want their relationship to be strained.

"Yes, but not in the way you're thinking." She leaned back in her chair. "They're—well, mostly my mom—are worried I won't be able to support myself down here."

That was not the answer I'd expected.

"And are you?" I asked.

"No." Her smile was wide, brimming with confidence. "Not at all."

That's my girl.

"Good. You shouldn't be. You're going to do great." I had no doubt.

It's what she came here to do after all.

"They want to meet you," she said, making my heart jump to my throat.

"What?" My voice came out all dodgy and high-pitched.

She laughed, reveling in my discomfort. "After I explained to them you weren't some random hookup—"

"I do not like those words coming from your lips."

"Context, Macon!" she scolded me, obviously amused, and I couldn't help but laugh. "I suggested we could all make dinner together."

"All of us?" I raised an eyebrow.

"Well, maybe not all of us." There was a brief pause before

her expression turned more serious. "I'm sorry I didn't tell them about you."

"It's—"

She held up a hand to halt my words. "Don't you dare say it's fine. It's not. It wasn't, and I knew it. I am not ashamed of us. Not of the way we met or the timing of it all. Anyone who wants to judge us for being happy? Well, they can simply fuck right off."

A slow smile spread across my face. "Well, all right then."

She smiled back. "So, dinner tonight?"

"I'd be honored."

"Okay, but, Macon?" She looked suddenly embarrassed. "Can you take me to the market? I hate that place."

The sound of my laughter filled the whole fucking coffee shop.

Marin wasn't kidding.

She really hated the grocery store.

After grabbing our food at the coffee shop, she dropped my tired ass off at my house to shower and change. We met up at the grocery store a few hours later while her parents went back to the inn to rest.

Walking down the aisles, I tried not to laugh. It was like watching an alien visit Earth for the first time.

"Do you really live on takeout?" I asked. "Like, all the time?"

She shrugged. "There's the ramen. But I have that stuff delivered."

"Good God."

When I started picking out tomatoes for a marinara, she frowned and asked, "It doesn't come from a jar?"

Fucking adorable.

"I'm gonna have to give you cooking lessons one of these

days," I stated as I grabbed a bulb of garlic and threw it in a bag.

"Okay, but only if you do it naked."

"That sounds dangerous." I laughed, tossing in another.

She poked at a bundle of basil with a frown. "We'll get you an apron. Something frilly and pink."

"Only if we get one for you that says, *Macon's favorite dessert*, with a big arrow…" I made sure to gesture with my finger, dragging it from her chest down to her—

She laughed, grabbing my hand before it could reach its destination.

"Insatiable," she reminded me.

I pulled her hand to my lips, kissing her palm.

A loud crash jerked my attention behind us. Someone had run into our cart with a string of apologies, and when I turned around, I found the bright red face of my ex.

"Kristy."

"Sorry, my cart must have gotten away from me for a moment."

That happens when you're not paying attention to it.

Marin tried to pull her hand away. It was still palm up, just inches from my mouth. I would not make her think I felt guilty for being caught by my ex in public.

Very purposely, I curled my fingers through hers and then tugged her hand to my side.

"For someone who doesn't live here, you seem to be around a lot."

I had seen her less when I was married to her.

Her face hardened. "The sheriff has commitments, remember? He serves the entire county."

Kind of weird she had referred to him as *the sheriff*.

"I remember," I answered, "But I didn't realize you had to come along, too."

"I—" She let out a huff. "I like coming. It gives me a break for a night." Her eyes widened before she added, "I mean, it gives us both a break. Together."

It was then that I noticed it.

The tiredness in her voice.

The dark circles.

I didn't know why I cared, but the words came out anyway. "Are you okay?"

She took a step back, a flash of surprise that was quickly replaced with anger. "Of course I am. Why wouldn't I be? I have everything I want."

She thought that blow would hurt.

It used to.

"Have a nice day, Kristy," I said before turning my attention back to Marin. She placed her free hand on our cart, and we started to make our exit.

"Macon," a soft voice called after me.

I turned to see my ex-wife standing there, looking more like the woman I had married. Only this version of her was difficult to look at. She looked stripped bare and utterly wrecked.

"You have to stop pushing him," she said.

"What?" I didn't know what the hell she was talking about.

"He doesn't like to feel threatened. And lately—"

He feels threatened? Since when?

"He's never been able to control me," I said. "You know that."

It's why I lost you.

"He's only going to put up with it for so long," she said.

"Are you saying my job is on the line?" I felt my throat tighten.

Her gaze searched mine, and then suddenly, it was like a wall came down. "Just...be careful," she said, straightening her spine before turning and walking off.

I turned back to Marin, and I saw the fear in my own eyes staring back at me.

I was trained to do one thing on this island.

What would I do if that was taken away from me?

I tried to relax. I tried to plaster a fake smile across my face.

"Well, that was weird," I said, pushing our cart as far away from Kristy as I could.

"You're not worried?" she asked, the lines on her forehead deep with concern. "About what she said?"

I shrugged. "Sheriff Hayes is harmless. If he wanted to fire me, he would have done it years ago. Besides," I added, feeling like the worst kind of liar, "he can't afford to lose another one of us right now."

"That's true," she said, nodding her head in agreement, although she didn't seem any less scared.

"And," I said with a toothy grin, "everyone loves me. There'd be a riot if I left."

She laughed.

"I think you overestimate your appeal." She rolled her eyes.

I felt the tension break between us, but it didn't stop the fear inside me from building.

Because I didn't believe a word I'd said.

If Sheriff Hayes had it out for me...

I was fucked.

Buying the flowers wasn't necessarily a bad idea.

Buying her flowers on the night her parents were going to be here?

Maybe the worst idea ever.

"Stop staring at them," she said moments after she came out of the bedroom. She'd changed again, choosing an emerald green dress and black tights. Her hair was in a loose braid, and she'd freshened up her makeup.

"Make me," I challenged, wagging my eyebrow in the most obnoxious way.

"If my parents knock on that door and I'm naked again—"

I laughed. "You weren't naked," I reminded her. I hopped off the stool next to the island and walked over to her. A stray hair had gotten loose from her braid, and I tucked it behind her ear. "You were just mostly naked. Do I need to show you the difference?"

But before she could answer, the doorbell rang.

"Saved by the bell," I joked. "But not for long."

"Are the flowers going to be a distraction?" She motioned to the vase on the island. "Should I put them in my room?"

I wasn't sure how attached Marin was to her vases, so when I'd bought the flowers on the way over, I got a vase to go with them.

It was clear and made of simple glass, something you definitely wouldn't miss…

If it were lost.

Or maybe accidentally broken.

"No, I'll be good." I answered, deciding it might be fun to keep them around.

"You better be. Otherwise, you're gonna have to explain to my parents why you have such a fervent infatuation with floral arrangements."

"Think of it as foreplay," I said with a wicked grin as she headed toward the door.

She faltered a bit at the mention of foreplay, tripping over the edge of the rug. I chuckled under my breath as she caught herself and gave me a dirty look.

Control yourself, she mouthed before pulling the door open.

It creaked open, and her parents were on the other side. Her dad held a bottle of wine, and her mom carried a bouquet of…flowers.

I nearly died.

The two of them came inside, and Marin took the gifts. Her cheeks flushed the second her hands wrapped around the vase.

"The innkeeper gave that to us," Marin's mom said. "She

told me to tell you to be careful with it. Marin, are you breaking people's things?"

Marin paused a second, looking down at it, shaking her head.

"No, Mama." Marin bit her lip, trying not to laugh. "It's a joke. She's a friend. Never mind."

She walked everything over to the island and set it down, careful to place the new bouquet on the other side of the counter, next to the fridge.

She turned around and noticed the large gap between her parents and me. They looked at their daughter, waiting.

"Oh, um," Marin said, looking ten shades redder. She took a step forward to stand next to me. "Mama, Papa, this is Macon. Macon, these are my parents, Henry and Margarete Mueller."

I was relieved to see genuine smiles on their faces, especially Marin's mother, who I knew was the more skeptical of the two.

We shook hands, and I offered to take their coats. Marin opened the wine and poured everyone a glass, excluding me, of course.

If her parents were curious, they didn't ask.

I grabbed a Coke out of the fridge, and everyone sat around the sofa while I headed to the kitchen.

"Macon offered to cook if that's all right, Mama?" Marin said.

"You found a man who can cook for you?" Margarete's brow raised. "No wonder you're staying."

"Did you know she lives off of takeout?" Henry asked, to which Marin rolled her eyes.

"And ramen," I chimed in.

"Cooking is hard." She pouted. "DoorDash is not."

I looked over at her, and I felt every ounce of tension leave as I started prepping for our meal.

This I could definitely get used to.

"They loved you!" Marin declared with a jolt of enthusiasm.

We'd just watched her parents drive away. They were headed back to the inn, and tomorrow, they would drive back home.

They had seemed satisfied with Marin's decision.

"You sure?" I asked as I cleared wine glasses from the coffee table.

"Yes. My mom even leaned over at one point and said, 'He's so handsome!' " She grinned, swooping in to grab the glasses from my hands. "Let me take those."

"I'd better not meet your sister," I joked as I watched her snag the rest. "I'll have all the Mueller women wrapped around my finger."

She rolled her eyes.

"I'm okay, by the way." I gestured to the glasses stacked in her hands. I then proceeded to prove my point by taking the leftover wine and moved toward the kitchen. She gave me a dubious stare. "I told you, it doesn't bother me."

"Are you sure?" She walked to the sink and set them down. "Like, not even a little?"

I shrugged, handing her the bottle. "Maybe a little, but I never really drank until…" I let out a staggered breath. "My dad didn't set the greatest example in that area, you know?"

Of course she did. She'd met the guy. Not exactly father-of-the-year material.

I nervously ran my hands through my hair as Marin turned to face me. "For the majority of my life, it was mostly like this." I motioned toward the living room. "When others drank, I wouldn't. I had a load of bullshit excuses to give people, but really—

"You didn't want to be like him."

I nodded.

"I kept that up for a long time. But then I found Kristy bent over Hayes's desk, and, well—"

I'd always wondered if his plan was always to marry her or if the surprise pregnancy had just pushed him into it.

"Macon." She reached for me.

I hadn't even realized I'd turned away.

"At first, it was just a little. When I went out with friends, I'd order a beer. Then two. I figured, why the hell not, you know? But then the friends slowly started to disappear, and drinking only got worse."

"Pretty shitty friends," she muttered.

I was leaning against the counter, and she stepped between my legs, wrapping her arms around my torso.

"I don't know if it was necessarily all their fault. We had never been very close to begin with, and I was kind of a mess."

"Not too much of a mess for Billy," she reminded me.

"No, but that's because Billy is a stubborn asshole." I gave her a sad smile. "We weren't even friends then. I just happened to show up at his restaurant one night, right before closing, demanding food. I was a fucking train wreck, and rather than call the sheriff's office—which was probably what he should have done—he made me food and drove me home."

"That sounds like Billy."

"Yeah," I agreed. "The next day, he showed up at my door with more food and told me he wasn't leaving until I sobered up."

"Did it work?"

"No." I shook my head. "He tried and failed. And then did it all over again. Pretty sure I threatened to arrest him on multiple occasions." I grinned. "But he never gave up. No matter how many times I fucked up and relapsed."

"Get out, Martin," Billy hollered, pointing to my front door.

"He already told you, he doesn't want you here," my dad sneered as his words sloshed around in my addled brain.

"I don't give a fuck what he wants," he roared, making my head snap back. "Now, take the booze and leave. This open bar is officially closed."

I closed my eyes. "Never again."

She cupped my chin, and my eyes opened and found hers staring into my damn soul. "You're incredible. You know that, right?"

I tried to look away, but her fingers locked around my chin. "I'm a fucking tragedy."

"No." She shook her head. "I see you, Macon. All that pain you try to hide, your strength, your passion. I see you. You are a miracle and…" Her voice cracked with emotion. "I love all of you."

My breath caught.

The earth tilted, and the stars realigned.

And my entire world became her.

Just her.

"Say it again," I whispered.

Her face softened as her fingers dug into my hair. "I love you. Only you. Just you."

I grabbed her waist and whirled her around, pressing her body into the cold granite. My hand tilted her head upward, and her gaze met mine.

"You know I love you, too, right?"

She nodded, her eyes brimming with tears.

"You are it for me, Marin. You are *my* miracle."

She reached up on those damn tippy-toes, grabbed the back of my neck, and kissed me hard. I didn't hesitate.

I needed to touch her.

I scooped her up and placed her on the counter, parting those pretty thighs as her feet dangled over the edge. I pulled her against me but growled in frustration as layers of fabric brushed against me.

We were not naked enough for this.

I made quick work of my shirt and ditched my shoes and socks. Bending down, I pulled Marin's ankle up to my chest and unzipped her boot. I watched as her dress slipped down her thigh, and suddenly, I forgot all about her shoes.

"What is this?" I asked, seeing the tiniest bit of lace peeking out from the hem of her skirt.

Heat stained her cheeks. "That is a surprise," she said, motioning back at her feet. "One thing at a time."

I licked my lips in anticipation, but went back to the boots, sliding each one off. I hooked her foot over my shoulder, running my hands over the silky fabric of her tights. Her dress slid down further, and I caught her staring at me, waiting for my reaction.

"These are staying on," I demanded, the moment my fingers touched the delicate lace of her thigh-highs. "Any other surprises for me?"

She bit her bottom lip and nodded, reaching for the hem of her dress. She pulled it over, and the fabric fell to the floor. I swore my eyes fell out of my damn head.

I didn't know what the hell it was called, but it was black and lacy and cut down to her navel. And, God, it was sexy as hell.

"You had this on the whole night?"

She just smiled.

"It's a really good thing I didn't know that." I tried to clear my voice. "I don't think your parents would like me nearly as much right now."

"Have you always been this dirty?" she asked, dragging her foot down my chest.

"No, definitely not."

"Good."

"This stays on as well," I said, unable to look at anything but her in all that wicked lace.

She didn't argue.

My eyes drifted over every inch of her as I tried to decide where to start.

There were a hundred things I wanted to do to her right now.

But I needed to be inside her.

Right. Fucking. Now.

I stepped away from her just long enough to shed my jeans and boxers. That heated stare she gave me only fueled my need for her. By the time my clothes hit the floor, I'd shoved that tiny scrap of lace between her thighs aside, and with a single thrust, I buried myself deep.

It felt like home.

She let out a loud moan as our bodies became one.

"Say it again," I demanded, knowing she understood.

"I love you."

I'd never get tired of hearing that.

My hands settled around her waist as her head fell back. Her arms splayed out over the counter.

That was a sight to behold.

I pulled out and slammed back into her. She let out a loud gasp as her ass moved back and forth over the cold granite.

"Yes. Oh God, yes," she cried out.

Music to my fucking ears. I let go, plunging into that wet heat over and over, as her cries of passion filled the room.

She *loved* me.

She loved *me*.

I kept saying the words over and over in my head as I claimed her body and soul.

"Let go," I said.

I could feel her growing more frantic as her breathing picked up pace. My hand tightened on her back, jerking her upward and deepening the angle.

Her hands slipped as her orgasm swept through her, those tight walls clamping down around me.

"Fuck," I groaned as I came with her.

I heard a loud crash.

Both of us, winded and slick with sweat, turned and

found the wood floor littered with glass and water. There were roses everywhere.

"Oops." Marin laughed, her eyes filled with amusement.

I'd forgotten about that damn thing, and from the look on her face, so had she.

But a broken vase was a broken vase.

"Well, I guess that's one fantasy we can say came true." She laughed.

No, not just one.

All of them.

All of my fantasies had come true.

Because of her.

CHAPTER NINETEEN

Marin

"Okay, hold on," I said, taking my phone and placing it on the dresser. I angled it just so and then took a step back. "I just need to get the zipper up."

I heard a gasp and froze.

"What? Is it bad? I feel kind of naked."

"No," Elena insisted.

I turned to find her staring back at me on FaceTime with her hand covering her mouth. I could see a look of awe in her eyes.

"You look hot. Like, really fucking hot."

"Yeah?" A sly grin spread across my face as I caught a glimpse of myself in the mirror.

The dress was made of a lush gold fabric that had the tiniest shimmer to it. I felt like a Grecian goddess with the way it draped over my body. Delicate gold roping circled the waist, and the neckline plunged so low that I had to use tape to keep everything from falling out.

"Can you even wear a bra?"

"Oh, no," I said. "Believe me, I tried."

"Lucky Macon." She laughed.

"You're sure it's not too much?" I turned around again. And again.

I'd gone to galas and charity events for work and whatnot, but I'd never worn something like this.

This dress was luxurious and designer and *expensive*.

God, I hoped I didn't spill anything on it.

"No," she answered. "It's a gala."

"Yeah, but it's a gala in Ocracoke. What if I show up and everyone is in sundresses and board shorts?"

She snorted and then made a face that looked like she smelled dirty cat litter. "If that happens, you should riot. No, just fucking move. Seriously. Board shorts? Gross. That's a crime against fashion."

She sounded like Elle Woods from *Legally Blonde* when she said shit like that.

"I'm serious," I stressed. "I'm new here, and I—"

"Are you afraid you're going to embarrass Macon?"

"A little," I admitted. "He's the captain of the sheriff's department."

Now, instead of a snort, she rolled her eyes. "When Macon sees you in that, you're gonna be lucky if you even make it there."

I grinned, remembering just how insane he had been last week when I revealed the black lingerie under my dress.

That man was an animal.

And he was all mine.

"You know I'm still here, right? And I can see you?"

I blinked several times, pressing my lips together to keep the laugh from bubbling up.

"Does this guy have a brother?" she joked. "Or even a sister? At this point, I'm not even that picky. I just want to have a bite of whatever you're having—please and thank you."

I laughed before saying. "Oh, he does have a brother." But then added, "But he's kind of MIA, and he's a roadie."

Her nose scrunched. "Oh, no, thanks. I already had my bad-boy phase."

"What happened to your dating app?" I started rifling through my jewelry, trying to decide on earrings.

She sighed. "No time. It's just me and my vibrator for now."

"Well, my offer still stands. We could be roomies." I put down the hoops in my hand and held my hands out to my sides like I was a game show host. "All this could be yours."

"I'm pretty sure I would wither and die in a town that small," she said. "I feel smothered in Richmond."

"No, you feel lonely. There's a difference."

My words must have cut a little too close to home because her expression stilled, and then she looked at me with sadness in her eyes. "I can't believe you're not gonna be down the street anymore."

I pulled the phone off my dresser and took a seat on the corner of my bed. "I know." I tried to smile, but couldn't. "You're going to have to drive a long-ass way now if you want to have a sleepover."

"At least the view will be better."

I gave a choked laugh, trying not to cry. "That's so true. That apartment was the worst." I'd already let it go, canceling my lease and bribing my brother and sister to move my shit into storage at the end of the month.

No turning back now.

"I'll come visit," she assured me. "You can't marry this guy without my blessing."

"Just because we got together quickly doesn't mean we're going to get married quickly." *Although I do look amazing in this dress*, I thought as I caught a profile of myself in the mirror. "There is so much more we need to learn about each other before that."

"But you do?" she asked. "Want to marry him?"

I swallowed down the ball of anxiety in my throat. "Yeah," I answered, knowing all the risks. All the ways in which I could get hurt. "I really think I do."

"Well then, let's get you ready for this gala," she

suggested. "If you're gonna be the future Mrs. Hot Cop, we gotta make you look good."

I snorted, wiping away the unshed tears under my eyes. "Really wish I'd never told you that nickname."

"I'm not. Now"—her eyes sparkled with excitement—"how do you want to do your hair?"

***

I nervously smoothed my hair, knowing it was useless. Every curl was perfect, and my makeup was flawless. Elena had made sure of it.

I was ready.

The doorbell rang.

I am so not ready.

I gave myself one last look in the mirror, and my stomach flipped.

Why was I so damn nervous?

I walked out of the bedroom and down the hall, thankful the strappy heels I wore weren't terribly high. Tripping would not be sexy.

When I got to the door, I went to grab the handle, giving myself a second to breathe before opening it.

"Holy fucking shit." The words tumbled out of Macon's mouth the second he saw me.

But I was having a hard time processing them.

Because holy fucking shit was right.

Macon had two styles. Casual and work, and there wasn't much of an in between. He was either in his uniform or he was in running shorts or jeans.

But now…

Now, he looked like he'd just stepped off a damn movie set. He was in all black. From his suit to the vest, all the way down to the tie, and it all fit him like a damn glove.

Where did he even get that?

"We're not going," he announced, pushing his way into

the house. "No one can see you like that. I'm very possessive."

I laughed as he grabbed my waist, taking another look. The way his eyes roamed down my body sent a shiver down my spine.

"Damn," he breathed out. "I am a lucky man."

"Oh, I know,"

"So, you agree?" His hand crept up my back, finding bare skin. "That we should skip it and just stay home?"

"That is not what I said, and you know it." I shook my head, feeling ridiculously happy. "Besides, do you know how long it took me to get ready?"

"I don't, but do you want to find out how quickly I can get you…un-ready?" That scarred brow rose as his fingers played with the strap of my dress.

"Yes," I answered, my voice low and sultry. I slid a hand under his suit jacket, and his breath hitched. "But later."

"*Marin*." My name came out of his mouth like a groan with a bit of a huff at the end.

"Oh, come on," I stepped out of his embrace, offering a hand. "How bad could it be?"

If only I had known…

"Stop staring at my ass," I scolded him as we walked up to the inn.

"Never gonna happen."

The grin he gave me as I looked behind me was infectious. He seemed to have gotten over his temper tantrum and was now either okay with me being seen in this dress or he was just planning on being glued to me the entire night.

My guess was the second one.

But I was okay with that.

I knew, like, five people on this island. I needed the moral support.

Molly had truly outdone herself with the decorations for the event. The path was lit with lanterns, and all the trees had been covered in beautiful, twinkling white lights.

"Is it inside?" I asked, realizing I'd never asked Molly for a single detail.

"No," he answered, as we walked onto the patio. The lanterns curve away from the door and around the house. "I believe it's out back, under tents."

Well, that would explain where we were headed.

If the entrance was impressive, the main event was enough to take your breath away.

White tents covered the expansive green lawn. The bay sparkled in the background, lit with torches and cozy seating along the shore.

Waiters wove through the crowd with trays of hors d'oeuvres, and a small quartet of musicians set the mood.

"And I was worried people would be in board shorts." I snorted.

"No." Macon laughed. "Not when Molly is running it."

A couple I didn't recognize walked up to us, and I felt Macon's hand slip around my waist.

Possessive bastard.

"Macon," the man said. He was young and attractive. He also seemed familiar in a way, and I didn't know why. "Didn't expect you here."

"Marin doesn't know many people yet since she just moved back." I could feel him squeeze my waist as he said those words, and it warmed my heart. "So, I'm suffering through. For her."

The humor wasn't lost on them.

"Well, we're happy to meet you." The man offered his hand. "I'm Taylor. This is my wife, Leilani."

She gave him a sweet nudge of her elbow. "You can call me Lani."

Good Lord, she was gorgeous. With silky, dark hair and

bronze skin, she had the body of my dreams. Curves in all the right places. Her red dress fit her like a second skin.

"Taylor is Dean's younger brother," Macon explained. "They own one of the oldest commercial fishing companies on the island."

Oh, okay. That's why he looks familiar.

"Well, one of the oldest still operating," Taylor commented, and he took a sip of his beer. "We do a lot of tourist-based business now."

"How's the baby?" Macon asked.

Wow, he really did know everything about everyone.

"Good," Taylor answered, a hint of surprise in his voice. "Driving me crazy, like his mom."

Lani rolled her eyes.

As I laughed, Macon watched me with an intensity I couldn't decipher.

We let Taylor and Lani go mingle elsewhere after that and headed for the bar. As we were standing in line, his thoughts seemed to drift elsewhere.

Finally, he said. "The last time I saw those two was on the side of the road."

I angled my head, brow furrowed. Before I could ask what he meant, he continued.

"They were on a walk. I had no reason to pull them over. No reason at all." His voice was soft, nearly a whisper. "Marin," he let out a sigh. "I wasn't sober. I swear, it was like I was trying to get caught."

I grabbed his hand. "It's in the past," I reminded him.

I could see it in his eyes. *Not far enough.*

Needing to change the subject, I asked. "You seem to know a lot about everyone."

"I'm the captain of the town." He said it like it was an obvious answer.

"Knowing who people are and asking about the welfare of their children are two very different things.

He shrugged. "I like kids." His eyes met mine. "Don't you?"

"Are you asking in a general sort of way? Like do I like the existence of kids or do I want some of my own?"

He blanched slightly before asking, "The second one, I guess?"

I silently laughed, loving how uncomfortable he'd just become.

I took a step forward, grabbing his lapel. "Everything," I whispered, recalling the last time I'd said that to him. His eyes flared with heat. "I want everything with you."

"Can we go *now*?" he begged, his hand sliding down my ass.

"Nope." I grinned.

"You're killing me, Marin."

"Think of it as foreplay," I said, repeating the words he'd once said to me. "Really long foreplay."

"That's just mean."

"Was it mean when you suggested it right before my parents walked in?"

His expression turned wicked, and I knew he was thinking about that damn vase again.

"No, that was fun."

We finally reached the front of the line, and to Macon's surprise, I ordered a virgin cocktail. He turned to me with a quirked brow.

"I don't always need to drink." I shrugged.

"You don't need to change for me," he stated after ordering his usual Coke.

That man's liver might not be in jeopardy anymore, but he could do his heart a favor and order a diet soda once in a while.

"I'm not changing," I stressed as we paid for our drinks and walked away. "I'm supporting. There's a difference."

He didn't say anything, but he looked at me with a mix of awe and affection.

We did our fair share of mingling after that, to Macon's dismay. He always pegged himself as an outsider, but the more people we met, the more I saw how well he fit here.

He knew these people.

It wasn't just their secrets he kept.

He knew about their lives, their families, and their passions.

He cared. Deeply.

And as much as he wanted to deny it, they cared about him, too.

He'd come back to make a difference, and he had.

I just wished he could see it.

CHAPTER TWENTY

Macon

"If Gavin looks at her one more time, I swear I'm gonna kill him."

Billy chuckled next to me, shaking his head as he sipped on a gin and tonic. "Gavin is harmless."

The local business owner was young, well off, and was one of the last single men on the island.

Harmless was not a word I would use to describe him.

I'd been hanging out with Billy for the last couple of minutes while Marin went to chat with Molly. I couldn't help but smile as I watched her, so animated and happy.

God, that dress looked good on her.

I caught Gavin across the lawn, checking her out.

He wasn't even trying to be discreet about it.

"He is gonna lose a fucking eye."

My burly best friend snorted and then gave a friendly pat on my shoulder. "Do you need to go piss a circle around her? Mark your territory?"

I gave him a scowl. "Like you'd be any different."

"Probably not. But then again, I don't get much of an opportunity, do I?"

"You could," I told him as I looked at him. "If you chose to."

Billy's confident smile fell. "It's not that easy."

It wasn't, and I had no right acting like I understood anything he was going through.

"Incoming." Billy's warning came a split second before the old woman was standing in front of us.

Her gown was dated and smelled of stale perfume, and she made my balls feel like they were crawling back up inside my body.

God, she was terrifying.

"If you're here and the sheriff is here, who's out there, making sure no one ransacks my garden?"

I cocked an eyebrow. "Do people regularly ransack your garden, Terri?"

"I'd like to see them try," she said with a wicked gleam in her eye.

All righty then.

"Lucas is on duty, and we brought in backup from the mainland," I offered as an explanation, hoping that'd be enough to make her go away.

"The mainland?" she grumbled. "A whole lotta good that'll do."

Terri was the kind of O'Cocker who could trace her family back to the days when Blackbeard had roamed this island. And anyone who couldn't say the same was a dingbatter in her eyes.

"You dating the new girl?" She looked over toward Marin.

"I am," I answered proudly. I didn't give a shit what Terri thought of Marin.

She gave her a long, appraising look and finally nodded. "I've got some extra tomatoes this week. Come by and grab 'em. Bring your girl."

And then she walked away.

"I think that was Terri's version of approval."

"Wasn't sure I was asking for it." I laughed.

"Well, you got it—and tomatoes." Billy shrugged before adding, "Wait, can I have those? Terri's produce is amazing."

"Get your own damn tomatoes," I teased.

"You know, a little gratitude wouldn't hurt."

It was meant in jest, but I couldn't help but sober a bit. "You know I am though, right? Grateful?"

My eyes settled on Marin once again.

So damn grateful.

"Yeah, man, I know."

Marin turned back, giving me a megawatt smile, and suddenly, I couldn't be away from her any longer.

I was drawn to her. Connected. Tethered.

"I'm gonna head back over to Marin. You good?"

He held up his beer and gave me a reassuring smile. "I'm good. Everyone loves me, remember?"

It was because of that love that he was so damn scared.

"I'll see you later."

I walked up to her just as Millie was joining them.

"You look amazing," Marin said, giving her a quick hug.

Millie had always been pretty, and the sophisticated black dress she had on showcased all that beauty perfectly.

But it didn't hold a candle to Marin.

No one did.

"Every time we're even remotely alone, Aiden tries to untie the laces on the back," she said, rolling her eyes, but the sly grin on her face told me she wasn't mad about it. Not at all. "And then he'll say, 'Faulty dress, love,' and act completely innocent." She mimicked her husband's accent with surprising accuracy, motioning toward a table where he sat with Jake and Dean. "He's been trying to get me naked all damn night."

I coughed into my drink, causing Marin to chuckle.

Really didn't need to know that.

"Thank you for letting me borrow this," she said sincerely. "I feel like a movie star."

"Well, you look stunning in it. You should keep it."

"What?" Her eyes went wide, looking down at her dress. She'd looked up the designer when Millie loaned it to her.

When she told me the cost, I nearly fell out of my chair. I hadn't known clothes could cost that much. "I couldn't."

"You can," she insisted. "It sat in my closet for years, and I never wore it. Consider it a welcoming gift."

"Usually, people just bring over a bottle of wine or a pineapple," she joked.

"Well, I'm a little extra." She held up her wineglass, saluting us as she began to walk away, but then paused. "Oh, and, Macon? Try not to rip it."

She didn't bother waiting for a reply and instead headed for her husband, placing a hand on his shoulder before she slid into his lap.

"I have a feeling this town is gonna get a lot weirder with you in it," I muttered, completely baffled.

I'd been nearly invisible in this town for years—only brought up when something went wrong—and now, I was having dinner parties with my classmates and being ordered around by old ladies.

All because of her.

I don't think I'd ever been so damn happy in my whole life.

Her hands wrapped around my waist. She looked up at me and grinned. "No, I think what you meant to say was, it's gonna get a lot more fun."

"If you want to have a little fun—"

"Come on. Let's go dance." She laughed.

"Okay." I winced at the thought. "But I'm warning you, I'm not great at this."

And by not great, I meant horrible.

Like really fucking horrible.

The moment we got on the dance floor, she turned and wrapped her arms around my neck. "Well then, I guess it's good that I am."

My hands instinctively went to her waist, and I nearly groaned when I came in contact with all that exposed skin.

"Do you have any surprises under here for me?" I asked, remembering the lacy lingerie.

She bit down on her lip and grinned.

"Yes," she answered as we began to move. "Absolutely nothing."

"Jesus," I swore as my hand slid lower. Dangerously lower. I heard her breath catch as I pulled her close. Close enough to feel how much I needed her.

"We can leave now," she promptly announced, her voice barely a whisper.

"Thank fuck."

I grabbed her arm and tugged her off the dance floor. She laughed as I pulled us toward the exit. I was very motivated.

"Macon!"

Dammit. So close.

Every bone in my body tensed as we turned to see Sheriff Hayes and Kristy walk up to us. The sheriff was all smiles in his stupid bow tie as he extended a hand toward us.

"Good to see you." He beamed.

All I wanted to do was walk away. He deserved nothing less.

But I knew better than to make a scene.

So, instead, I reached out and shook the bastard's hand, not bothering to say a word.

"Marin, is it?" he said, barely giving a glance in her direction.

She gave a curt nod. The asshole knew her name. Marin smiled politely at Kristy, who did the same.

Her dress was elegant and simple, but she looked downright uncomfortable in it, and I couldn't help but notice the cavernous gap between her and her husband.

His arm was snaked around her, but she was as far away from him as she could be.

It was like watching two mismatched magnets being forced together.

It made me feel the slightest bit of sympathy for her, but she'd chosen this.

She'd chosen this over me.

"So, I guess everything worked out, huh?" He leaned back on his heels, seemingly pleased with himself.

"What?" I asked, a bit taken aback.

"It's just"—the sheriff motioned between me and Marin—"you seem pretty happy now, right?"

Was he taking credit for our relationship? For Marin and me?

I nearly lunged for him, but a slight movement from Kristy kept me from lashing out.

Her eyes were wide. *Don't*, she mouthed.

Her words from the grocery store came back to me.

"You have to stop pushing him."

"He doesn't like to feel threatened."

"I've never been happier," I said, steadying myself.

I felt Marin squeeze my hand, silently giving me strength.

"Well," Hayes laughed, throwing his hands in the air, "water under the bridge then, wouldn't you say?"

"Indeed," I answered through gritted teeth. "Now, if you'll excuse us, we were just on our way out."

I caught Kristy's gaze just then, and I saw it—the regret, the guilt, and the deep sense of remorse.

A couple of weeks ago, I would have considered that proper payback.

A genuine triumph for all the pain I'd endured.

But now, it just felt like a damn tragedy.

We started to walk away, but Hayes's voice stopped us once again.

"I meant to tell you," he said, causing us to turn. "I took your advice."

"Oh?" *God, what now?*

"On getting more involved with the community. You know, like the kids at the marina?"

My jaw tensed, and I felt an overwhelming sense of dread.

Hayes sauntered forward, his happy-go-lucky attitude a complete affront to the menacing grin plastered on his face. "I hated the idea that this event might not be accessible to the working class. Like those kid's parents," he went on. "So, I bought several extra tickets and gave them away."

I tried to control my emotions. "Very kind of you."

I started to walk away, but a loud crash brought our attention to the opposite side of the lawn. The small quartet that was set up there was now in disarray. Musical instruments were on the ground, chairs tipped over, and in the middle was a man—

"Did I mention I gave one to your father?"

My head whipped around so fast.

"He doesn't like to feel threatened."

"He's only going to put up with it for so long."

"He's always been a hard worker, right? Plus, there's nothing better than family." He gave me a charming smile. "Sweetheart, let's go get you another drink." He wrapped an arm around his wife's shoulder and started to pull her away. "Green, you might want to take care of that." His gaze fell to my father.

I caught Kristy glancing over her shoulder, an apologetic look on her face.

"Get off me," someone shouted.

That someone was my father.

"Fuck," I swore under my breath.

My dad was pushing people as they tried to help him off the ground. His suit was wrinkled and covered in grass stains, and he was clutching a bottle of beer like his life depended on it.

"I've got to—" I tried to say, my expression turning grim as I turned to Marin.

"Go," she simply said, knowing I had no other choice. *Fucking Hayes…*

I walked over to him, collecting myself as I did.

"Dad." I kept my voice calm, controlled, and most of all quiet. "Come on. Let's get you out of here."

I held out a hand while his ass was still firmly planted on the ground. Those glassy eyes looked up at me and he tried to focus.

And then his head fell back, and he cackled.

"You expect me to listen to you?" His laugh was borderline manic. His free hand gripped his belly, and tears fell from his eyes. "You?" he shouted.

"This is not the time or place for this." I gritted my teeth.

"Oh, I'm sorry." He struggled to stand, sloshing beer onto his hands and clothes. No doubt it was just an accessory at this point.

He'd probably shown up like this.

"Am I embarrassing you? Captain Green?" His words slurred.

I suppressed the urge to roll my eyes. I'd been so close to leaving.

So close to this being someone else's problem.

But it was never going to be someone else's problem, was it?

He would always be mine.

"Come on," I urged. "Let us take you somewhere."

His eyes flared. "Us?"

He looked past me toward Marin. The moment his gaze locked on her, he seemed to realize the hush that had fallen across the lawn.

He looked around, noticing the number of people watching us, and he visibly winced.

Finally.

He took a step forward, but then stopped. His defeated expression turned heated. "You think you're better than me?"

Here we go.

"You and your no-good brother think you are so much better than your old man." I reached out to grab him, but he shoved me. "Your girl know the real you? She know you're a drunk, just like me?"

I tensed. "You need to stop talking and leave."

His smile turned deadly. "So, I'm only worth talking to when you're drinkin'? That it? Well then, come on, son." He motioned with his beer. "Grab a drink. Let's enjoy ourselves, like we used to."

My eyes darted around as people started shifting around, looking uncomfortable.

And then I found Marin. She was standing there, her expression a mixture of confusion and horror.

I wasn't the only one who noticed it.

"Come on, boy. I just want to spend some time with ya. Like we used to."

I swallowed down the lump in my throat.

Like father, like son.

"But now, you're too high and mighty for that, aren't you? You dried out and kicked your old man to the curb, like I didn't even exist."

So many mistakes. So many failures.

"It doesn't matter," I muttered. "None of that matters right now."

"I think it'd matter a hell of a lot to her." He grinned.

"What the hell are you talking about?" I stepped forward, my face mere inches from his.

"Well, see, the thing is, I remember stuff from those days. Stuff you probably don't."

I tried to think back to those nights when he'd come by, looking for money and booze. They were hazy at best.

And even the hazy memories I'd tried to forget.

"You're very chatty when you've been drinkin'." He chuckled. "So very chatty."

"I think you've said enough," I told him. "If you won't leave, then I will."

"You think the townspeople will forgive you once they find out you've spilled all their secrets to the town drunk?"

I sucked in a breath.

He turned toward the crowd like he was onstage and they were his audience. "He told me all about your drug troubles, your family squabbles. Did you know our very own Billy Radcliffe is gay?"

Oh God.

My eyes snapped to the crowd.

Billy was standing there, his hand clasped over his mouth, frozen in fear.

Everyone was looking at him.

Everyone.

I'd outed my own best friend, and I didn't even remember it.

I started to lunge for my father, but the crowd parted as Billy stormed toward the exit, his face a brutal mixture of fear and panic.

Millie quickly rushed after him.

I was going to kill my father.

"I think that's enough, Martin," Dean said, stepping forward, his large frame looming over him. "Go with Macon, or we're calling the sheriff's office."

My dad's gaze lingered on Dean, his eyes fixated on his crossed arms. "You know Macon blames himself for that arm of yours?"

My heart stopped, and then it started hammering in my chest.

No.

No, no, no.

How much had I told this man?

"What are you talking about?" His eyes darted from me to my father.

"He told me he let Raymond on the ferry when he shouldn't have. Said good old Ray was probably hammered when he sank that boat right into the sea."

"What the hell, Macon? That true?" Dean's hard gaze fixated on me.

I let out a ragged breath. "Yes," I admitted. "I ran into Raymond right before he boarded that day. I asked him if he'd been drinking. He swore he'd been sober for a while."

My dad snorted. "That man was never sober a day in his life."

"His wife told a different story," I remarked, remembering the hours of work we had done after the accident. "But I'll never know for sure. I let him go, and, well"—I looked down at the grass—"we all know what happened after."

A moment passed and then another as Dean processed what I'd just said.

Before he could say anything, someone came stalking through the yard.

Someone had already taken it upon themselves to call the sheriff's office, and Lucas walked up to my father.

"Come on, Martin. Party's over," he said, taking my dad's arm and hauling him toward the exit.

He went willingly and flashed me a grin.

"Take care, son."

"Yeah, fuck you."

He chuckled, walking away, knowing he'd gotten his revenge.

I'd walked into this gala feeling like I finally had it all.

And now…

Now, my life was ruined.

My job, my friendships, my—

I turned.

I looked around the lawn, searching everywhere.

Marin was…

She was gone.

CHAPTER TWENTY-ONE

Marin

"*We all know what happened after.*"

Those words screamed in my ears so loud that I could barely think.

He blames himself…

The second I heard those words, the moment they fell from Macon's lips, I couldn't breathe.

I had to leave.

I felt myself backing away, my feet faltering as I tried to flee.

I turned and ran headfirst into Molly.

"I need to…" I tried to say. "He never told me."

Her eyes widened slightly, but she simply nodded. She turned to Jake and whispered in his ear. A second later, he pulled out keys from his pocket.

"Go," she insisted, handing them to me. "Go get some air."

I didn't even thank her. I was in such shock that I just stumbled down that lit path, the one I'd been so enamored with earlier.

Now, it felt like an emergency exit, and I was definitely in crisis.

I found Molly's car with little difficulty. I'd seen her

around town enough that I knew what it looked like. My hands were shaky, and my eyes were teary. I started the engine, and I pulled out of the packed driveway.

Where to now?

I had no plan. None.

So, I just started driving.

I drove down street after street. Turn after turn.

I didn't think. I just focused on the street signs, the road, and my speed.

Finally, I ran out of road. I was on an island after all.

I pulled into the ferry terminal and shut off the engine. The parking lot was empty. In the distance, the inky-black water glistened under the moonlight.

I opened the car door and took a step outside.

The wind rushed up and tossed my hair. It was cold but quiet. I took a few steps toward the ocean. A light caught my attention, and I turned to see the memorial out in the distance, standing tall along the shoreline.

Maybe I hadn't been driving around aimlessly after all.

There was a long path that connected the terminal and the memorial, and I slipped off my shoes to walk it. My steps slowed as I reached the base. From afar, it looked so much smaller.

As I stood in front of it, it was quite impressive.

Aiden was a talented artist.

Flowers and small trinkets and mementos surrounded it. Some of the bouquets were new. Some were wilted and old. I noticed a few notes stuffed wherever there was a crevice or a space.

It made it so real.

So, so real.

And there, among the names, I saw it.

Daniel Mendez.

I heaved a sob and felt the tears fall from my eyes.

"Sometimes, I think it's easier for me to try and forget you were ever here," I said, hating myself for even admitting it. "I think that's why I've been avoiding coming here. Because then I have to confront all the ugly memories of you I've tried to forget."

I sat down next to the memorial, for once not caring if the dress got dirty. That was what dry cleaners were for.

"When I think of you here with me, I think of that phone call and…" My words faded as my head fell back on the cold stone.

"I thought coming back here would be hard, but I think this is where I'm supposed to be." A ghost of a smile spread across my lips. "You always said the island life looked good on me."

My thoughts turned to Macon.

"I didn't think I could ever love anyone the way I loved you." I looked up at the stars and felt my eyes close. "When you died, I felt like that part of me died with you."

For years, I'd been going through the motions. I'd said yes to that date with Curtis, hoping that my heart would open up to someone.

But friendship was not love and I'd inadvertently put my life on pause.

"I met someone," I told the heavens. "Someone special. Someone different."

My heart leaped at the thought of him. But then his father's words came back.

And I felt it.

Betrayal.

"I didn't think," I tried to say before tears stung my eyes once again. "I didn't realize I could get hurt—like this."

My heart had been broken in the most devastating way. My husband had died.

I had forgotten that your heart could break in all sorts of other ways.

Secrets.

Why had Macon never told me?

I looked back down at those names.

All thirteen of them.

Did he really think he was responsible for their deaths?

Did I?

I shook my head. No.

No matter what choice he had made that day, it didn't hold him accountable for the lives etched on this memorial.

But it didn't change the fact that he'd kept it from me.

That he hadn't trusted me enough to tell me.

He didn't believe in us.

Had he been drowning in guilt since the moment he had seen me? Terrified I would run the minute I found out?

And you did, that voice in my head reminded me.

Just a week ago, I'd declared my love for him, swearing I saw him—the real him—and then at the first sign of trouble, I had left.

Oh God.

I bolted upright.

He'd been running for years, trying to keep himself sober.

He never wanted anyone to find out.

And his dad had just outed him in front of the whole town.

I had to go find him.

I had to go find him now.

I tried his cell, but he didn't answer.

I went to his house, but no one was home.

Where is he?

It had been less than an hour since I had left, so I decided to head back to Molly's. Maybe he was still there.

At the very least, I could return the car I'd so swiftly confiscated from her.

As I drove back through the streets of Ocracoke, I prayed he was okay.

The parking lot around the inn was nearly empty. The gala

had either come to an end or it was about to. Did I go around the back like before or knock on the door? I looked at the lanterns, now mostly blown out.

I decided to be polite and go for the door.

But after a few knocks, no one came.

Finally, Molly's thin frame appeared. She was dressed in leggings and an oversized sweatshirt and holding a large mug.

"Hey," she said the second the door pulled open. "You okay?"

I nodded. "Yeah," I answered. "Thanks for the keys." I handed them back to her.

"Anytime. You want to come in?"

"Sure." I gave her a once-over. "Although I think I might be a little overdressed."

She laughed, throwing a flippant hand in the air. "No, I'm definitely the oddball. Everyone else is still outside. But I pulled the pregnancy card and came in to rest."

She motioned toward the back, where a few stragglers were. Jake and Dean were huddled together, laughing. Dean's brother was talking to Aiden while Millie spoke to—

"Macon's still here." I didn't bother to hide the relief in my voice.

She nodded as we both looked out toward the lawn. "He kind of lost it after you left."

I tensed. "What do you mean?"

"He went after the sheriff."

My eyes nearly fell out of my head. "What?"

Molly laughed. She freaking laughed. "I know. Welcome to Ocracoke."

"Please tell me Macon isn't going to be arrested," I said, looking out at him while he chatted with a few people.

He looked calm.

Calm people don't get arrested, right?

"No," she assured me. "But Macon accused the sheriff of some pretty awful things."

I turned to her, and she wasn't laughing anymore.

"You think he's going to get fired?"

"I think it wouldn't hurt to go talk to him," she suggested.

"Are you okay?" I asked. "I mean, about the ferry? And Macon?"

She looked out toward the lawn. Her gaze turned speculative. "Macon said Hayes purposely invited Martin?"

I nodded. "He probably knew Martin would be the perfect weapon against him. Get him in the right place at the right time."

Tick, tick…boom.

"If I'd known that was his plan with those extra tickets—"

"You didn't know," I told her.

"I don't hold anything against Macon, Marin. If anything, I feel for him. There's only one villain here tonight. And it's not him."

One villain and one very sad old man.

"It's true, what Ray's wife said. He had been sober for a while," she went on. "Of course, we'll never know. And I'm sure that's what Macon has struggled with. Jake has the same problem."

"Why?"

"He asked Dean to stay back and catch the last ferry with him. Dean almost died. So, he feels like it's his fault."

So much guilt over the same event.

"We should have a support group or something," I joked.

She looked at me and blinked. "You know, that's actually not a bad idea."

"What?" I laughed. "I was kidding."

"I know, but I'm not. It's been five years, and the people in this town are still messed up because of that accident. It wouldn't hurt."

"No." I blinked, slowly agreeing. "I guess it wouldn't."

Just then, Macon looked up, and our eyes met. Whatever he was saying stopped and he excused himself, stalking forward. His gaze never left mine.

"Well, I'm going to go wrangle my husband away from the festivities," Molly said, quickly making herself scarce.

Macon's expression was a mixture of emotions as he slid the patio door open and walked straight toward me.

Apprehension, fear, guilt.

His steps slowed as he closed the distance between us.

He was still dressed in that midnight-black suit.

Still devastatingly gorgeous.

Still mine.

"You left," he stated.

"Yes," I said softly.

A silence settled between us.

"Are you okay?" I asked. "I was worried…" My eyes drifted back toward the lawn to where the bartenders were cleaning up.

He swallowed, but there was a hesitation in his voice. "I'm all right."

"You fought with the sheriff?"

His throat worked slowly. "Not my finest hour."

"If he fires you—"

He cupped my cheek, hesitantly at first, as if he wasn't sure he was still allowed. "Then, he fires me. I'll find other work. I'll sell fucking ice cream. I don't care, as long as I still have you."

His eyes rounded, and I knew what he was asking.

Do I still have you?

"Why didn't you tell me?" I asked.

"How do you tell someone that, Marin? Until tonight, I thought I hadn't told anyone." He took a step back, a frustrated hand running through his hair.

"That was not fair of your father."

"I don't remember any of it."

"How did he know all that?" I asked, trying not to sound judgmental. "You spent time together?"

"He—" He let out a frustrated huff. "He'd stop by from

time to time over the years. Mostly when he was strapped for cash. He happened to make one of these visits when…"

He didn't need to finish the sentence.

"Oh God."

"Pretty much like winning the fucking lottery for him. He not only got to see me at my worst, but he got to cash in on it, too."

"He bribed you?"

He shrugged. "Empty threats—or so I thought—but at the time, he was the only person around. Some real fucked-up father-son bonding time." Every word was laced with pain. "When I finally sobered up, I told him we were done. Offered to get him help to get clean, but made it clear I wasn't giving him any more money."

"And you don't remember what you told him?"

"I don't even remember being conscious half the time." The devastation on his face…it broke me. "God, Billy."

"We will take care of Billy. If the town doesn't support him, they will learn to."

"Does that mean you're staying?" His eyes met mine.

"I wasn't aware I was leaving."

"You—"

Left. The word hung in the air.

It was why he'd never told me. Why he'd kept that guilt bottled up inside him for so long—because he was terrified I'd blame him for something so completely out of his control.

I just wish he could understand that.

"Did I ever tell you why Daniel was on that ferry?" I asked.

He shook his head, guilt swimming in his eyes.

"My last conversation with him was a fight," I explained. "I yelled at him. I was angry and so damn lonely. I loved it here, but I hated that he had to sacrifice so much for it."

I breathed out a shaky breath at the memory.

"My island fantasy wasn't turning out the way I wanted,

and when he called to say he missed his flight and wasn't going to be home for our anniversary, I lost it."

"Marin…" His voice was gentle and soothing.

He reached for my hand, and I took his.

"He tried to make it up to me by renting a car so he could drive here. He caught the last ferry. But he never made it. If I hadn't yelled, if he had just caught that flight."

"It wasn't your fault."

I looked up at him. "It wasn't your fault either."

His eyes squeezed closed. "It's not the same."

"It is exactly the same," I stressed. "Did you send Raymond on that boat with the intent of causing harm?"

"No," he answered, his voice barely a whisper.

"You made a decision, just like Daniel did. You can't predict the future. No one can."

"I feel—" He paused. "I feel undeserving of you because of it. I tried to push you away at first. I tried to deny these feelings, but I couldn't. I can't—" He let out a breath. "I love you so damn much, Marin."

This man…

"I can't explain why things happen," I told him. "I'm not even sure I'd want to if I could. But I do know a good thing when I see it, Macon. You're my good thing. My one good thing after a long, endless sea of bad. And I don't want to waste any more of my life, swimming in grief and guilt. Do you?"

He looked down at me, those eyes blazing into mine. "No," he finally answered. "I don't."

"Good." I smiled. "Then let's go home. I'm dying to get out of the dress. Wanna join me?"

His expression changed, a large grin spreading across his face. "Always."

CHAPTER TWENTY-TWO

Macon

I couldn't stop staring at her.

I'd been awake for over an hour, just watching her sleep.

The sheet was draped over her naked body as the breath slowly moved through her parted lips.

I'd thought I'd lost her.

The moment I turned around and realized she was gone…

The panic in my chest as I searched the lawn.

Gone.

She was gone.

I didn't know how long I'd stood there in utter disbelief as everyone around me began to chatter away.

The gala went back to normal, as if nothing had happened.

Meanwhile, my life fell apart.

Gone…

I didn't know how or when, but I started walking. Moving.

And suddenly, I was in front of the bar.

My eye twitched. My fingers itched for something to hold.

And then I saw him.

Fucking Sheriff Hayes.

He looked over at me and gave a triumphant smile.

I won, it said.

Fuck that.

I came at him with everything but my fists. I knew my limits. I would not end up in jail because of this guy.

We yelled. I tossed quite a few accusations his way. People gasped. He laughed them off.

And then, with a look of malice in his eyes, he had stormed off with the promise of retribution in his wake.

Yeah, I was fucking screwed.

At least I wouldn't be working for that asshole anymore.

And I still had her.

Plus, there were no more secrets between us.

I let out a sigh of relief as I dragged the back of my palm along her cheek. She made a little noise and shifted to her side, brown curls falling around her face.

That moment in front of the bar had been a wake-up call.

I needed to make some changes.

I needed to—

The doorbell rang. I checked my watch and raised an eyebrow.

A little early for someone to visit.

I threw on a pair of flannel pants and ran toward the door, hoping whoever it was didn't require Marin awake.

I had not expected to find Kristy on the other side of the door.

Her eyes traced over my bare chest, and a flash of longing zipped across her face.

"I figured you'd be here," she said stoically.

"I wasn't even aware you knew where *here* was."

Her lips pursed together as she gripped the handle of her purse. "I got the address from Molly."

"Molly?" My brow rose.

"I called her," she explained. "I needed to see you. I wanted to tell you—"

"What?" I asked, the frustration clear in my voice. What could be so damn important that she had come all the way—

"The sheriff was arrested this morning."

"What the fuck?" The words fell from my lips.

The serious look on her face told me she wasn't kidding.

Maybe I needed to sit down for this.

I took a step aside, and she stepped inside.

"Have a seat," I told her. "I'm gonna—I'm gonna go grab a shirt."

'Cause sitting shirtless in the living room with my ex while my girlfriend slept naked down the hallway was way too weird.

I jogged toward the bedroom and headed straight to the dresser. The tiniest grin tugged at the corner of my lips as I remembered the conversation we'd had just days earlier.

"Put your stuff in my dresser, Macon."

"Are you sure?"

"I like seeing your things when you're not here."

The next day, when I had come over after work, I had found her at the door in nothing but my shirt.

Marin seemed to have a knack for sexy surprises.

"Why are you putting a shirt on? You know how I feel about shirts this early in the morning."

I turned to see her sitting up in bed, the sheet dangerously close to falling to her waist.

"That they're better on the floor?"

"Exactly." She grinned.

I couldn't help but chuckle. "Kristy just showed up. I thought you'd appreciate me being fully clothed when I spoke with her."

Her mischievous grin turned confused. "Kristy? Here?"

She used her pointer finger and pressed down on the mattress.

I nodded.

"Oh, well then, yes." She waved a hand toward my chest. "Cover that shit up. Did she say why she was here?"

I threw a T-shirt over my head. "She said the sheriff was arrested."

"Are you serious?" She threw the covers off. "I'll be right out."

I let out a sigh. *So very naked.* "This is not how I planned the morning."

She shooed me away. "Later."

I left before I changed my mind.

I walked back to the living room, noticing the way Kristy sat, so rigid and uncomfortable. She glanced around the room, checking out the artwork and several photos.

"Did Marin do that?" she asked, pointing to a painting near the door.

"Yeah," I answered, folding my arms across my chest. I suddenly felt very protective of it. Of Marin.

"It's really very good," she commented, almost as if it pained her to admit it.

I relaxed a little and walked to the seat Marin always favored. No sooner had I sat down than Marin came bouncing down the hall. She'd hastily put on a pair of leggings and a long sweater.

"Good morning, Kristy," she said.

"Morning," she answered through tight lips.

Marin came and placed a hip on the side of the chair. Kristy's eyes lingered on the casual way my hand rested on her thigh.

"So, how did this happen?"

She bit the inside of her cheek. "The things you said yesterday at the gala," she started. "How long have you known?"

I shrugged. "I've suspected for years. But I never had proof. Still don't."

"I do," she stated very matter-of-factly. "You aren't the only one fed up with him. A deputy on the mainland contacted me a year or so ago, and we've been working on a case against him ever since."

My eyes widened. "Against your own husband? Why?"

She looked down at the floor. "I think you know the answer to that. He treats me very differently in front of you. Everyone else gets to see the real Hayes and it's not the fairy-tale I imagined."

I let out a sigh. Unfortunately, it seemed she had learned the true nature of her husband a little too late. "Why now?" I asked.

"He was going to fire you, Macon," she explained. "Or worse."

Or worse…

Meaning he would have pinned his crimes on me. It could have been me sitting in that jail cell.

I tried not to think about that one too long.

"We had enough to back up your claims and then some. Bribes, drug smuggling—yeah, he's in serious trouble."

"I can't believe—" I breathed out a sigh of relief before looking up at her. "Thank you."

"No." She shook her head. "Thank you. If you hadn't taken that first step"—her lip quivered—"I'm not sure I would have ever gotten the courage."

"So, what's next?" Marin asked. Her voice was gentle and supportive.

"I don't know." She sniffled. "But I'm leaving. I can't stay here."

"Your parents?" I guessed.

She nodded, and I knew it was a good choice for her, for her kids.

For all of us.

She didn't stay long after that. She tried to apologize, tried to say she was sorry for all the hurt she had caused.

But I told her it was in the past.

I'd found my one good thing.

Now, hopefully, she could find hers.

"Do you think she'll be okay?" Marin asked after we watched her pull away.

"Yeah," I said confidently, "I think so."

"So, no selling ice cream then?"

I grinned, wrapping my arm around her shoulders. "Not yet. But there's always retirement."

She laughed. "Good, 'cause I can't think of a sexy nickname for an ice cream man."

My brow rose. "What's this? I have a sexy nickname?"

"No!" She scoffed. "Shit. This is gonna go straight to your head, isn't it?"

I grinned. "Oh, it already has."

"That's it. I'm never telling you." She walked toward the kitchen.

I chased after her, grabbing her around the waist. "How about I try to guess? And every time I get it wrong, I owe you a favor?"

"A favor?" Her brow lifted. "What kind of favor?"

A single finger trailed down her collarbone. "Anything."

A wide grin spread across her face. "Deal."

"Oh, for fuck's sake, Macon," Billy's voice boomed through the restaurant.

I turned to see him storming through rows of tables, and I flinched.

"You've been here every day of the week. Every damn day."

I casually nodded, sitting back in my chair with one foot

over the other. "And I'm gonna keep showing up every damn day until you talk to me."

"I am—" He huffed, looking incredibly annoyed. "I'm talking now."

"No," I corrected him as Marin peeked over her menu, trying not to grin. "You're yelling. Pretty loudly, too."

We looked around at the packed restaurant as people diligently tried to ignore us.

He grabbed the towel on his shoulder and wiped his brow. "I told you the first time you were here that I didn't want to talk to you."

"And I told you that was fine, but that I'd just keep coming until you did."

He let out a frustrated growl and then proceeded to walk away. He hadn't served me in a week. He'd let me sit at a table, but that was it.

No menu, no drinks.

Not a single French fry.

Nothing.

Sometimes, when Marin joined me, he'd serve her—just out of spite, but never me.

He'd made himself clear the first time I came to apologize.

He did not want to talk to me.

And I understood that.

He had every right to be mad at me. I'd fucked up. More than fucked up.

But that didn't mean I was going anywhere.

I'd sit at this table for a month, a year, a fucking decade if that was what he needed. But I'd still sit here and show him that I was here for him, no matter what.

'Cause that was exactly what he'd done for me.

Of course, I was hoping it wouldn't take nearly that long.

Especially since…

"What's the ETA?" I asked Marin in a hushed tone.

She looked down at her phone. "Mmm. Ten minutes maybe."

I nodded. "Good."

Billy was so busy being mad at me that he didn't seem to notice how packed the restaurant was—or who it was packed with.

Since the gala, there had been a record turnout—a silent show of support from the town. Not from everyone, mind you—this wasn't *Schitt's Creek*—but a lot more than I'd anticipated.

If Billy noticed, he didn't say anything.

But he'd see soon enough.

"Five minutes," Marin said.

"Jesus," I muttered. "He's either going to kill us or—"

"Us?" She scoffed. "As far as he knows, *I* had nothing to do with this, okay? This was all you. You're already in the doghouse anyway."

"All I did was logistics. It's not like it was my idea." I grinned, sitting back in my seat as we waited for our secret surprise to get here. I looked around the restaurant, seeing the friends who had turned out.

Jake and Molly sat with Millie, Aiden, and his brother, who was visiting from New York. Dean sat with Taylor and their wives. Gavin even managed to find a date—some leggy blonde. Probably a tourist. I was just glad he wasn't ogling my girlfriend for once.

Everyone sat in nervous anticipation, talking among themselves.

Waiting.

Finally, Marin got the text.

She nodded, and I pulled out my phone.

Go time, I wrote in the group chat.

Me—in a fucking group chat.

Billy better appreciate this.

Everyone—and I mean, everyone—reached under their seats and pulled out individual candles, supplied by Millie. We all placed them on the tables, and while Billy was being distracted inside, they were lit.

The patio was instantly aglow in flickering flames.

"It's so pretty," Marin said, her eyes a little misty as she looked around.

Someone pulled out a speaker, and music filled the air. It was one of Billy's favorites, and like a moth to a flame, he stepped out onto the patio.

"What the hell?" his deep voice said.

I watched his eyes dart from person to person until they finally landed on…Eli.

He was standing at the entrance of the patio, all decked out in his designer duds. A shit-eating grin plastered across his face.

Never in a million years would Billy have expected this.

"What the hell?" His voice was much softer this time as everything started to shift into place.

A chorus of chuckles echoed around me.

Billy nervously took in the scene as he saw all the love and support of his friends. His hands covered his face as he turned his attention forward. They met halfway, and before Billy could say a single word, Eli dropped to one knee.

Words were said, and tears were shed. But all I could focus on was Marin.

Her smile, her joy.

Our eyes locked as a chorus of cheers erupted around us.

"Thank you," I said as everyone celebrated.

"For what?" Her eyes danced.

"Everything," I answered.

Everything.

EPILOGUE

Marin

"Does he look okay?" I asked, a note of concern in my voice as we all sat around Billy's, watching the mounted TVs. " 'Cause I swear he looks like he's gonna throw up."

"No," Billy scoffed, looking relaxed and unfazed. He sat back in a chair, sipping soda. The restaurant was closed to the public, so he was enjoying a bit of rest. Although, since Eli had moved in, he'd been looking a lot less stressed in general. "I've seen him throw up. Lots of times. He's fine."

I glared at him. "Seeing him heave his guts out when he's drunk is not the same thing."

Billy shrugged as we watched Macon nervously pace back and forth while we waited for more results to pour in.

We had thought it'd be an easy race.

As Ocracoke's captain, Macon was a shoo-in, and it was just a special election.

He'd probably run unopposed.

None of those things happened.

Macon's opponent came in from left field and was brutal. He dragged him through the mud and then some. But Macon weathered all of it—the digs against his alcoholism, his rough upbringing, even the ferry accident. The community in Ocracoke had supported him through all of it, and he was finally embracing it.

"You all right?" I asked, walking up to Macon as he stared out the window toward the water.

"What?" He looked at me, his eyes blazing. "Oh, yeah. I'm fine."

"Is this like when you used to say you were fine and then go out and run a bazillion miles?"

A grin tugged at the corner of his lips. "It was never a bazillion. And that's what I have the meetings for now."

I smiled. One good thing from his father's gala rant, besides the bastard finally moving far away. Macon didn't need to hide anymore, and he could truly take care of himself.

Now, he just ran for the fun of it.

And to make my life miserable.

He was the worst running coach ever.

"Let me take your jacket. You don't need this anymore," I offered.

He'd had a few last-minute stops today, trying to get as many people to the polls as possible, and played the part, suit and all.

He didn't mind the people, but absolutely loathed the suit.

"No!" he said suddenly. "I mean, I'm fine. I'll need to make a speech soon, good or bad, so I might as well keep it."

I looked at him, those hazel eyes doing their best to avoid mine.

"You're not fine," I protested.

"What?" He scoffed, running a hand through his hair. "I'm totally fine."

I gave him an incredulous stare. He never used the word *totally.*

Which meant he was *totally* not fine.

Macon

Marin was looking at me like I was a caged lion at the zoo.

And I understood why she might be concerned.

Running for the special election had been stressful. And crazy.

And downright nuts.

But I could win this race for sheriff by a landslide or lose miserably, and it wouldn't make a difference either way.

My janky nerves had nothing to do with those numbers scrolling across the screen and everything to do with the tiny ring box currently sitting in the pocket of my suit jacket.

I was going to ask Marin to marry me tonight.

And considering the reaction she'd had to her last proposal…

"Hey, Marin, why don't you get Macon a plate of food?" Billy suggested as he walked over to us. "He's looking a little peckish."

"Oh, sure!" she answered, happy to make herself useful.

I gave him a miserable stare.

"Dude, you gotta calm down," he stated as he stood next to me, his hands in his pockets.

"Easy for you to say when you were on the receiving end of this."

He grinned, taking his left hand out to look down at his engagement ring—a solid platinum band with a row of diamonds. "Yeah, that did take the stress out of it. Thanks for that."

"Still didn't talk to me for a solid week afterward though," I said dryly.

"Oh, that had nothing to do with me being angry at you," he explained with a wicked grin. "I was busy celebrating."

I rolled my eyes. "I know. I practically live next door, remember?"

"Yeah, about that. Are you going to sell your house? Seems like it's just sitting around."

I gave him a pleading look as I gazed over at Marin. "Yes, but *she* doesn't know that."

My house meant jack shit to me, and I'd be happy to get rid of the memories and everything else attached to it. Plus, the extra income from selling it wouldn't hurt.

"Oh, right." He made an *oopsie* face and continued to drink his soda.

"Sorry Eli couldn't be here," Billy said, changing the subject. "Handing over the reins to the new management has taken a bit longer than he anticipated."

"I'm just glad he's finally moved here."

"Me, too," he agreed. "Although I do worry he's going to die of boredom."

"He's wealthy. Just tell him to buy a boat."

Billy snorted. "He is considering trying to buy that fancy restaurant down by the water—the one right across from me."

I knew which one he was talking about. It was the one Marin and I had been to right before we…

"Is it even for sale?"

Billy shrugged. "No, but Eli can be very convincing."

"And so, the Radcliffe restaurant empire begins."

"Radcliffe-Rivas empire," he corrected me with a grin. "We've both come a long way, Macon."

My eyes flickered toward Marin. She was over by the food table, chatting with Elena, who I'd just met tonight. Their laughter drifted over, and I couldn't help but smile.

How did I get so damn lucky?

"Yeah. Yeah, we have."

Billy patted me on the shoulder. "You've got this. You're going to win, and she's going to say yes."

"Thanks, man," I said, swallowing down a well of emotions.

"And if you lose, maybe she'll say yes just out of pity."

"Great pep talk. Thanks."

"Anytime, man."

Marin

"Why do they look so guilty over there?" I asked as I grabbed a plate and started piling it with food.

Elena looked over at Macon and shrugged. "He's a politician now," she said. "They always look guilty."

I laughed, shaking my head. "Is the sheriff really a political office?"

She gave me a face, the *I know everything* face she'd perfected since law school. "Did you vote on it?"

"I guess I did."

Kind of weird to think of Macon as anything but Hot Cop. Hot Sheriff just didn't have the same ring to it.

I tried to hide my smile as I remembered all the many delicious favors he had done, trying to guess that nickname. It'd taken a while, so long that I had started to wonder if he was failing on purpose.

"Your dad seems to be enjoying himself." She gestured over to where my father was talking to Aiden, while my mother got drinks. "He's really proud of you."

I pressed my lips together, feeling my cheeks redden. "I know."

My artwork had only been in Aiden's gallery for a short time, but I'd already sold enough to keep me afloat for a while.

A long while.

"Does that embarrass you?" Elena asked.

"No," I answered. "Kind of? I don't know. It's just surreal, you know? I've wanted this for so long. And now, it's happening, and it all feels a little too easy."

"Why would you say that?"

"I guess I just feel I lucked out, meeting Aiden. If I hadn't—"

"I saw lots of artists in that gallery, Marin. Your art is selling because it's good. None of this has been easy. You lost your husband and suffered through years of grief. You worked in a career you hated. Don't pawn your success off as luck. Own that shit."

I pressed my lips together, trying to contain my smile. She never beat around the bush. "Okay."

"Okay, good. Now, are any of these men in here single?"

I laughed as we huddled together, looking out at the crowd.

"Everyone!" Billy's loud voice boomed through the restaurant. "The final results are coming in."

I looked over at Macon, just as his eyes met mine.

I didn't even bother saying good-bye to Elena. I just set the food down and ran over to him. My heart hammered in my chest.

"No matter what," I said, my eyes meeting his, "I love you."

He grinned, squeezing my hand. "I love you, too."

We both looked up at the screen and waited.

Cheers erupted around the restaurant.

I looked over at Macon's shocked face as he stared at the screen.

"You won!" Billy hollered. "You fucking won!"

Macon's arms wrapped around me, and he lifted me as everyone cheered.

He set me down, his eyes blazing.

"I'm so proud of you!"

"Speech!" someone yelled.

A few others echoed the sentiment as a chorus of laughter echoed across the restaurant. I stepped out of the way to allow him a moment in the spotlight, but he grabbed my hand, keeping me in place.

"I know you all want a speech," he said. "But I had a little something else planned."

The room went silent as he turned toward me.

He looked at me with a mixture of anticipation, joy, and love.

Before I could ask what he was doing, he dropped to one knee.

But this time, I didn't panic.

This time my heart quickened for an entirely different reason.

And this time, I said…*yes*.

ACKNOWLEDGMENTS

It has been four years since I published a new book. There were periods of time when I thought I'd never get back to this point.

I can still vividly remember the day I pulled up a job search engine, the reality of my situation finally settling in. But, as my cursor blinked and blinked in that search bar, I had no idea what to type. I tried to think of what I wanted to do next.

I closed my eyes and tried to visualize a new job…

A new career.

And I couldn't.

I knew at that moment that no matter how bleak things got—if I had five readers or five thousand, I'd always come back to writing. It's where I belong and I'm immensely grateful for a family who supports that.

I don't know how many different ways I can thank my husband. He's a superhero among men. Seriously, guys. I won the lottery. And even though they drive me crazy most of the time, we have pretty cool kids too.

There are a few people who helped make this book possible. Without them, I would have never gotten to the finish line.

Jovana Shirley—my lifelong editor. Thank you for braving my hot mess of rough drafts.

Katy Nielsen—my proofer. Thank you for your accuracy, but also for your friendship over the years.

Juliana Cabrera—my cover designer. Thank you for

bringing Macon and Marin to life and creating this beautiful series of covers.

Wildfire Marketing (especially Melissa)—Thank you for all the help with marketing.

Berg's Readers Group—This group (formerly Berg's Bibliophiles) was dormant for years, and I truly appreciate the individuals who have helped bring it back. Social media is the crux of this introverted author's life, and I cherish all of you.

Lastly, thank you to all of my readers—both old and new. You make my words come alive.

ABOUT THE AUTHOR

J.L. Berg is the USA Today bestselling author of the Ready Series, the Lost & Found series, and many more. Originally from California, she now resides in central Virginia with her high school sweetheart, two children, and three dogs. When she's not writing, she enjoys spending time with her family or indulging in her love for Doctor Who. J.L. Berg is represented by Jill Marsal of Marsal Lyon Literary Agency, LLC. For the latest book updates, audio news, and more, be sure to visit her website.